In 1970 **Jennifer Potter** was born in Leeds, England to an English father and Californian mother. At six months old Jennifer went back with her mother to Los Angeles. They moved to Las Vegas in 1976. In 1987, Jennifer returned to England to study and get to know her English father. She planned to stay in England for the summer and is still here. She now lives in Camden, London.

Although the heroine of these stories was also born in Leeds in 1970 to an English father and Californian mother and at six months old returned with her mother to Los Angeles, the author would like to make it clear that she herself has never had facial warts, excessively long pubic hair or some of the experiences described here.

GREEDY MOUTH

GREEDY MOUTH

Jennifer Potter

First edition published in 1998
by Arts and Commerce

Printed in England

All characters in this publication are fictitious and any resemblance to real persons, living or dead, is purely coincidental.

A CIP catalogue record for this book is available from the British Library.

ISBN 1902 053 036

arts & commerce

Tales of mama's milky breast

Finger fuckin adolescence

The juicy bits

Airplane. June 5, 1987 ✈

Right now, if I close my eyes, I'm there lying on my mail order personalised raft. It says "I love Jesusa" all over in silver and gold. I'm sipping Diet Coke from the drinks holder attached to the pillows as the sun sizzles slowly through my eyelids, peeling deviously away at my corneas.

What can I feel? Physically, it feels like a 1000 microscopic insects are multiplying on the inside of my eyelids. The pumping water is gently buoying me towards the deep end. The occasional firefly is trying to free itself from my coco-greasy skin. My extended arms float on the surface of the water, keeping my temperature from boiling. I feel slightly turned on as I sacrifice myself to the manly sun: he is my evil master.

Beneath the skin? Oh, there's ain't much goin' on in there except for maybe NutraSweet cancer. My hypnotized head is full of hopeful movie-star daydreams but the inside of my body feels hollow, like a cheap ceramic statue of Jesus pinned to the cross. I feel like Californian cement, already cracked but still holding out for the Big One.

What can I hear? In my left ear construction workers are pasting pink condos and, in my right, airplanes are landing and taking off. When I was 14 and brushing my eyebrows up like Brooke Shields, I thought airplane passengers could see me in my bikini, so I'd wave to them. That. Is. How. Narcissistic. I. Am.

That's what my long-lost dad called me the other day, on the phone. He's a bloody psychotherapist dude and I'm gonna go live with him for a while. He goes, "You suffer from narcissistic rage". Whatever. He thinks he can fix it. Anyways, it's not true cos most of the time I hate myself. But I like the way "narcissistic" sounds.

I'm gonna learn one new word a day and add it to the list at the front of this shitty journal diary book my Mom gave me before I got on the plane. It's all a part of my mission to get smart. The only way to get smart was to get the hell outa Vegas...

So, for the first time in seventeen years, I am writing. The sensation kinda reminds me of the first time I smoked a doobie when I was 10. I feel nervous... drained... and furry around the edges... calm and strangely tired, but racey. For the first time, I can actually feel my brain thinkin'.

I've never really written anything, apart from stupidly folded letters in class, yearbook signings, what I did for summer vacation and fill in the bubble tests. Next, I'm gonna write a long letter to my Mom - tell her what I think of her poor excuse for parenting... but I'm not sure it's her I should be blaming.

My brain's not very big but I know one or two things. Greediness begins at birth. You come out screamin' for mama's milky breast, and you know to suck, suck long and hard as you can cos, just when you get used to it, they'll take it away and push you into the world like the tiger does with her cubs.

I was born Jesusa Whitby in hospital three weeks premature at four pounds in a recently converted mental asylum in Leeds, England. What happened that month after my birth, before she bundled me on to my first outta the womb, ear-popping flight to America, I'll never know for sure. Like all old stories, mother and father have different versions.

Mom says: a few days after my birth, he confessed to bein' in love with someone else. Pop says: she had an affair with his best friend so he then slept with the girl in question. Who knows for sure? I don't really care cos I'm well aware of what kind of shit hippies got up to in those heady days of "free love". So I don't do that line,"Well why did you have me in the first place?"

That's not even why I'm goin' in blame U-turns.

She'd go, "Parents aren't supposed to be good. Why should they be? We didn't have good parents either. Get over it and get on with it."

She always shocked me when she said shit like that. More than once through the years, my mother told me how depressed she was after my birth and how much she hated England, with its unending grey days, and how poor she was, and how cold it was back then in the 60s, without central heating.

Mom didn't have it in her to marry a millionaire like Howard Hughes. I wasn't really disappointed with her, I just thought she wasted all that beauty. She was up there with Bridget Bardot and Marilyn Monroe.

Unfortunately for me, offers of stardom made her sick to her hippy stomach. She hated the way L.A. was full of fame-seeking desperadoes and capitalists obsessed with money and the movie business – especially the Beverly Hills crowd.

She'd go, "Beverly Hills is cursed and I'll never live there again!"

"But Mom, we could have lived in Grandma's apartment complex." I violently wanted to reside in Hollywood cos our family had lived there for three generations.

Whenever I would get on this trip she'd tell the Charles Manson story, which was my favourite. We were stayin' in my Grandma's house four down from Sharon Tate the night she was murdered. Sharon Tate was pregnant, just like my mother was with me. The following day the whole neighbourhood was terrified that their house was gonna be next.

She thought this story and others about her wild days with Tina Turner and The Doors would put me off L.A.'s scent, but it didn't.

Nagging was the only way I could get her to talk about the past and when she did I memorised every word.

✈

THE SOUND OF SEX

Aged 6.
you read me my favourite book "Where the Wild Things Are"
I nestle into my bed with my floppy rabbit
I tell you not to read so fast as I brush my puffy hands across the grainy pictures
your voice is like baby powder when you try
I want you to mother me forever
I stroke your long blonde hair

I explain to you there are some nice monsters like Puff the Magic Dragon
I've worked out most monsters have two sides to them
the gentle side which only budding flowers and charming children see
and the horrible side which they save for grown-ups who attempt to destroy his power
all monsters are ashamed males
they have a thingy
your lamplit profile shows that you're impatient
you wish I would just go to sleep so you could go roll a joint and pour a glass of wine

Mommy, put my plastic record player on
the red 45, Molly the Monster
leave the door open a little bit
and I fall asleep almost immediately after-

"...if I ain't feedin my empty heart is bleedin... "

you wake me with that gross sound of bones mashing
ehh... ehh... ahh... ahh... ohh... ohh... baby... oh yah... ahhhhhhhhhhhh!
gurgling noises from the sex room
no matter how much it repels me
I always smell the sheets in the morning
making sure there is no blood
then I strip the sheets tie them into one big ball and dump them on the kitchen floor
I hate you Mommy
the way you take me from sleepy dreams of purple castles and talking reindeer
Rumpelstiltskin, Jack and the Beanstalk and Pismo Beach

you pull my head from the pillow
a pervert sent from the devil
I go to my bedroom door
I listen harder to be sure you are actually doing it
and it's not just the Northern Californian wind blowing the shed hatch open and shut
or it's not one of the hippies up from L.A. camped on the front porch meditating
I close the door and plug the gap between the door and the floor with unfavoured stuffed animals

you won't be considerate will you
you don't think about my thoughts
I'm not really a person yet
what could be going through a 6-year-old's mind
children don't understand sex at that age
not until you tell them

over my head I layer my handmade pillows
1. 2. 3. to muffle the sound and suffocate my cries
why does the sound upset me
the sound of sex pumping at my eardrums
but it's good hippy sex
if it feels so good why does it sound so painful
like a cut-throat squealing pig in the slaughter yard running in circles
chasing the spurting blood hoping to recycle it
or a dying rabbit caught in a farmer's trap
the sound still seeps in through my air tunnel

the shrieking and the panting
writhing and the rumping
bumping and humping
nothing keeps the sound outside
not even my baby blanket or the army of stuffed animal against the door
which leads to your bedroom where HE, the monster has taken over
his big black body thrusting between your legs

I start the record over again
wait till you finish
try and think about something else...

Mommy, do stuffed animals come alive at night
because at the bottom of the bed they all seem to be laughing at me
with their sharp white teeth chattering
I wish I could train my stuffed animals
build them into an army and then they would march through the dark house
into your bedroom and assassinate HIM
take the gun he keeps under the bed as a warning to you
"if you leave I will kill you"

the sound of sex is ugly, UGLY
so when I hear your cries of pleasure
I wonder if he's twisting your arm behind your back
or bruising your cheek, holding you down
and the sound of the bed knocking against the wall

it's going on too long this time
I pee the bed and wail loudly for you
MOMMY. . . MOMMY. . . MOMMY. . . MOMMY. . .

I bang my head against the wall
you still don't come
I'm angry as hell now
I invent my own monster
I paint him on the wall above the bed with my poo
Mommy hates this the most
I scream as loud as I can
so everyone in Santa Cruz will know my pain
how can a girl of 6 know about love making

you never come
too tired to scream anymore I cradle myself underneath the bed
you know my tantrums
you know it's a trick to get you to come to me
all you grown-ups say I do it for attention
I do it because I have no choice
when children have tantrums they are giving birth to monsters
and the monsters stay there forever

Airplane. ✈

I've had 1000s of grey days but they've all been painted over in technicolour.

It's almost impossible to shut memories out, especially when you're staring out grey, airplane windows. Strapped into this little window seat, I pretend I'm bein' tortured in prison. It helps me feel more like a victim. All you got is a room and a bunch of stabbing memories. Some weird brain experimenter is masturbating in another room with a stack of TV monitors. He's electrocuting me with a remote control. And these memories are buzzin' in and out of my head like flippin' channels. It's drivin me lacucharacha cos the remote control ain't in my hands and I can't decide when to change the channel.

I wish I had a remote control for my fucking memories. I'd put them on mute forever. But that's exactly what I can't do. I've got ten hours on this plane that's headin' for London Heathrow. So I'm writing in this diary. It's got a cheerleader in the corner of every page...

I'm tryin' to think of how to describe my Mom on paper.

Rollercoaster and Hippies

I wanted to punish her for pullin' me off her tit.

One minute she was laid-back hippy, suckin' on a joint and the next she was serious PTA mother "gettin' over it and on with it." She danced, baked cookies with me, and pushed me on the swings but every now and again she'd accidently feed me to the sharks.

The first five years of my life I can only piece together from photo albums and fragmented stories. Los Angeles Mom meets English Dad at University in Dublin. They marry and live in a council flat in Leeds. Young love goes wrong. Mom takes baby back to America.

The earliest memory I have is blowing palmtrees, flashing metal and booming car sounds. The full story, which Mom liked to tell at the Thanksgiving dinner table after a few glasses of wine, was more matter of fact. One day while we were living with my grandparents in Hollywood I, at terrible 2, wandered out the front door and down the street in my diapers. I walked a hundred yards to the end of the street until I hit Hollywood Boulevard. About ten minutes later my mother found me in front of the House of Pancakes, in the arms of a policeman.

When I was 3 we found ourselves in a hippy commune just outside of San Francisco. That's where Mom met Leo Brown, her first long-term boyfriend after my dad and her split. Leo became the first and last man I ever called "Daddy".

Leo was one of the head honchos at this Black Panther kinda ranch, but he wanted total control so we moved a few miles down the road to Santa Cruz to set up his own throne. Santa Cruz was the first home I can remember. It was a hippy town with a beautiful beach and huge surfer waves.

It all started when my Mom disappeared into the waves. That day, I stood on the shoreline crying for her to come back. She swam further out, at least a mile. She then swam all the way across the bay. I followed her along the shore, trying to keep my eyes on her bobbing blonde hair. I cried until Leo threw a stick in my direction which sent our German Shepherd Blacky toppling on to me. When I stood up again I lost sight of her. Surfers and boogie boards blocked my view.

I sat down on the wet sand underneath the *Beware of Sharks* sign and let the foam tickle over my feet. People and seagulls flapped in the distance as Blacky licked the salt from my toes. On the seventh wave the water reached my crotch.

I have two holes.

Scooping up sand and sprinkling it like sugar into the breeze, I played guessing games as to which direction Mom would appear. I leaned back and gave into the sun's breezy ways. The Californian sun wasn't like the Vegas bastard. It was soft, not too hot.

The happiest I ever saw Mom was when she dragged herself out of that thunderous sea, readjusting her string bikini, stumbling through the pull of the tide who wanted her back as much as I did. She held her arms out for me to come to her. Weepy eyed, I climbed up onto her hip bone. As we stood in the lush foam, I made her promise she wouldn't go out so far next time. She laughed and carried me towards the waves. I kicked and swung on her hip.

"I wanna go back." She was waist deep and the waves were coming for us.

"Swim into the base!" Mom's bathing suit bottoms slipped through the wall of water, her voice dissolving as the roar of the waves closed in over my head.

Within seconds, I was gulping in a washing machine of foam, sand and sea weed. Somersaulting, not knowing which way was up, the ocean floor sandpapered my eyes. Little shards of glass against my 6 year old body. I struggled to the surface.

Just as I managed to inhale air, I felt the suck of another tidal wave. White-knuckle ride number two. This time I closed my eyes and mouth and curled up into a tantrum ball, arms tightly wrapped around knees.

Wave three kicked my ass on to the shore. Blacky Dog stood barking at me like Lassie, not knowing what to do. Open mouthed, I waited for someone to give me air, too pissed off with Mom to do it myself.

Leo came up behind me, turned me over and patted me on my back. I spat the seashells out and looked around to see where my birth giver was. She was still out in the ocean, carefree, diving like a teenage dolphin. I hated lovin' her so much... I threw a fit when she did something wrong. I saw her as a beautiful angel so when she fucked up I couldn't understand it.

Leo wrapped me in a big towel and laughed, "I bet you're not scared of the big red wave". Next thing I knew we were strapped in the front car of a kiddy rollercoaster. Chugging up the hill, one wooden plank at a time, I tried to finish my ice cream. Leo had his arm around me in case my tiny body lunged forward. As the trickly cream dried on my chops I giggled and let out a rodeo "Yahoo!"

I am American. I am American.

We nose-dived over the peak. I gazed out at the ocean to see if I could spot my mother's bleach blonde hair. Just as our front seat car accelerated over the first hill I dropped my cone on the passangers behind us. For a few seconds I stopped thinking of my mother and was transfixed by the controlled rush. As we plummeted once again my rosy cheeks wobbled in the stampeding wind. This was bolting bliss, in the arms of a big black Daddy, not left alone in the sea to learn how to wrestle the five foot waves. I was here on a man-made wave of dashing red bolts, metal and oil. In the glowing sunset my new home town spun round like a mini Hollywood with its zipping metal and distorted faces below.

This first rollercoaster ride was just a taster of what my mouth would water for from then on - trying to recapture the throbbing wind on the face, never wanting the ride to end, to feel tingly tingly all over.

Airplane. ✈

The more memories I scratch at, the harder it is to stop itching. And so the more obsessed I get with trying to fish them out of my sewagey brain. Once I get all the fuckers out of my head I'm gonna go to the toilet and flush them over the Atlantic Ocean. I'm not gonna be one of these retarded talk show victims feelin' sorry for myself.

WIZARD OF SANTA CRUZ

I love walking my cat Sam down my street barefoot. Avoiding the glass, cracks, spit, ground-in poo, bumpy gravel, oily potholes and scary neighbourhood dogs. My little yellow brick road is paved with gold. I'm really in love with myself today. I have my brand new, yellow summer dress on, it tickles my knees. I'm not used to wearing dresses, but when Leo gave it to me wrapped in bunny paper I fell in love. It's sunny and I can smell fruit in the fresh air. It's Easter morning and I have a huge basket of chocolate. Sammy Cat is allowing himself to be pulled along by my Mom's best belt. Me and my Mom are the only white people in our neighbourhood. I know almost everyone on this street with no sidewalks. We live in "The White House" opposite Hiawatha's dirt garden. There's a sign in her yard saying "Children Welcome Anytime! No Adults!" She brings us slices of watermelon while we play with her ant hills and crawl in and out of massive truck tyres.

Hiawatha, the Big Mama, kept chickens in her dirt yard. Hiawatha made my mouth water. Hangin' out with Big Mama was like eating an entire Betty Crocker triple-layer chocolate cake with double fudge icing. She'd emerge from her oven-like screen door warm and yummy. When you touched the flesh on her arm it was like holding a velour teddybear. She was the coolest old person I ever knew, most of em' seemed so cranky. Not Hiawatha, her boobs bounced when she burst out in laughter, and then she'd look down at them and start chuckling even harder, which prompted all us kids to fall off the tyres in hysterics. Whenever I'd whine "I want my Mommy", she'd go, "I want my Mommy too, but you gotta let go... can't be no baby forever child".

Although our home was small, it was the best kept on the street. It could have been in one of my picture books. When my school bus pulled up in front of the house to drop me off one day, the driver said it was "unbelievably symmetrical". Once I found out what that meant, I agreed. It was painted perfect white with a red porch. A daisy-lined pathway of marshmallowy stones led up to the face-like shack. With three giant sunflowers on both sides of the porchsteps, two swinging loveseats underneath a pair of eyeball-windows either side of its mouth-like door, it looked like a pretend house built outa' disappearing glue. The Big Bad Wolf could have blown it over in one breath.

I was known as Leo's kid. We were too poor to live anywhere else and Leo thought it would be good for my Mom, seein' how she grew up in Beverly Hills and all. He always preached that white people should be thrown into an "uncomfortable environment" so we could know what it was like for black people trying to move into all white neighbourhoods. Leo was my Mom's first and only black boyfriend. He always seemed to have hundreds of kids and ex-girlfriends waiting in the backs of Cadillacs. He had that vacant stare that passed right through you for miles.

Leo was the Big Bad Wolf but he was also Peter Pan and Gepetto. One afternoon he would be playful and sweet, just bubblin' with goodness and then that same night he could turn into a brute with mean snarlin' teeth. I never knew when he was gonna make me jump with his roar. He was a man, all mixed up on the inside. Good, bad and neither. The hunter and the hunted.

Big Bad Leroy Brown, the baddest cat in the whole damn town. When he spoke everybody listened. He was poetic, smart, and bossy as hell. He wanted people to know he was a real cool, wheelin', dealin' "nigger" from South Central. He seemed more comfortable around white people, probably cos they paid him more respect out of fear and admiration. And, although he was so proud of what he was, I saw from the way he rubbed his face with his hands really hard, that he wanted to get away from what he had been – which was just another poor black man from the ghetto.

After two months of lovin' him, Mom started to see the signs of a controlling and violent man who had the habit of keeping a gun under the mattress. By then it was too late to change anything. They were both enrolled at the college in Santa Cruz. We belonged to the Big Bad Wolf for three years. No backing out. His rule was when a man becomes the head of the house, he owns everything in it.

Still it was a cute white house. I was the other cute part of the package, I never nagged him like my mother did for all the bad things he was involved in. Just give me an ice cream and Jesusa's happy. Leo never laid a finger on me. He spoilt me with presents and took me on his small time adventures, picking things up, and dropping them off.

The Angel Dust weekend was a perfect example of how their relationship worked. It was 1976 and not many people knew how to concoct the drug. One of Leo's friends from L.A.

was a science and chemistry major, which meant he could put any drug together. Leo did his smooth talking to my Mom, explaining it would pay for the next four semesters of school. Mom still protested but in the end Leo was Mr Veto.

Leo and his hippy friend were out in the backyard making it up in the shed near the orange trees and pot plants. Leo showed me how to look after the little green trees of marijuana when I first met him at the hippy ranch. He told me they were laughing trees and in the middle of the night you could hear them giggling when the wind tickled their leaves. I had to water the pot plants everyday in the summer so I was very proud when they got to be nearly as tall as the sunflowers.

It was a Saturday morning and my mother had a list of chores for me. I didn't mind doin' the chores cos I was always rewarded with her praise and a McDonalds. Besides goin' to the beach, havin' a glass of wine and a joint there was nothin' that made my Mom happier than a clean house. There I was out back in my own little baby talk world stroking my plants when Miss Priss came running out of the back door in her long cheese-cloth flowered dress bitchin' at Leo.

"Leo, you know damn well there could be an explosion if anything goes wrong."

I put my watering can down and observed. Leo just stood, arms folded with his big Afro and his flared jeans flappin' in the breeze; Mom, all in his face with her braided hair and her lit cigarette, making patterns in the clear, sunny air. She looked over at me and sharply directed me to collect all the rotting oranges from the grass. So there I was in my underwear, racking up mouldy, ant-infested oranges with a wreath of daisies in my hair. As I bobbed around in the long grass I looked through the dusty shed window. Leo's shifty friend was there with a bottle of acid in his hands. He was funny lookin', like a cross between Dr Jekyll and Wolf Man Jack. The four of us looked like we stepped off one of my Mom's album covers.

I was scared there was gonna be a fight, I only ever saw one fist fight before. I knew they happened in the sex room.

Please don't hurt her. Maidens shouldn't have to fight the monsters.

Mom was too angry to stop, shrieking for the whole neighbourhood to hear. A shopping list of insults lingered in the hushed air,

"Low-life, drug-dealing con-artist".

And then, as if it were as normal as the sun, The Big Bad Wolf whacked my Mom upside the head, knocking her off balance. She got back up and strutted towards me. Pulling me to her waist, like one of her tie-dyed scarfs, she sashayed into the house, clutching me as her trophy. Leo knew I'd always take my mother's side. I gave him a dirty look as I swung on my Mom's hip bone. I was their ping-pong ball.

Mommy put me down on the kitchen floor. "Go water the sunflowers in the front yard."

As I hosed the erect soldiers I could hear her crying inside. I didn't want to fluster her so I got on with my job. There were six soldiers, three on either side of the brick-red steps that led to the porch. My mother and I planted the sunflowers when they were babies. Now, they were six foot tall. We gave 'em names and talked to 'em in our secret language, which Leo didn't understand. Besides cleaning, and swimmin' in the ocean, there's nothing my Mom liked better than puttin' Joni Mitchell on the outside speakers, getting stoned and doin' gardening.

Whenever Leo Brown upset my Mommy, we worked on the garden. As the flowers grew I thought they looked like guards on Buckingham Palace duty. So still and erect. I informed my Mom the beds of daffodils and tulips were our allies and the sunflowers were our protectors and that I knew all their battle strategies.

When my Mom came out of the hospital for fractured ribs and stitches the year before, we planted the sunflowers. I remember sippin' ice tea, perched on the red steps, admiring her as she sowed the soil scuffing her hospital manicure. I could tell she was planning a strategy behind her mirrored sunglasses which covered most of her stitches.

Mom tried to leave Leo a few times, problem was she loved him madly. One time we flew to New York to hide out with relatives. And, once, my dad in England sent us plane tickets and we sat in a Manchester pub garden for a few weeks. My Mom and Dad would briefly fall in and out of love. But then she would pine for Leo, we both would.

After most fights we'd drive over to Cockroach Nora's who lived in Pismo Beach. I called Nora that cos her house was crawling with them. Nora studied bugs at the University. She fed them coffee grains and all kinds of shit... another hippy taking too many drugs, anyone who chooses to study cockroaches all their lives has got to be on drugs. Sometimes I would refuse to sleep in her house so my Mom would let me sleep in the Volkswagen.

Leo would drive up in the morning with a Cadillac full of Winchell's Doughnuts which sent me running into his arms. I listened and chomped, mocking his pleas, apologies and promises of change. We'd always go back with him. I think Mom felt she didn't have anywhere else to go. When I reminded her we could go back to Los Angeles, she told me her parents were alcoholics and that they didn't want us living there. I'd sit in kindergarten staring out the window wondering what she should do. It was too much for a 6 year old.

Although Leo was dangerous he was also safe, like a strict father she and I never had. At 25 she seemed kinda lost. I think she liked the way he told her what to do. He was the lesser of some other evil. I knew she was buying time though. I overheard her saying to Cockroach Nora one time, "I only have a few months left of college, then I can move to another city".

Even though they fought all the time I felt pretty content with the flowers, big Blacky Dog and Sammy Cat. There were block parties with hot dogs and potato salad relayed over fences. There were always lots of hippy kids to play with too, people coming and going while Leo measured out the dime bags. On Sundays, me and my Mom picked grapes with Steve the turkey farmer. I'd sit in the back of the pick-up truck counting my grape-pickin' money in the sunset.

Steve was a real live 6' 4' Indian with famous ancestors. Like Leo, he was proud of his roots. His great-grandfather was a warrior who tried to fight off the white settlers a hundred years ago. If I ever met anybody with a visible soul it was him, you could see it glowing outa' his chestnut skin. Like everybody else, I think he had a soft spot for my mother. Sometimes Leo would stop us from grape pickin with Steve. Leo was jealous of everyone except me.

And then one day the final fight took place.

I'm helping the ants in Hiawatha's anthills, feeding them and helping them build their empire so they can fight the cockroaches for the rule of the world. I hear a yelp, like when a puppy gets kicked so hard he can't cry the fullness of his pain. I see Mom stumbling out of the house holding the side of her face. Sobbing, she drops to the grass. I sit frozen like I'm in a drive-in movie, waiting for Jaws to attack. Now Leo is pushing, pulling and dragging her towards the white fence. Dancing a sick dance, they trample over my flowerbeds. My guards do nothing. This time Mom's not fighting back. She plays dead, like her Raggedy Ann doll.

The neighbours assemble on their porches like they're watchin' 4th July fireworks. Some gaze from their screen doors cowardly. Even though Blacky is officially Leo's dog he's barking at him. I'm rooted to my anthill.

Leo kicks my Mom in the the ribs he's fractured before. Swear words fly from his mouth like Vietnam bullets. He kicks her again and again, and again, and again, and again, and again, and again, and again . Now he's back in the house.

I'm still leaving you!" She screams. I snap outta my TV stare. Red ants are crawling all over my legs and up my dress. There's a gun. It's in her face. Leo smirks: "Now you still thinking of leaving me?"

I'm running. I have to protect her. He never hurts me. I can stop him. I wrap my arms around her shoulders, hoping to sheild her from his weapon, "Please don't hurt her, daddy". He flings me into the soft bed of lilies. I see the broken heart in his copper pupils. His eyes are miles away. My Mommy whimpers, "That's it! So if you want to kill me, do it now. Finish me. Just do it now! If you don't, I'm going. I never want to see you again". She's sobbing.

SMACK. He hits her again across the face with his free hand and lets out this awful caveman growl. He runs back to the house. I hug Mom to me and help her up.

The only part I remember perfectly was the Big Bad Wolf struttin' past us with Mom's clothes and hurling them into the dirty street. I enveloped my Mom's thigh with my useless arms. I wanted to be her knight in shining armour. We hobbled towards the white picket gate.

"Why won't any of you help us?" I cried. Blacky Dog followed, ignoring Leo's calls. A few minutes later we had retreated behind enemy lines to Hiawatha's yard. For the next ten minutes the whole neighbourhood observed in crisp silence as Leo streamlined back and forth dumping our belongings.

The breeze stood still and the clouds came to a halt. Nothing about this street seemed "cute" anymore. Not the neighbours and especially not our White House - it was an evil werewolf's cave with shit and blood smeared on the walls. There on my yellow brick road lay my Mom's discarded desk with our bedding, pots and pans, plants, toothbrushes, books, photo albums, stuffed animals, even Sammy Cat came flying over the fence.

All of a sudden, Steve pulled up with his pick-up truck. He had a shotgun.

"Look Leo," he shouted in his Red Indian battle warning. "That's enough now. Leave them alone before someone calls the police. It's finished now, let them pack up their stuff tomorrow. We've had to listen to you terrify this woman for two years and I'm sick of it. They're gonna stay with me tonight and then tomorrow they'll be gone from your life. Do you understand man? Just leave them the hell alone."

Leo stood there in utter disbelief, shifting from foot to foot, shocked that a man of 50 was brave enough to point a shotgun at him – the Big Bad Wolf. Now, Leo was one street-smart motherfucker and he knew none of this was worth getting in trouble with the law, not with so many people watching, not for a white woman. He stopped his house-wrecking mission, got in his Cadillac and screeched off.

Steve walked over and helped us into his truck. It was dusk and everything was outlined in lavender. We sat there while he and the neighbours packed what was lying in the street into the back of the truck. He drove us along the bumpy road to his house at the end of the street. I was still shaking as I curled up on his couch with Sammy Cat. Still shedding tears, Mom went into the back room. Steve got out his first aid box and a bottle of pills. He told me he was going to give my Mom a feel-better pill. I remember feeling this cold clinical fascination towards her wounds as I watched him dab cotton balls over the bumps. For some reason, I was surprised there was hardly any blood.

It had fallen dark outside and the crickets were buggin' out through the windscreen. Steve guided me back into the cosy living room and sat me in front of the TV. Framed pictures of turkeys plastered his walls. The Wizard of Oz was just about to start. I knew the book but I never saw the Judy Garland movie. A huge bowl of ice cream with hot fudge chocolate sauce appeared. Steve kept checking any outdoor movement, in case Leo came back.

I was still shaken but slowly relaxing. My eyes were puffy from crying and my t-shirt was ripped and covered in soil. During every commercial I checked on Mom, stroking her long blonde hair, the pretty locks she never let me touch when she was awake. I studied her bruises and the cuts on her cheeks. She looked so young. I sang her a melody and words that came from I don't know where. I can't remember the words.

I watched Dorothy's world turn upside down as I had watched mine that day. I understood how bad she wanted to go home. I was determined to be brave and look after my Mom.

I didn't know where we were going the next day, but everyone else did. I would have my Mom, Sammy Cat, and Blacky Dog to keep me company on my adventure.

I wasn't sure if I hated Leo. He was like the Wizard of Oz hiding behind macho steel. All I knew was that he loved my mother too much for his own good. It drove him crazy. When you love someone too much it makes you sick. I was soon to learn this.

Airplane. ✈

"Mom, why don't you marry one of those rich Jewish guys in Beverly Hills? Why do you fall for these super cool bad motherfuckers or these poetic dreaming scheming weaklings who can't make a decision to save their life? Mom, are we going to L.A.? I'll find you a man, I'll be your manager. With your face and my bullshit detector we can kick some rich Jewish ass. You do like Jewish men, Mom, Woody Allen is Jewish and he's God's gift to women...and I don't care if Beverly Hills' boys are screwed up, you'll have a lot in common."

I'm pretending this is what I said to my battered Mom as we drove away from Santa Cruz. From what I can remember, within the space of twenty four hours I changed from a flower child into this Tasmanian tomboy brat. I was heroic Dorothy on speed pills, quickly splattering red paint over the day before, "tuned in" on the edge of my seat, waiting for the next TV episode. Mother and child, two brave warriors, had won a small victory over what I decided was the enemy: MAN.

BYE BYE APPLE PIE HELLO HELL

Truth is I became the new enemy to my mother. The minute Leo was outta the picture-book I started stampin' around in his bossy boots, demanding attention. I was determined at age 6 not to be like her. Angelic saint she was not, in fact I was kinda disenchanted with her. I loved her but I didn't want to be like her. I hoped I'd be as beautiful as her... but smarter, stronger and richer.

Hippy mothers are the worst kind and the best kind. They're so mellow you get the feeling they don't care. They think it's cool for you to explore life on your own and they barely punish you. There are no barriers or barbed wire fence, no stop signals, no warning signs or indicating lights.

She was so exhausted thinkin' about survival - if I wanted to be the mother, then she was the child. If I wanted to throw a fit and bang my head against the TV she'd let me. But she wouldn't let us go back to L.A. Apparently, "all the smart people were moving out, to a golden land of eternal youth, no taxes, cheap houses, plenty of land and jobs".

Yah, right, follow the yellow brick road... No matter how sunny the sky was that day I felt like a dark shadow was right behind us. The day we left I killed Hiawatha's ants with the bug spray and smashed their front doors down with a brick, cementing them in. I pulled up the marijuana plants and sunflower soldiers and ripped them to shreds. They were useless protectors. Mom stopped me from pulling up the rest of the flower beds and the house plants. I barked at her, "Why?" and she just rolled her puffy eyes. Steve the turkey farmer pulled me aside and reminded me of all the vows of bravery I had made the night before as I polished off his carton of ice cream.

"There has been enough damage done and Dorothy wouldn't do it."

Great, another guilt trip. Not only did I have to worry about the plight of Blacks and the Red Indian, I had to feel bad about destroying plant life.

I perched myself up on my mother's history books in the Volkswagen's passenger seat and waved goodbye to the neighbours as we putted down the street. Sad. Sad. Sad. I knew that the simple, safe part of my life was over. We passed the grapevine yards where we used to work every Sunday... Steve's turkey farm... and all the other farm fields, surrounded by green, green, green. Transition blues. I looked in the side view mirror and observed coldly as the Californian wind pushed a tear across my cheek then disappeared into my hair line, a salty stain left in its path. A slug leaving its trail, a snake leaving its print in the sand. I was so sick of crying. I counted to ten and breathed out. And then again like Mom taught me.

Yoga Master, on the other hand, looked perfectly composed and relaxed. As we drove along the thin, weaving road lined with redwood trees, I went through her purse. Outta the habit of copying my mother, I applied some lipstick and blush in the flip mirror on the back of the sun visor. I gawked into the reflection long and hard, thinkin' I could outstare my twin with an evil squint. Nobody can Clint Eastwood the looking glass though, so I flipped the visor up. Again, I went rummaging through my mom's purse.

"What are you looking for Jess?" The opened windows made it hard to hear. I noticed a plastic bottle of pills.

"What are these for?" I demanded.

"Aspirin for my headache."

The child-proof gadget wouldn't budge so I flung them back in her purse. I'd work on them later.

"How do you feel today?" I wanted to know if her ribs were sore. I wanted to know if she missed Leo.

"I'm as fit as a fiddle... Oh wow! Look at the way the redwood trees meet over the top of the road, it's like we're driving underneath a huge grape vine. Oh, and the little pockets of sunlight on the road."

"Mom, why did you name me Jesusa, it's not a very hippy name?"

"I think I was feelin' homesick - ah, wanted something real American - so I named you after this famous 19th century cowgirl I read about in my *How the Wild West Was Won* book. She was a showgirl from back East who came out West to escape her mean husband. She ended up running one of the biggest ranches in Nevada and everybody loved her. Will you pass me my lipstick outta my makeup bag, Jess?"

It was obvious she was gonna try to erase Leo and Santa Cruz from her mind.

"What was your daddy like?" I enquired before giving over the erect red nipple.

"OK, I'll give you a quick history lesson but I'm tired and we've got a looong journey." She snatched her lipstick. "Do you remember when we drove down to L.A. for his funeral?"

"Kinda, we drove in the snow with the top down covered in clothes... you couldn't keep your cigarette lit."

"Ya, the top wouldn't go up... there was like no-one else on the road and I couldn't see more than five feet in front of the car but we had to get down in time for Daddy's funeral."

"What did he die of again?"

"He had a heart attack." she said, too casually.

"How old was he?" Much more attentive than she.

"Daddy was only 52."

"There were all those war people in uniforms and that band playing and getting up on the little step and looking in the coffin to see his face. "I never saw that much make-up on anyone ever."

"I drank so much I threw up. Oh my God, how outta control... And you stuffed your tiny face with a whole table full of finger food. I thought we were both going to end with our heads down the toilet. What a time to find your favourite food..."

"Eggs Benedict. Oh Mom, you got me hungry now."

"And you met your cousins for the first time. We're gonna see them when we get to our new home."

"Get back to Grandpa."

"Well daddy was a war hero, he got shot twice in the head, so that's why it was a big funeral. Do you remember the American flag they draped over the coffin? You can have it when I die."

"Why did Grandpa have a heart attack?"

"He mixed the booze and pills. Oh, I love this song!"

I took a picture of her with the Polaroid camera that Steve gave me. There she was with her Bud Lite in one hand and her cigarette in the other. Miss Lackadaisical, lookin' like a teenager. She was practically steering the V.W. with her knee.

"You should keep both hands on the steering wheel, and you're only allowed three cancer sticks an hour!" I could barely hear myself over the roar of the little engine and the swirling wind, "Maybe you wanna die like grandpa but I don't wanna get black lungs."

She took another dramatic drag and turned up the radio. Before I could help myself I was singing along with her to Don McClean's *American Pie*. It was my favourite song back then. My dad sent it to me on an eight track cassette in the mail. He never sent me toys, just music and books and some money for my Mom.

The books he sent weren't exactly in the same league as *Where the Wild Things Are*. They were "How to" colouring books: *How to be a good daughter* or *Marxism for Very Beginners*. As I curled up sideways and rested my head on the shoulder of the passenger seat, I watched the sun rays shoot through the trees. I thought about my real dad, Max. "Max the Marxist" my Mom called him. He'll be glad Leo's outta the picture.

As I drifted off to sleep I thought of the time when my dad flew over for a visit in Santa Cruz about a year back. I could barely make out his eyes through his beard, caveman hairdo and bushy brows. Every grown up I encountered tried to look like Jesus or one of his disciples but my dad won the Jesus look-a-like contest hands down. Max was an atheist, a Marxist and an anarchist. After they forced me to go to bed everynight I could hear him politely arguing with Leo and his Black Panther friends about Vietnam stuff.

I remember Max sunbathing in the backyard with his Speedo's swimming trunks on. Leo was so jealous I thought his Afro would light up in flames. Leo actually went outside and yelled,

"Brother, what the hell you wearin'?"

Max showin' the contours of his penis was like breakin' the big rule of American macho man -*Don't show your dick.*

Next thing I know Leo's showin' Max his five guns, like he was showing how big his penis was. Leroy Brown was layin' some laws down in his mock friendly manner, you know, a can of beer and a few back slaps. Max's beady little green eyes popped so far outta his John Lennon glasses they started steamin' up. Leo insisted Max attempted some target practice shooting. Sammy Cat in arms, I studied him as he stood there in his Speedo's firing at a tin can.

Max hated guns and war and practically everything American - except for Cadillacs, milkshakes and blue cheese salad dressing. He told me that's why he didn't move to L.A. with us after I was born. He was scared of getting drafted in the Vietnam War. Version seventy eight of Mom and Dad history...

When I woke up I turned around to see the dog and cat were resting easy in the back seat. I checked the U-Haul trailer was still attached to our Volkswagen. Mom had given the animals some downers so they were zonked, tongues hanging out. I wanted to ride with the top down but we were packed to the brim.

"Where we goin'?" No answer. I tried counting telephone poles but they went by too fast. My neck jerked as my eyes snapped back and forth. My mood changed as we entered the freeway. Goodbye Santa Cruz, California. I knew we'd never see Hiawatha, Steve or the beach or the red rollercoaster or our street paved with gold. Put it behind you, little girl, like the telephone poles, clock it like the miles on the speedometer.

After I locked the car door, I pushed my head out the window and screamed the lyrics to *American Pie* . Air punched at my gaping hole. There I was mindin' my own business, wavin' my little hand in the backwash of air. All of a sudden a big bug hit me in the forehead.

"OH MY GOD, DID YOU SEE THAT, MOM?" I flipped the mirror visor down. There was a big red dent but no bug.

Our VW, Betsy, took a deep breath and began climbing the Sierra Nevada mountains. Sunset came and went. Landscape blistered and drooped. Mean ol' mountains so jagged with their scary faces and gorges, angry and bossy, flexing their muscles as if to say "You will not level me out, and put tunnels through my gut, motherfuckers!"

The freeway was coiling itself around a curvacious mountain. As Betsy crawled in first gear in the outer lane I peered over the cliff. Rows of ancient redwood, pine and oak trees reached to the sky for miles, hill after hill, valley after seemingly untouched valley.

A sign. Watch Out! Bears crossing the road!

"Mom, is this where we're moving to? Am I gonna be chased to school by bears?"

She gave me a clue.

"We're going to live in a valley, surrounded by mountains like these, it will be smog-free and sunny. It will never rain and you will have your very own pool to swim in."

That ruled out L.A.

Big ol' diesel trucks carrying Twinkies and Japanese cars zoomed passed us, tooting their fog horns, peeling their moronic eyes off the road to ogle my mother's golden blonde hair. Flirtatious as ever, Mom tipped her beer to them and they returned the salute. I stuck my tongue out at them and gave them the finger. They left us in the dust as we began our descent from the mountains. Mom let me do the gear change into second.

Once we were outta the dangerous crags, I rested my head in Mom's lap, like I always did with night-time driving. I liked the smell of Mommy, the soft jean cotton. I fell asleep to the cooing of Stevie Nicks. I don't know why Mom listened to her, it only made her blue.

I awoke to the sound of a woman's voice gargling from a speaker: "Good morning, can I help you?" McDonalds drive-thru.

"Mom, I want an Egg MacMuffin, hash browns, french fries, a chocolate shake and a Happy Meal with four packets of ketchup.

"You can't eat all that!"

"You wanna bet me five dollars?"

"Since when do you gamble?"

"What's gamble?"

She ignored me and gave our order to the brown sign.

I checked out the terrain. All I could see were cacti and fast food chains: Denny's, Burger King, Carl Jr's, Dairy Queen and a few stop lights. I yanked the sleep from my eyes and put Mom's sunglasses on.

"Is this where we're gonna live?"

Mom smirked as she lit her ritual morning cigarette.

"This is Bakersfield, honey, nobody lives here, it's just a place to get juiced up."

We all took care of our bodily needs and hit the road again. I looked between my feet and checked on my Mom's favourite fern. It was beginning to wilt. As soon as the speedometer clocked sixty, it slapped me. NEVADA HEAT.

"Mooooom, what's that?" I could barely swallow.

"What's what?"

The stabbing brown air choked my throat, as if I'd been hauled inside a blimp-sized blowdryer with the red button pushed for EXTRA HOT ACTION. Dog and Cat didn't know what hit them either. Blacky plunged his head out the window and his tongue wrapped around his head. Sammy was on his back with all four paws spread-eagled.

Mom burst out in hyperactive laughter. She was sweating like I never saw.

"That's just the heat, you're not used to the heat."

She bounced up and down hootin' like a cowgirl as she lit another joint. Prepared for the temperature change, she slung a bandana around her forehead and poured the rest of the ice from her McDonald cup over her head. I never saw anyone dump freezing cold ice on themselves. As usual I copied her, reachin' into the ice chest, scoopin' a cupful of melting slush. I sizzled in its short-lived waterfall. I was dry within seconds. Throat parched, I scrambled for the ice chest and gulped yet another can of coke. I threw a few cubes into the plant's soil and tossed one or two at the animals.

"Where we gonna live? In hell? What was that sign saying Death Valley... DEATH VALLEY!! Are we goin' to die in Death Valley? How could you do this to me?"

Mom kept pulling me further and further out into the waves. My inner thighs were stuck together. I felt dizzy...unwarrior-like. The only green was the backdrop on the destination signs. Apart from that just dirt. Ash. Fall out. Shrubs. No trees, just these sorry excuses called cacti. So evil and deathly. Enter at your own risk. Angular pointy arms crying out for a drop of water. A desert full of Medusas, snakes in their hair, turned to stone. *I wanna go home. I wanna go home. Toto take me home.* I passed out.

Within a few, sweat-drenched hours, I worked out from the green signs that we were headin' for a place called Las Vegas, not Death Valley. As I shifted in my seat I demanded "some history stuff". Being a history major, she was like a talking encyclopaedia.

"What does 'Las Vegas' mean?"

"It means 'The Meadows'. The Spanish explorers named it when they found it like two hundred years ago. Beneath Las Vegas is an underground lake, it's in a valley so in the winter, when the snow melts, the water trickles down to the valley and stays locked underneath the desert. The water saved their lives."

"Woopie doo..." I was not impressed with Mom's history lesson.

"Honey, you know this place is gonna be sooo much better than L.A. Lots of famous entertainers do shows like... Elvis... Frank Sinatra, Jerry Lewis, Sammy Davis Jr., Barbra Streisand, Diana Ross and Tom Jones... oh and Liberace, you're gonna love Liberace - he drives a pink Cadillac and plays a pink piano..."

These names meant nothing to me.

"Oh and Howard Hughes, the richest man in the world lives in Las Vegas!"

"Is he Jewish, Mom, like Woody Allen... I mean, could you marry him?"

My Mom turned me on to Woody Allen when we watched *Everything you Always Wanted to Know about Sex* . I fell in love when I saw that big boob coming over the hill.

"No! I'm not sure what he is... except for old and crazy... I think he might be Mormon. Anyways he's practically dead, he lives at the top a hotel and shoots pain killers into his groin."

"His what?"

"You know between the legs, those sacks between the dog's legs."

"In his balls ? Ewwwww!! you ain't marryin' him Mom. Ewwwww."

"Jess, you're so crude, stop askin' so many questions and turn that awful Don McClean song off, I'm soooo sick of it! We haven't got long to go now, just a couple more hours."

"At least the sun is starting to melt away. Mom you know what, the sun is a man and the moon is a woman."

"They're neither, they're just stars."

"No, everything is a girl or a boy. Just like this car is Betsy and that cancer stick is a Marlboro Man."

For most of the trip we just sat in the blowdryer silence, occasionally driftin' in and out of conversation. I liked the quietness of driving, just me and her and the drugged pets. After a few short hours, I stopped caring where we were headin', I could just drive like this forever.

Mom,
breathe in,
hold and count to ten and breath out for twenty,
and put it behind you.

SLEEPING INDIAN

I can still conjure my first Nevada sunset. We'd been overtakin' sky scrapin' billboards advertising motels and hotels for the past ten miles. In the middle of nowhere, sexy showgirls in diamond-studded bikinis made no sense.

"What's a buffet, Mom?" No answer.

"What's a Chicken Ranch? Is it like Steve's turkey farm?" No answer. I later learnt a chicken ranch was a whore house.

The car was overheating so we pulled over. As we waited for the engine to cool down so Mom could put water in the radiator, we stretched our sleeping legs. Blacky led the way, pissin' on as many tumbleweeds as he could. We squatted behind a real tall bush.

"Mom, what kind of cactus is this?"

"That's a real life Joshua tree, the only tree that grows in the Mojave desert."
The temperature had dropped about ten degrees. No more panting and sweating for the day. Sam was staring with disgust from outta the car window.

Within minutes the sun had set like a pot of gold. It was just like one of those airbrushed paintings Mexicans sold at the flea market back in Santa Cruz. Rising out of the base was not a rainbow but a bonfire. My tired eyes moved further up the gigantic sky. Waves of mountainous arches, silhouetted in purple cotton-ball clouds blanketing the sky for miles, were framed in an orange glow.

While hippy Mom poured water into the radiator, I scooped up a handful of warm dirt. It was smoother than Santa Cruz sand. There were so many little scrubs and plants. They were kinda ugly and pretty at the same time. Without warning Mom rushed up from behind and lifted me towards the fiery sky.

She stumbled a little and pulled me to her waist, fixing me there.

"Now that was a sunset!" She mellowed into her Woodstock sway.

"Ya, it ain't bad, not as good as a Santa Cruz sunset."

"That's a Nevada sunset. Half a billion years ago this was all underwater. Ahh! Look at those mountains. You see that one over there?" She pointed just left of the skyline, "I think they call that mountain The Sleeping Indian."

"Oh yah, it does look like one, his nose is just like Steve the turkey farmer."

What came next was silence. We musta looked like the front of a 70s Hallmark card, swaying in a mother-daughter moment without the awkwardness that would rear its ugly head in the next few years. As she rocked me from side to side, the skyline see-sawed. When my mother danced with me, all distrust left my body and I fell madly in love with her all over again.

The highway was black. The Big Dipper and the zillion stars headlighted the sky. We piled back into the car and Betsy sputtered on down the yellow brick road.

"You should try and stay awake to see the Las Vegas lights when we go over the final pass - they say it looks like a pile of diamonds on black velvet."

I was too worn out. Last thing I remember was another billboard glittering: Lady Luck. As I laid my head down on my Mom's lap, I asked my last innocent question,

"Who's Lady Luck?"

"She's you and me, Jessie."

Airplane. ✈

I'm trying to remember my first impression of planet Vegas. Everything seemed to be melting or dying. I was sure I had rabies. I developed facial contortions: grinding baby teeth; peeling the right side of my lip like Elvis and chewing on the inner cheek of my mouth to draw blood.

It wouldn't have been so bad if I lived above Sassy Sally's Saloon downtown where I could watch people get killed over gambling debts but I was marooned in between ticking time with only a sly digital clock on the microwave to remind me I was growing up.

Static, the evil sun made everything static in Vegas. Immobile. Too hot to play outside unless you stay in the pool but then you start to shrivel in the chlorine. The dead air was so suffocating it was like bein' squeezed outta real time - waiting for the NASA spaceship to take me back to civilisation, away from this weird ghost town.

Searching for nuclear mushroom clouds through pretend binoculars, my eye slits zoomed across the desert... there it was, the same as the day before, cooking away, steamy oil bubbling and shimmering in the distance like a Clint Eastwood movie. At midday, when the sun was its brightest, my eyes mistook mini tornadoes for a dusty warpath of Indians twirling tomahawks above their heads.

Five deadly species crawled around on the other side of Grandma's tinted sliding glass door, invisible to the human eye, hunting for food and death.

THE SADDEST SMOKER

Every Monday morning the whiskey crate arrives at 8:30. My job is to put it in the garage next to the trash compactor. At 8:40 I empty your ashtray in the den. With barbecue tongs, I pick up your snot rags that have been stuffed in the cracks of the couch cushions. I sprinkle carpet freshener and vacuum around the area you sit. No matter what latest product Mom buys, I can't budge the permanent stench of the stale smoke. Dirty, sloppy woman, what's wrong with you? The wrinkles in your face tell me nothing, they don't map together like your Swiss Alps puzzles on the coffee table. Each crevice splinters into another one giving no clues. I can't take my eyes off the loose, purply skin folded tightly around your chunky rings. Hiiiiii Grandma.

Las Vegas, the *Unforbidden Planet*. It should have been forbidden to human habitation, seein' how nuclear bombs were being exploded left, right and centre. Nothin' was forbidden in this town. Anything rode into town and very rarely did it leave, including us. We had landed safely in Grandma's surprisingly small three-bedroomed bungalow on the outskirts of town. Even though my mom's Mom was officially a millionairess, her concrete tent was crammed full of penny-pinching relics. Grandma was a travel agent and regularly went on cruises around the world at a discount price.

The shadowy house was rammed with ornaments, voodoo dolls, ceramic statues and cuckoo clocks that didn't work. Most of the slanting walls were plastered in mirrored squares with this turgid marble effect making the mirrors look like they were cracking. The only good thing about living with ol' Grandma was that we ate in the den on the coffee table in front of the huge TV and not underneath the dining room chandelier. To keep the temperature cool, every window was tinted, adding to the spooky atmosphere. I'd just seen Amityville Horror so, of course, I was convinced both house and grandma were possessed.

My Mom promised me a pool and I got one: an algae-infested, mossy swamp. You couldn't even see the bottom. Just to entertain my cat Sam I'd stick Grandma's declawed cat, Seymour, on the raft and push him to the centre of the pool in hopes the *Swamp Thing* would devour it. It never happened. Nothing ever happened except for the sunset... and grandma refilling her glass.

Grandma wouldn't let Sam in her house because he attacked Seymour the minute he got there. Soon after Sam lost all of his ambition. In Santa Cruz he killed mice by the dozen and even one of Hiawatha's chickens. But here he just slept all day. He had no desire to be king of the cats. Flies fed on the corners of his eyes. He had become so undignified, so cowardly lion, and not very sexy with his hair falling out.

Seymour was a 17-year-old Hollywood has been. My Mom said she was used in a few movies but it didn't wash with me. Teetering on four knotted paws, this old bag looked like an over-stretched balloon ready to burst. We never saw that fat cat travel more than five inches, a bit like her owner. But at least Seymour didn't drink and smoke.

It was still summer vacation and I knew zero kids. The only place I ever saw them was the store or the Mall. I called them the reptile kids cause their leathery skin was withered with sun spots and snakey tan lines. Every kid's hair was chlorine-and-sun-bleached. Soon I'd be a sun cancer kid too. My Las Vegas cousins were up in Seattle still visiting their dad. Mom was always gone working and going to summer school so she could be a teacher. Some nights I could hear her crying alone in her double bed, next door to mine.

I really had nothing to do apart from watch TV and do my chores. I didn't mind doing chores back in Santa Cruz cos we were perfecting our White House but this stucco tent was like a roadside mini-museum: cold, dark and tacky. I resented having to wipe up after my grandmother like she was some kind of queen. We had spoken maybe four sentences since we had moved in. She wasn't outwardly mean and, when she was drunk and listening to Irish songs, she even smiled sometimes. Our dislike for each other was unspoken.

Seymour was another one of my duties. Whereas Sam's living quarters were outside by the lawn chair, riddled with Black Widow eggs, Seymour's 'house' was stored under the Hollywood drinks trolley in the dining room. Wedged deeply in the plush two-inch carpet were the three components that made up Seymour's sad life: the waterbowl, the crusted food bowl and the litter tray. I had never seen a cat content to lie next to his own shit. I'd never seen a woman content to live in an indoor yard sale for that matter. Like her cat, Grandma had three obsessions - booze, cigarettes and escape.

Every weekday at 5:00 p.m. I hear your blue-rinse, battleship Cadillac pull into the driveway, interrupting my afternoon movie. You think you're an MGM studio star with your routine. First you turn up the air-conditioning and then you change into your night-gown-housecoat-momo thing and collect your drink. By the time you finally plonk yourself down on the brown couch with your glass of brown bourbon you're out of breath. At 5:15 p.m. you light up and down your first drink of the day. I think. You'll sit there for the next six hours, playing solitaire and watching Hollywood Squares, only moving to refill in the kitchen and discharge in the bathroom. We never say hello, just flash the fake smile we both copied from Bette Davis. You and I are TV partners. Whether we like it or not.

The only TV in the house slumped like an old marble grave stone underneath grandfather's war medals and sword mounted on the wall. Kennedy was assassinated on it and my grandfather died in front of it. The TV was the one object in the house I paid respect to. Along with Sam, he was my afternoon playmate. My love affair with black and white movies started with this TV. I preferred old movies to colour cos it was more soothing to be in the past. The movie stars charmed me into a glamorous adult world full of drama, winding roads and clean Beverly Hills ranches. A beginning, middle, and end with characters who were black and white, good or evil.

I remember one particular afternoon, during the last five minutes of *Baby Jane* with Bette Davis and Joan Crawford was hell. I could barely see her pasty face through the rising cigarette haze. It wafted over to me and crept up my nose, infecting me with her addictions. Grandma bit her nails like she hadn't eaten in days, gnarling away, unblinking, alternating ice cube crunch crunch with extra menthol cigarette drag drag. I turned the volume up as she sat there, legs apart hunched over, no longer sexual, chewing and spittin' ice back into the whiskey water. Her limp wrists and sunken neck said "I'm so tired of this world".

Oh there goes grandpas' sword flying off the wall, slicing through the thick air. How can you smoke a hundred cigarettes a day? How do you drink straight whiskey grandma? Why don't you go down town and drink with the slot machines like normal people your age do? How can you light up a cigarette before you eat and let it burn throughout? Well, go on, Bette Davis, drink yourself to death. As long as you pay me my allowance, I'll clear it up in the morning.

My concentration moved down to the ice cubes swimmin' in the tumbler. White knuckled, I watched the condensation trickle down the glass tumbler, soaking into the coaster. I thought of Howard Hughes injecting pain killers into his groin. Was he starin' at the same fancy whisky glass a few miles away in his Desert Inn penthouse? Rotten-toothed and bitter, bedsores eating away at his skin down to the bone of his shoulder blades.

After the movie ended, Grandma changed the channel over to *Hollywood Squares* as I went to refill her drink. It was another one of my chores.

"Not too many ice cubes please," Grandma called after me.

I tried to imitate the way Grandma walked outta the den, all rickety-legged and drunk. She was afraid of heights and the five-inch step scared her. I lifted my left foot a little and then put it back down. Lifted it again and put it back down. I held on to the walls for dear life, swaying in the orange carpet. Stopping every couple of feet to catch breath. When I got to the dining room I pretended to have a heart attack. I fell against her crappy dolly ornaments and finished on the floor, staring dead-eyed at the chandelier.

My nose crinkled as I struggled to pour from the gallon-sized whiskey bottle into the glass. The fumes were like my Mom's cleaning products. The weight of the bottle forced me to tip it too far and the whiskey overflowed from the counter, dribbling down the cabinet on to the rust-coloured linoleum floor. Dying to know why the brown liquid was so yummy, I held my nose and took a sip. While Blacky licked it up and I downed a glass of milk, I tried to piece Grandma's puzzle together.

After the war, Grandma and Pa worked together in the Technicolor department at Paramount painting film stills. They worked hard, saving up and planning the family.

The drinking started off casually at 1950s cocktail parties. Grandpa finally became a lawyer and made lots of money on some big case. The minute they got serious money, that's when things got bad. After he achieved what my dad called the "American Dream", he quit working altogether. Mom said she'd be leavin' for school in the morning and they'd still be passed out in the front room, with their dinner plates all over the coffee table. They never cleaned the house or did the grocery shopping. She was left to do everything.

When my Mom and her sisters became teenagers, their parents became affluent escape artists, travelling around the world. For a while they settled in Dublin, drinking guilt-free, all day in the pubs. I'm guessin' Dublin didn't cork their holes so they returned to L.A., the worst place to be if you're dyin' of thirst. Without knowing what war he was fighting or what side he was on, Grandpa finished himself off quickly. A true hero.

Grandma fled to Vegas, to blend into the escalators of jewelled, widowed women. Nobody would bother her in Vegas. She became a travel agent, an escape route expert helpin' other people do the same.

Imitating her alcholic hand-shake, I set the drink on the coffee table. From then on I decided Grandma was Baby Jane. The heroine and the villain. I invented all kinds of black and white tragedies from her past, so instead of plotting her death I tried to pity her.

I looked at her and thought if it takes all these daily addictions to get through life, what's the point. There we were, three mute generations of lonely hearts, all stuffing our mouths with pills, food, drink, cancer sticks and telephone receivers. I'd long since given up on *The Wizard of Oz*. It really was like that movie *Forbidden Planet* - each of us stranded prisoners being tortured by our own head monsters.

Airplane. ✈

The thought of the sun brings back bad memories, but each one lasts a millisecond and they all blend into one so it no longer feels like... They. Are. Mine. Like it might be a false TV memory. Same with the shit I'm writing - it reads like I got every single sentence off the goddamn TV.

O.K. I've had two lives; my real one, which seems banal. That's my second new word I've learnt on this flight. Anyways, this 'real' life I had back in Vegas was like a cartoon or soap opera of *Apple Pie* clichés.

My other TV life was lived vicariously through boob tube characters. I can pathetically map those years by listing the TV shows of my youth. Like when I think of *Little House on the Prairie* I remember my Mom's wedding and with *Cheers* I remember sneaking out the window during canned laughter and *Charlie's Angels* and *The Cosby Show*... the list goes on and on. So I was a TV kid, but that is the least of my complaints.

The girl sittin' next to me is fuckin' weird. She's buggin' the shit outta me, biting her nails and breathing too loud. I'm sure she's trying to read what I'm writing. I'm gonna punch her if she starts striking up a conversation. She's already asked me if I wanted my extra gin bottle. She's drinkin' like a fish... readin' some stupid book about the soul. She looks like a hippy cos she doesn't have any make-up on. I haven't seen a person without make-up on since the last time I flew to England.

She orders another drink so I ask for one too.

Memories could be kinda what make up your soul. Now, I don't give a shit about souls. I never gave them a second thought. I'm as soulless as a microwave. The first time I ever heard that word was when I was sitting in church and the priest was sending me to sleep. Even when I watched all the devil movies in the 70s, I figured the soul only had something to do with religion and I hate anything to do with religion.

On to the next goddam memory.

SUNDAY SCHOOL AND CHAMPAGNE BRUNCH

Aged 7.

My two favourite words this 1977 summer are bloody and bugger.

First of all, who wants to be sittin' in a classroom on Sunday morning reciting lies when the best cartoons were on? Secondly, I ain't slept for two days cos I've been scroungin' extra meals on a plane for twelve hours. I puked up over Kansas and had diarrhoea over the Grand Canyon and now I am BLOODY jet-lagged. After Sunday School I have to drag my flower-dressed butt through the courtyard and into the cute crappy church where my whole god-fearin' family will be bent over in a row sayin' sorry for wife-swapping' and skinny-dippin'.

My Mom's pretending she's Mrs Little House on The Prairie now or somethin'. She's always trying to give me the slip. Just when I think I got her pegged as a cross between Marilyn Monroe and Joni Mitchell, she decides she wants to be Saint Teresa. She was like this when I was born. I mean givin' me a name like Jesusa when my dad was an atheist. I'm surprised she hasn't gone Mormon on me. Miss Priss is trying to be a respectable Las Vegan by puttin' me into Catholic School, hopin' she might meet Michael Landon... I should inform the congregation that only a year ago a bunch of hippies were brewin' Angel Dust in our backyard.

If she's gonna send me to England every summer, she's gonna suffer like Christ on the cross for it. Little does she know, I'm a swearing punk rockin' atheist. And I'm gonna tell her as soon as I decide to speak to her again. For now I have to pretend I'm mad when all I really wanna do is jump up on her hip and beg her "never make me go away again". The truth is I had fun on my summer 'holiday' in England, but not enough to make up for the pain of missing her.

I can't believe I have to sit and listen to an hour sermon by some bald priest who's too scared to get naked and have sex. What gives the priest the right to get up there and tell me about abortion being murder. I AM NOT IN THE MOOD FOR THIS SHIT. All this when I can barely keep my eyes open. And I'm so hungry, the only thing I can look forward to is the tasteless sliver of wheat the priest sticks in my mouth smugly.

Up and down. Up and bloody down. Bloody Hallelujah, put another quarter in the basket, baby. Church is crazy, you don't get a moment's rest. O.K. Now we are down on our knees, praying head on hands, against the wooden pew and I'm falling asleep. Until my aunt tugs on my punk haircut. Now we are sitting again.

The reason why it's so important for me to be here this morning is because I have to get up in front of the church members and say why I want to go to their amazing school from Monday to Friday and pray all day and pay for it. I don't care if my cousins go to this school. They're brainwashed, uniform-wearing clones. They wear gold necklaces with crosses on them.

I have invented games to keep myself awake which include counting the different colours of congregation hair, how many old people, how many fat people, how many ugly people and then I imagine what they look like naked. I'm surprised I don't have to go to confession. She knows she would have a serious tantrum on her hands. The only reason I don't throw a tantrum about this church business at the airport is because I discovered we're going to Caesars Palace Great Champagne Buffet – Two For the Price of One.

Caesars Palace Champagne Brunch Buffet made Willie Wonka's Chocolate Factory look like a Salvation Army soup kitchen. All those cheesy sauces, burbling away for hours, greasy scrambled eggs, mashed, fried, scalloped potatoes, bacon strips and sausages, machines pumping out swirls of chocolate and vanilla pudding, strawberries and whipped cream, cherry cheesecake, Belgian waffles, toffee-custard pie, Eggs Benedict, rows of chocolate cupcakes stacked in pyramids. Centre stage in the buffet hall towered magnificent ice-sculpted statues of dolphins and unicorns and at their hooves, fruit salads overflowed from water and honeydew melon bowls. This was my house of God. Charlie's Angels waitresses draped in mini skirt togas slaving away for me. Not to mention countless giddy trips to the frothing champagne fountain where you can dip your glass below the spurting jets. I called it the Jacuzzi of Love Juice. I may not have liked the taste of grandma's whiskey but I acquired a taste for champagne. Plums, kiwis, grapes, cranberry juice, boysenberry syrup, strawberry mountains, blueberry hills, cinnamon valleys, imported apple trees and raisin muffins for the picking, jello umbrellas, banana boats sailing down the river of rootbeer floats. Shirley Temples, tangerine tarts and lemon sherbet...

I woke up when my mother passed me the basket. Before Aunt Erica yanked it from my hands I tried to guess how much money there was. The basket is hot potatoed around church three times in one hour. This church didn't even look like a church, more like a brand new school cafeteria or a concrete barn. There were no stained-glass windows or echoing bronchial coughs like you get in English cathedrals. It stank of newness. From the outside, it's just a Spanish-styled fort standing in the middle of the desert with a huge cement cross telling the airplane tourists that good church-goin' folks live in Vegas. We're not all gambling sinners, just hypocrites. The worst part of church was when you had to clasp hands with some Bob Hope look-alike stranger, raise locked hands in the air and then hug everyone, whispering "God Bless" with sincerity. Grind. Grind. Grind.

It's time. My Mom nudged me onto the stage altar. The microphone was lowered. Beneath heavy eyelids, my pupils widened as they raced from face to face. Culture shock. I'd been suffering from it since I moved to Vegas.

I'd been back and forth between England and America since I was 4, but now that I was 7 I noticed the "Vegas lopsided smile". We all know Americans smile bigger and brighter than any other nation, be it dentures or expensive caps, but these Vegas smiles stretched and strained from ear to shining ear. Unevenly. False.

Although English folks generally had yellow teeth, at least they possessed natural smiles which weren't lopsided and twitching. British smiles looked like the bricks from buildings they walked in and out of. What you saw was what you got - chipped, worn in and sensible, part of ticking time. In this church they look like they'd come straight off the golf course dressed in white cotton and yellow polyester culottes. Rows of lopsided curves smirked at me as if they were all in on some stupid secret, like they were waiting for pig's blood to drop on my head.

As my eyes skimmed across the sea of white, pink and yellow, I shouted in my best *Coronation Street* accent,

"I AM A BLOODY ATHEIST!"

I hightailed it down the centre aisle to dodge the choruses of oohs and aaaghs. I didn't care what they thought and to prove it I dipped my finger in the Holy Water, mock gesturing the sign of the cross and then bolted out the front door.

Now, this outburst sounds like some kind of false memory bullshit, but that particular summer my dad had totally brainwashed me into being a rebel. With all those Manchester prostest marches he dragged me on, I blame him for my revolt.

Outside, I did some rock hoppin' in the dirt driveway. I slid my Uncle Bruce's van door open and stretched out in the backseat. That was one good thing about church parking lots, you could leave the door unlocked. My mouth watered when I saw his mini-bar refrigerator. Bruce built a whole travelling bar with leather, swivelling stools and beer holders. Bruce was the mellow one out of our crazy family and that's cos he wasn't related, he was my aunt's second husband.

I got the key from underneath the fake fur dashboard cover. Nothing to drink but beer so I cracked one open, it couldn't be as bad as Grandma's whiskey juice.

Mom jerked the sliding door open, snagging her pinky nail on the latch. She had lipstick on her teeth. This was bad cos I couldn't take her seriously.

"What the hell was that?" She'd gone from hippy big sis to PTA wannabe.

"Is your nail O.K.?"

"Answer the question!" she demanded, shakin' her pinky.

"My dad is an atheist. Why can't I be? All his friends laugh at me cos I believe in God and they tell me how stupid Americans are. What do you expect if you send me away to live with a bunch of Communists."

"Don't raise your voice to me, little girl. Who the hell do you think you are? You had no right to embarrass me!" Tears swelled in her eyes. "Now there is no way you can get into Catholic private school" she whined.

Another one of those Vegas silences filtered through the van as she tore the rest of her painted nail from the fresh white skin.

"You don't have to always try and be bad on purpose, I'm only trying to give you a decent education. If you go to Paul Sage, you'll be surrounded by trash."

"Mom, the priest didn't want me anyway. We don't have enough money, that's all they're interested in. Your bloody money."

"Do you want your mouth washed out with soap, young lady?" Her threats were never scary. But still all I wanted was to keep punishing her for sending me to England.

"I hope it's strawberry flavoured and not lemon" I squealed back.

She cuffed me across the head as gently as humanely possible. I blocked her and flailed my arms in retaliation, accidentally knocking her in the eye.

"You're going to get restricted again, young lady, if you don't watch that sewer mouth. Jesus, Jesusa, you wonder why I have to send you away, you're too much to handle. You don't listen to me." She lit a cigarette and took a few yoga breaths.

"It doesn't matter what your dad believes in, it's what you believe in... and it's clear you don't believe in respect. You went to a Catholic school in Santa Cruz, you even played Mary in the Christmas play, you loved receiving First Communion and now you don't believe in God! I give up!" She said it all the time.

"We should be spending our money on findin' a house of our own. You know I hate living with Grandma."

"Grandma is gonna be gone for the next two months on that cruise."

I'd forgotten that she was sailing around the world with her new boyfriend.

"These church people are a bunch of bloody hypocrites, Mom."

"Ooh, big words for someone who does so bad at school. What's with 'bloody', is that all you learnt over in England?"

We stopped arguing when the rest of the clan climbed into the van, glowin' beneath their polished halos. Uncle Bruce winked as he spotted the empty beer can under his swivel chair. He took it, flattened it with his rubber flip flop and tossed it in his crushed can recycling bag. He then cracked open a few beers for the adults.

Bruce whispered in my ear, "I hate church, too, but for one hour a week it keeps the wife quiet".

"Bloody hypocrites" I said underneath my breath. Lucky for me the grown ups smoked a joint on the way downtown so Mom was a chilled-out hippy again.

My freshly acquainted cousins Kat and Dona were baggin' on my new hair cut, and pretending to be mad at me for dissin' their church.

"You're gonna go to hell, Jesusa!" Kat sniggered, half serious, half not giving a shit.

"I'm already in hell." I rested my untanned cheek against the cool-tinted bubble window. Hello, brown home.

Once we piled out of the van, our oddball family unit worked up a trail of sweat trudging in and out of cars and campers melting in the mile-long parking lot. Oblivious to her appetite, my Mom launched into another lecture, this time slurring her words with stoner gaps. Stoner gaps were what you get when you've smoked too much weed. The brain slows down. I held her bag as she applied her lipstick and tugged on the seam of her shorts like a teenage hitchhiker.

"To be honest I don't like going to church either but it's a way for the family to come together. You know... It's like... It's like the yoga breathing technique I taught you. It's a way of meditating, switching off... It's a form of release, honey. Where people can go and sit still, switch off from the noisy world outside and be grateful for what they have. Where people are reminded of what's important in life, like being loving and understanding, to forgive and do good things for other people."

Normally I would have said, "You're such a pothead!" but I kept my mouth shut. As she rambled on I thought, I can't believe we go to this casino every Sunday and she doesn't ever get dressed up. How in hell is she gonna find a rich man in hot pants, thongs and a boob tube?

What I was really worried about was her pining for these average truck driver types like Denny. She tried to sell me on him cos he planted flowers in the desert for a living and liked backpacking. But he didn't come round no more after I kicked him in the balls. I managed to scare away every low-life guy who pulled into the driveway with his pool cleaning techniques. It was the same every summer but I'd soon shoo away any seasonal sniffers with long-term designs on my mother. I wasn't going to take any risks after Leo. I was still in charge.

As we each opened an automatic door to Caesars Palace, the best hotel casino in the world, I toked on a deep breath of money and musty air. Cool goose pimples shot through my body. We had left the heat and entered the refrigerator. It was a well known fact cold temperatures kept customers table-hopping and handle-pulling. It would keep us eating. Up the escalators to the buffet rooms. We took our places in the zigzagging line cordoned off by gold tasselled ropes and mini Roman pillars.

My Catholic cousins wouldn't talk to me at first in the buffet line.

"I'm sorry, I do believe in God, I was just joking," I blurted out.

My Aunt Erica turned on me. A blur of diamond and cigarette ash scraped against my face, leaving a scratch. I added her to my list of screwed up grown-ups.

"Jessie, will you shut up for once. You always have to be the centre of attention. You're such a spoilt brat. I'm sure you were dropped on the head when you were a baby."

She was always calling me a spoilt brat. I heard it so many times I thought, fuck it, that's what I'll be.

TOMORROW THE DIET
TODAY THE GREAT BUFFET

That's what it said on Aunt Erica's t-shirt.

So anyways I'm standin' there, rubbin' my thighs together in anticipation with a torn palm tree held up against my face to sooth the scratch. It was like waiting for the best ride at Disneyland. What I love most about buffets is that once you're in, you can start eating before you even sit down. None of that "What can I get for you today". It's all you can eat, for $3.99, help-yourself-buddy service. At Circus Circus, you could get a whole buffet breakfast for $0.99 but the food was nasty and cold.

Us kids got our own table so we could spread and organize our numerous plates, drinks and stacked trays. We paced the pigging out, breaking for a game of Ring around the Roses, circling the well-endowed, plaster, Roman gods pillared between waterfalls. We'd get so full our bellies bulged over our bathing suit bottoms. If we were too full to move, we unbuttoned our Ditto's and played electronic Bingo. On the wall there was a big screen and each table had its own cards. Of course, if we won, us kids couldn't cash in.

The grown-ups sat at the opposite table, hollering and hooting over racist jokes and mortgages. The moms would have their white purses in their laps stowing food in Tupperware. Roast beef for the dog, smoked salmon for the cat and cookies for the kids' packed lunches.

Our family adopted this buffet style of eating at every home gathering we had. Christmas, Thanksgiving and birthdays we'd just lay out buffets on the table and stand around, eating continuously all day long in between swims. We never sat down around the table like my family did in England. If we did, it would mean we'd have to converse for more than one minute and that was too much like hard work.

After the Champagne Brunch Buffet, me and my cousins were always instructed to wait outside the casino area while the grown-ups gambled. Sometimes we'd sneak into the pool but they could tell we were local hillbillies by our sun-spotted tans, so we'd get thrown out. Us kids weren't allowed to be near the slot machines so we had to either wait in the van or sit out on the kerb or we could walk to Circus Circus, but by that time we just wanted to lie down somewhere cool. All we wanted was some TV, maybe a game of Operation, or Monopoly and then a game of Marco Polo in the pool.

On this Sunday we played hide-and-go-seek. I never liked playin' when I was 'It' so I gave up and wandered in and out of the slot machines, spying on lounge shows. When I was really starved for attention, I'd inch up to a slot machine or a table and wait to be told to move along by a security guard.

Sometimes I'd hang out at the bathroom entrance watching all the rich women swan by in sparklin' floor-length gowns, kinda hopin' that I might run into Howard Hughes. I never saw anyone famous, just mean lookin', baby-blue-suited Mafia types, giving signals with their ringed fingers cupped suspiciously over their groins. It was like watching a baseball game. Plain-clothed security men stuck to their bases ready for any fast or foul balls.

It always felt like something important was about to happen. It was all so James Bond, like these men were passing secret messages across the room on how the world was going to be blown up. The Mafia dudes frowning and gold penning codes on pads of paper, the hidden cameras, the quick flick of the dealers' hands. These people took gambling so seriously - casinos are kinda like churches. Lavish temples of faith and praying, buckets of change being passed around, so far removed from ordinary nine-to-five life. Gamblers throwing their hands up towards the ceiling for guidance and the only guidance they're getting is surveillance cameras.

In spite of the heavy atmosphere, Caesars Palace was my favourite casino cos it was the classiest and had the richest people. These folks were so different from the locals you ran into at Sassy Sally's on Fremount Street.

Sometimes I'd get a little blue walking around those casinos. Envy would get the best of me. My life seemed so small compared to all this action that took place just a few miles from Grandma's house.

No-one in our family had any class. I mean come on, they wobbled around in cut-off shorts and tank tops saying, "I stop for all Buffets", talking about sales, bills, down payments, content to work at the same job all their lives, planning vacations, road rallies and Christmas presents. This was supposed to be the city where people came to build their dreams out of one pay cheque, swarming here in Hondas and Winnebagos, their entire belongings beneath the ice chest of Coors and soggy grapes. People like me and my Mom, escaping from monster men in some mid-western town. It's like when all them starving folks headed out in the gold rush days... all thinking Lady Luck would change their lives and then they end up just making do.

After I snapped out of my jet-lag daydream, I headed over to the marble shopping land next to the brass elevators. My cousins found me in the Walt Disney shop staring at fake signed autographs of Judy Garland and Betty Boop. They snuck up behind and pinched my butt.

"Stop day dreamin', Jesusa."

I'm led yawning over the slippery floor. In the gift shop, we played with the plastic-bubbled tarantulas encased in sand dunes. Through the windows we watched the rich ladies trying on fur coats, LAS VEGAS jackets and the sequinned tennis shoes like the local peasants.

When we finally found our birth givers, my Mom was moronically sticking nickels into the slot machines. Uncle Bruce was flirting with the cocktail waitress as he ordered more free drinks. I went to my Mom and forced myself to mumble an apology. As a security man rushed us I asked her to carry me to the van.

"You're too big."

"Are you still mad at me, Mom? I'm soooo tired. I wasn't thinking right."

"You really don't want to go to Catholic school?"

"No, I can't explain very well, but trust me, Mom, when I get in that church I feel like Megan from *The Exorcist,* I feel possessed. I think I might kill someone if I go to Catholic school. "

"OK, but look, you have to get a normal hair cut."

"Mom, can I have one of those cookies in your bag?"

On the way back to my aunt's house, my mom let me put my head in her lap. All I wanted to do was watch Monthy Python on Uncle Bruce's raft as the pool shadowed over.

CHARM SCHOOL

I already knew everything there was to know about being charming at the age of 8, but I was curious to see what they did at "Charm School".

There are two kinds of charming chicks. The ones who act smart like Katherine Hepburn and Bette Davis; and the ones who act stupid and innocent like Marilyn Monroe and Shirley Temple. To charm someone you have to know what that person wants to hear and what their tastes are. You can usually work it out by the shoes a person wears or the type of haircut. The only rule is you have to coldly study the person you're trying to charm. Pick on weakness. Sometimes you act precocious, sometimes you act retarded, it all depends on what sucker you're dealing with.

I said O.K. to Charm School only because my cousins Kat and Dona were forced to go and we could cruise around town on our skateboards without having a babysitter monitoring our eating. WE were the "Ditto Butt Angels". Ditto jeans were all the rage cos they had a fake pocket at the front to rest your hand as you yelled at your mother. From the top of our heart-shaped bubble butts ran a big M seam all the way down to the bell-bottoms. Because our Dittos were so tight, our flowering sex was split in half in a W shape.

Me and my cousins became almost like sisters watching *How to Marry a Millionaire* and *The Story of O* over and over again at their house. They'd moved to Vegas a year before I did and they had a big TV out by the pool. We fought whenever the three of us got together. Me and Dona swapped the slave role. Kat was 10; Dona was 9; I was 8.

Being the oldest, Kat never got picked on. We made up plays and charged kids in the neighbourhood to see them. Sometimes we'd put on our own version of the *Gong Show*. The plays were just re-enactments of various *Charlie's Angels* episodes. No matter what, Kat always got to play Farrah, I was Kelly and poor Dona was Sabrina. Nobody ever wanted to be Sabrina. Nobody wanted to be the smartest one, just the prettiest.

I'd never seduced a man, so if Charm School could teach me a bit more about sex, I figured it would be time well spent.

I wanted to learn how to:
silence a room with my entrance
get my revenge on a cheating man
be a "10" like Bo Derek
smoke like Rita Hayworth
marry a millionaire
end up in Hollywood
cause a car crash with a wiggle
arch one eyebrow
throw up and get gifts
win friends and influence people
charm snakes and scorpions

Instead they taught us how to:
set the table and bake a cake
select a bra size and wax bikini lines
paint a French manicure and walk with a book on our head
cheerlead and dress dolls
be a good sport and make small talk
set and curl our hair
say please and thank you and control our PMT moods
make our own vanity table out of cardboard boxes
sew a hooknail seam
apply make-up so it looks like you have none on

...all the things I hated most about being female.

So us girls made a pact to:
not wear underwear and sit with our legs wide apart
let air come out whenever and wherever we wanted
wear a ton of make-up like a prostitute
to skateboard and get scars all over our legs and pick them for weeks storing them in our scab box

to wear sooo tight jeans we couldn't have babies
to be rude and crude and gutter-mouthed
to say "Fuck that for a bowl of Cheerios" when the prissy Mormon teacher told us, "This is how a girl should act".

It was fucked up cause we were watchin' stuff like *Wonder Woman* and *Bionic Woman*, thinking that's what we had to look like and act like in order to have adventure. Pretty much like *Charlie's Angels*, they were the role models of the day, them and the Dallas Cowboy cheerleaders.

O.K., so Charm School sucked big donkey dicks! But the concrete Mormon temple had excellent shaded ramps and smooth, crackless hallways to coast over. There was nothin' worse than sailing full speed ahead down the street and, because of one lousy desert rock, wipin' out. After Charm School we'd hang out with all these skate boys, practising stunts for hours.

I was famous for my Farrah Fawcett hair flip trick. You had to have a long smooth runway for this one, at least a hundred yards of fresh cement. After lipgloss touch-up, you start low, butt on heels, like she does on that one episode when she's chasing the bad guys. Then slowly rise to surf position. Pull the vent brush from your Chemin de Fers. Toss head upside down, brushing the hair from the base to gather lots of volume. As you flip the hair back, do a half-turn so that you're skating backwards. You end with a cheesy Farrah grin and puffy hair-do and the boys go wild. That's charm.

We met every Monday after our separate schools had finished at the end of my street. Brand new Vans, board in arm, comb in the back pocket, bangs feathered with just the right amount of hairspray and blue eye shadow and two bucks to play Pac Man at Smith Food King after Charm School.

On the second Monday, we had to decorate a shoe box so "we could have our own personal Beauty Box to keep under our pillows". We had to make sure all the "essential ingredients" were in our Beauty Box like needle and thread, comb, lip gloss, lotion, tampons, clear nail polish, deodorant, baby powder, travel toothbrush and paste, pencil, diary and band-aids. I made my box into a cat with a few tampon applicators, cotton balls and toothpicks for whiskers. It looked like shit but I didn't care cos it was going in the garbage as soon as I got out of there.

After I started making money, I was really O.K. with the Charm School deal. Every year it was the same. When I got back from England I was full of Max quotes... atheist this, Communist that, but I was the biggest hypocrite of all them church goers, being the little capitalist I was. All the Charm School Mormon nerds paid me a dollar to curl and set their stringy locks. My hair had finally grown out of the spiky, punk rock look and was like a Santa Cruz wave. A mixture of Kelly and Farrah, curled but not too curled and highlighted just enough to look unnatural. They loved my hair and wanted to know my secret. Like any American, they paid for it.

Our final project for the term was to create something that "best represents the qualities and assets we acquired from the six week course". We were just going to do a skate board show or a *Charlie's Angels* play, but we didn't think it would be shocking enough for our self-righteous, Mormon teacher.

I decided I hated Mormons more than I hated Catholics. They all came from Utah originally and, before it was outlawed, the men were encouraged to have as many wives as they wanted to boost the population. The women couldn't even drink Diet Coke and had to have like ten kids each. On Sundays they sat in church all day long. Uncle Bruce informed me the Mormons got money from the Mafia and Howard Hughes in the old days. There were 1000's of Mormons workin' in the casino's makin' good money outta sin! What hypocrites.

I'd had enough of this woman telling us to be "lady like". We decided to do a disco dance to the hit song *More, More, More* , dressed up like prostitutes, throwing Monopoly money around the stage in the cafeteria. After rehearsing every day for a week, we stole some polyester evening gowns, gold stringy belts and stilettos out of our mothers' closets. We did the show and the girls in the class loved it, but the adults were freakin' out. Our moms weren't upset about us dressing up as whores, it was that we were wearing their best casino clothes.

As we snuck out the back door, Dona-Sabrina goes,

"I told you we should have done *Lucy in the Sky with Diamonds."*

"We gotta get back home as soon as we can," called Kat Farrah as she pulled her mom's high heels off and jumped on her skateboard.

"Ya, we'll hang the clothes up and plead ignorance and, if that doesn't work, we'll just accuse them of hallucinating from all the weed they smoke."

So we started riding as fast as we could, swooping in and outta road kill on the newly spread pavement.

"Come on Sabrina, come on Kelly, faster!" I shouted out.

Kat growled as she overtook me,

"Don't be callin' me Kelly, I'm Farrah!"

I was a little over-excited about bein' on a life-or-death mission for once in my sorry life. Assigned to rearview, I kept an eye out for my Aunt Erica's Pinto. Due to the lack of roads on the outskirts of town the hippy moms would surely be taking the same route.

On my twentieth head turn, the skateboard hit a crack. My body propelled five feet through the air like the Bionic Woman. Unlike my heroine would do, I smacked into a parked camper van. As the skateboard rolled on, I impaled my stomach on a nail sticking outta the side of the camper. The rusty nail sliced through the flesh as I slid to the ground, leaving a four-inch gash more impressive than Megan's "Help me" stomach carvings. My skateboard flipped over and came to a halt in the middle of the road – it had gone right under the camper and out the other side.

Kat and Dona slammed on their breaks, turned around and boarded back to gawk. Hands on hips, shakin' their heads, the two sisters chomped on their gum in disbelief. I'd never bailed like that in my life, but far worse I had torn my mom's new disco dress. The cut didn't hurt much but I never saw so much blood. It was like I'd just given birth. I felt strangely proud and fascinated, lifting my head off the ground to get a peek inside the wound. Like a true tomboy I laughed and attempted a joke to suppress the tears,

"I let Charlie down". Farrah would never have bitten the dust. I was destined to play Sabrina forever.

The PTA buffet-stealing mothers were heading right for us like two sharks high on the scent of blood. Busted. Cigarettes flailing, they jumped out of the car and cleared their throats for an onslaught of bitchin'. I was dreadin' the sting of my aunt's diamond-clad hand but, when my mother saw me lying there looking like I was in the middle of surgery, she rushed up to me full of concern. I was carted off to the hospital for a tetanus shot and stitches. The attention was well worth the lifelong scar.

We didn't get yelled at, at all. Afterwards when we all were sitting in Carl Jr's the adults couldn't help laughing when they reminded us of how we "Ditto Butt Angels" looked skating down the street in their off-the-shoulder dresses. We got put on restriction for a week and my board was taken away. We didn't care though, cos we were all excited about these skating sandals we ordered - they had wheels that popped in and out for when you wanted to skate or just walk.

That night my Mom let me sleep in her bed. As we lay there with our small bowls of ice cream watching *Cagney and Lacey*, I told her it wasn't right what those Mormons were teaching us at Charm School.

"They're trying to turn us into Mormons, Mom."

"Mormons aren't as bad as you think."

"Mom, the women are slaves. Why do men get to rule everything? Why do they always get to be the boss? It's like when I used to go skateboarding - they always get to go first at everything."

"Yah, but it's all changing - look at *Cagney and Lacey*."

"Well, Charm School's bullshit-training for how to be a wife-slave."

"Jesusa, one day you will be a wife-slave."

I skateboarded a little after that, but I never went fast, I stopped doing the stunts. I became a sideline girl posing in pussy pants, just watching the boys.

Airplane. ✈

I'm on my fifth gin and tonic... still goin' around in blame U-turns. What use is it scratching at a scab to re-open it over and over again? Except that I've got all this anger - I feel like jumping outta this plane right now or beatin' the shit out this girl sitting next to me. I don't want that feeling anymore, it makes me too tired.

I reckon the girl next to me is a few years older than myself - maybe a college student. She's in black and I'm in pink. Her hair is flat, mine is puffy.

"Do you want another drink?"

"Uhh wha... ya... ya, um. a gin and tonic please." I try to be as monotone as possible.

"Can we have four double gin and tonics, please. Thanks. So is it a visit or do you live in England?" She reminds me of a fly. Her voice is squeaky and nervy.

"Um, my dad - I'm gonna stay with my dad for a while in Manchester." She passes me my drinks and peanuts. I don't want to encourage a conversation so I start writing again.

"Whatcha writing?" She opens a bottle of pills and swallows a few with her drink.

"Um, it's a letter to my Mom." I hunch over my journal as if she might grab it outta my hands.

"Nice or mean?" She is slightly cross-eyed. Her smile is crooked.

"It's personal."

CANNED FOOD CAPITALIST

Aged 9.

"O.K., O.K., jeeeez, get over Charles Manson. God, you're a weird kid... I don't know, maybe it was growin' up in L.A., like I said. People with money get all screwed up. You remember what I told you about my mom and dad. I don't give a damn about money. I mean we're poor right now but I feel so... liberated and you know I'm goin' to school and I'll be able to get a job teachin' and I'll be able to pay Grandma back and we'll be fine. Just you and me... and Lady Luck."

"But Mom, you should have found a rich man for my sake. You have to learn to sacrifice like Jesus did."

She raises her eyebrow at me.

"I tried going out with rich guys but in L.A. they're all weird. This Rolling Stone photographer stopped me in the grocery store one time and asked if you and I wanted to be featured in a spread called "baby-boomer hippy chick and baby". I agreed and eventually I started hangin' out with this hip Jewish guy. His name was Ralf, or Raff, I think. He reminded me of Woody Allen."

"We love Woody Allen."

"No, you love him. Anyways, he came from the best family in the city. But he did a lot of drugs and... you know, I had you to take care of... and this guy was talking marriage proposals."

"Mom, he would have been perfect, then we'd be livin' in Beverly Hills right now."

"I blew that set-up the first and only time I met his parents. A Jewish girl was what they wanted, not a Catholic. He lived in a mansion in the seeerious hills of Beverly Hills. Before we got there, he gave me a pill. So we got to the mansion and I started walking down these marble stairs that were like a mile long. About half-way down I saw all the glamorous-lookin' people sipping Martinis, just staring in my direction. All of a sudden, I felt dizzy and like completely stoned and the next thing I know I'm rolling down the stairs, laughing and crying. Somehow I wasn't hurt but I could not stop laughing at all these faces leaning over me. I took off my heels and hightailed it out of there. I never heard from him again."

"Wow!"

"Thing is, I think he gave me that pill to trip me out on purpose, so they could all laugh at me. Rich people have a mean sense of humour."

OK, so rich people were assholes, but I still wanted to be one. Poor people were assholes too, who had the better deal? I used to love it when she talked about Beverly Hills. She never wanted to, but I always sucked it outta her.

Her childhood sounded so cool compared to mine. She would go to the beach every day and watch her boyfriend surf, she crashed cars into walls and laughed, threw parties when her parents were taking a cruise around Egypt and had the maid clean it up the next day.

The funniest stories were about her fat days. At 14, she was Big Bertha. On the way home from school, as she was passing Lucille Ball's house, she had to steal a palm tree leaf and put it between her legs to stop them from bleeding. Her inner thighs were rubbing that hard. She decided that was the final straw. The fancy Beverly Hills doctor prescribed the same diet pills Judy Garland got addicted to. By her fifteenth birthday she was Bridget Bardot with a little pill habit.

Somehow time started tickin' on the microwave clock. Grandma helped me and my mom find our own escape route, probably because she was so sick of seein' me snarling at her everyday. She bought another Vegas house and we paid her rent on it.

Mom was still working two jobs. During the day she taught history at Desert Rose High, telling tales of far-off places and years, in the evening she sold underwear at Mervyn's Department Store. Santa Cruz ferns hung everywhere in our medium-sized yellow home. We wallpapered and made a coffee table out of Mom's encyclopaedia case.

Although it was nothin' fancy, I loved our new house. I would've lived in a motel next to prostitutes if it meant I could watch TV on my own. We had a pool and a nice view of Sleeping Indian mountain out back. I had Mom all to myself. No more noises in the night.

When the sun reared its ugly head, it was a different story. Every morning I awoke to the sound of tractors and churning concrete machines. I'd look out my dusty window to see tanned, bare-backed men building houses. Those hunky guys were my alarm clock for years. It happened all over town. Houses just grew like weeds around flowers. One day you'd drive by a house all on its own and then six weeks later some developer would come in and put up a hundred identical to the first.

I thought about money a lot, probably more than a kid should. The Levis and Nikes I wanted were getting more expensive and the styles were always changing. Mom had me hooked on Clinique makeup so that all added up.

I looked at dust blowing into our pool and all over our deck chairs, and brainstormed. With my favourite magic markers I made some flyers and put them in the neighbours' postboxes.

I managed to get ten regulars. I charged ten bucks a job – that included mowing, weed eating and pool cleaning, minus the chemical treatments. Usually, this mostly white neighbourhood employed cheap labour, Mexican immigrants to do their yards. But I was even cheaper and more pleasant to look at through their sliding glass windows, I guess. I figured they'd rather give money to their own, that's what kind of people were multiplying in Vegas.

I didn't like them as much as Steve the turkey farmer or Hiawatha the watermelon mama. Just like the crooked Vegas smiles, small talk always seemed false and constipated. These grown-ups never had anything soulful to tell me, if they did, they didn't know how to get it out of their mouths. They were all like my grandma, tongue-tied and tight-assed. They used to explain just how they liked their cars shined and what kind of wax to use, the kind of mower stripes they liked on their lawns, how long they liked the grass and how they wanted the pool hose hung on the concrete wall in the garage. The neighbourhood was quiet and clean, nobody sat on their porches or had barbecues in their front yards. Any activity was kept in their neat little turfs of land. They gossiped and called 911 if it looked like their neighbour's tree was dropping leaves into their pool.

Even though I made money, I was sweating boredom buckets. Mom was always working or very tired so I used to watch a lot of TV on my own, about eight hours a day. I only saw my cousins at the weekends cos they lived on the other side of town, but even then we'd spend most of our time watching the boob tube in our boob tubes. Sometimes we'd get dropped off at the mall and I'd buy a jersey with my name on it or some Ditto jeans, some new Vans or Nikes or some new wheels for my skates. We would play pool games or go to the movies, ride our bikes and skateboards, watch the dirtbikers in the desert, but I remember thinking that all us kids were stranded out there in the middle of the desert miles away from real civilisation.

Even though the weekends were O.K., when Sunday night came, I was an only child again. From the minute I got home from school till bedtime I snacked every fifteen minutes. Mom could see I was bored and I was putting on weight.

I tried to keep myself entertained. I invented new microwave recipes. I'd bake cakes, Sammy Cat soufflés and meatloafs. When I was feeling really lifeless, I'd eat the cakemix and cookie dough raw, straight from the bowl. Spooning it in even when I felt like I was going to explode. After *Three's Company* I'd dress up in my Mom's clothes and high heels and blast through my list of chores. I'd run in and out of different rooms with my magical vacuum, turning on all the TVs and radios, talking to the plants and giving the cat a heart attack. I'd end up lyin' on the floor staring at the carpet wondering how it was made.

Something was wrong - the sun, or the nuclear energy, or the neon lights - some substance or chemical was making everything static. Whatever I touched gave me an electrical shock. I wanted to go outside and plant flowers or pick fruit but the only thing you could pick in Vegas was the tumble weeds out of the pool or coins off casino floors. Everything was either dead-looking or fluorescent.

Mom had a whim to be a good mom. She resigned herself to getting me out of my boredom doldrums. I told her that I wanted to learn to play the guitar and sing like Janis Joplin, so she called up a music store and they told her it was a good idea to start a 9-year-old out on an accordion first, because it got the child used to working both hands. I hated accordion lessons. It was like having a crate of Grandma's whiskey strapped to my waist. My mom said it was too expensive to buy a child's accordion so we bought a grown-up one from a yard sale. Everyone laughed at me, even the teacher, even my Mom, especially my cousins.

I wished I had never told my Mom I was bored. To show me she really cared, Mom enrolled me in Girl Scouts. Now I wasn't bored – I was depressed. I was a nerd, a real nerd. Every week we had to go pick up garbage along the freeway, in an effort to "Keep Las Vegas Clean".

How boring was it standing outside Smiths Food King selling Girl Scout cookies in 110 degree heat? I'd end up buying them all myself and stuffing them into my mouth in the desert as I watched the shirtless construction workers moving against the sunset and mountains. I was so ashamed wearing that green uniform with crap badges all over it. My accordion teacher was entering me in contests. My life was hell.

One good lesson I did pick up from the Scouts was how to be a canned food capitalist. I used to ring the rich-looking door bells in my little outfit and cutely ask if they had any spare canned food for the homeless and they brought a bag full. Rich people had the best brands: Chef Boyardee Ravioli, Kraft Macaroni and Cheese, Betty Crocker Vanilla Pudding and more.

I decided me and Mom could save money if I got cans for our household. I was "eating us out of house and home," as my Mom would say. I could never make the food last. And all the extra money I was making so I could buy my Chemin de Fer and Ditto jeans was goin' down the tube because I kept poppin' outta every pair of jeans. In order to put my jeans on, I had to lie on the bed and pull the zip up with a coat hanger.

So I was BORED! It was the first thing I said in the morning when my Mom stuck a vitamin under my nose. It was the first thing I said when my dad called from England. All the kids on my street were pretty much in the same boat as me. Our parents were doin' two jobs or they worked nights and slept all day. And what for? So they could buy that second car or house, or boat or build that pool. Meanwhile we didn't get shit for attention. We were just another piece of property. Whoops! There I go again playin' victim.

"Mom, why do people have babies?"

"Oh, I don't know, I didn't really plan it, I mean we wanted you but you know me, I don't ever plan things too much."

I thought people had babies on the spur of the moment because they were bored with their lives. I recall thinking there has got to be more to life then just making a living and spending it on trying to cure boredom. I'm sure we would have been better in L.A., or Santa Cruz or San Francisco, anywhere but "The Meadows".

JAMES SPRINKLER-HEAD

I was so glad I didn't have to go to Catholic school but public school was a real eye-opener. American public schools were the opposite to English public schools. The bottom of the barrel.

Walkin' home from school used to be like goin' through a battle field. There were fights on people's front lawns and dog attacks all the time. I had my first fight on my second day. Debbie Douglas cornered me against a wall a few blocks from school. I just stood there with my mouth open until she grabbed my luscious hair.

I wanted to say, "Please, anything but my hair". But I was too damn hot. The next thing I knew the owner of the house sprayed us with bug spray. Debbie just kept tugging while all the sun cancer kids howled. Finally I kicked her in the face with my Nike and she went whimpering off. School was rough but I did win some respect on the tetherball court. I was nearly champion so the boys in fifth grade had started to take notice of me.

James Sprinkler-head lived around the block from me. He terrorized the whole neighbourhood and was well-known at the local police station for pouring gasoline into peoples'pools. Daily, he twisted my titties. Even though I had to put icecubes on my nipples when I got home from school, I couldn't help likin' the little shithead. James was my first serious admirer. He had a habit of abusing me with sick words and dirty thoughts. He was Matt Dillon cute, but fucked up... like Leo, I guess.

One hot, hellish day, I was walking home from school with my brand new Las Vegas friend, Caitlin. She was coming over to my house to eat ice cream and swim for the first time so I wanted to impress her.

There was James, sitting on his stolen BMX bike, smoking a cigarette in the alley. As I strutted past he threw it at me. I ignored him. He got off his bike and pushed me against the hot wall. He tried to get his hand up my shirt. I fought back as hard as I could. Caitlin thought nothing of it, boys were always puttin' their hands in unwanted places.

As James attempted to secure my hands behind my back, I scratched him across the face with my painted claws. His pupils changed from brown to reptile orange.

"Run, Caitlin!"

We flew out the alleyway towards my house. I looked back to see James after us on his BMX. When we reached my lawn he pounced on top of me and pinned my arms out to the side. Jesus pinned to the cross. I was writhing underneath him. Blood from his scratch wound dropped onto my eyebrow.

As he pushed his pelvis up against my crotch, his pupils switched to shark-fin silver. I tried to squirm my hands loose but he had my wrists locked. At first I kinda like what he was doin'... *bein' tickled in new places.*

I couldn't move, his body was too heavy. He was hurting me. The circulation of blood wasn't getting to my hands. The shards of grass were scratching my naked torso. Shy giggles turned to angry tears.

He managed to pull my t-shirt up while the other guys observed my braless boobies. Nobody was laughin' now. I was screaming, desperate to scratch his eyes out. When he let go of my left hand to cover my mouth, I was able to throw him off, but only for a few seconds. Before I could get any distance, the prick yanked on my ankle and tripped me up.

"Caitlin, fucking help me!"

She just stood there. I was down again. He kneeled on my arms, with his crotch in my face, leanin' back, pinchin' my nipples really hard. Instead of screamin', I held my breath, as if I was diving into the pool.

He rode me rodeo style, laughing and grunting, "titty twister, titty twister" at the top of his lungs. I felt so humiliated with those boys watching, I wanted to cry - MOMMY.

He then grabbed a sprinkler-head from my lawn and proceeded to push it against the crotch of my jeans in a to-and-fro movement for a whole minute. Tears filled my eyes.

Finally my neighbour, Mr Hensen, came out wavin' his golf club at the sun. I prayed he hadn't seen the sprinkler-head. James jumped off and got on his bike. Fighting back the tears and shame, I opened my front door. My crotch ached. I was so angry, but all I could do was get in the house before I cracked.

Caitlin didn't say much, as if this sort of thing was as normal as going to the bathroom. I tried to laugh it off as I limped bow-legged to the refrigerator. I got two tubs of ice cream out. One for me, one for Caitlin. As I ate in front of the TV, I didn't feel upset, just numb and dazed. The cold ice cream and its chunks of caramel soothed my throbbing crotch. I closed my eyes as I took each bite.

Airplane. ✈

if you get too close I'll eat your insides out
I'll eat your home and house out
I'll eat your brains out
no-one will notice anything
except an unlady-like burp
I ain't gonna stop until
I vomit it all up
because if I ain't feeding
my empty heart is bleeding
love always,
Greedy Mouth

I've just finished my perfectly portioned dinner... for a bird. I'm still starving. The freaky hippy chick next door has barely touched her food. At this moment, I want her chocolate pudding more than I want to land safely.

She keeps lifting the fork to her mouth and then putting it back down again. I feel like force-feeding her just to get the luscious shit outta my sight. I'm just jealous of her self-control. Come to think of it, she looks like a skeleton. I bet she's got some food disorder. I wish I did. No. I don't mean that. I'm just sick of bein' hungry all the time.

When I was little, people were amazed by my greediness, they shook their heads in disgust but at the same time they wished they could show their desires in such a brash way. I guess my Greedy Mouth grew outta my desire for my mother.

"Ya, I'll have another gin and tonic please. I don't mean to be a big fat pig but are you gonna eat that chocolate pudding or what?"

GREEDY MOUTH GOBBLEDY GOO

Aged 10.

"Now Jesusa, there are five granola bars in the cupboard, you have to make them last all week. I'm not going to the store again, when they're gone, THEY ARE GONE!"

Over the next five minutes "GRANOLA BAR" flashes like a Fremount Street neon sign in my mind's watering mouth. My taste buds are baby chicks squawking for those honey-coated nuggets surfing through a wave of milk straight from the carton, down to the whale's inner cave.

Within an hour I eat all five of 'em. First I take one bar, then , after ten minutes of trying to distract myself, I snap the second one in half, agonising over which is the biggest half as the gooey caramel stretches and hangs stiff in the air. Again I try to divert my mind from the craving. I go to the bathroom and stare in the mirror, flick through the TV channels, rearrange my rows of Nikes and Levis, sit in my mom's closet, torture the cat, but this nagging voice in my head orders me to march to the kitchen. "You weakling piece of shit, you fat lazy pig!" How do I spell relief? I take the whole box of granola bars into my room and finish them off as quickly as I can.

Big ol' Hiawatha watermelon mama used to say, "The kitchen is the heart of the house". The kitchen was a black hole and the fridge was as evil as Darth Vadar. I was getting fatter and fatter and I couldn't stop it. I stocked up on Tab Cola and Grape Nuts cereal. I'd even taken up exercise. I used to crank up the outdoor speakers and swim fifty laps a day to Queen's *Another One Bites the Dust* but the minute I got outta the pool I was famished.

As the math teacher explained equations, all I could think about was getting home to a big bowl of ice cream. Sadly, the fun in eating only lasted five minutes. After that it was just like you have to stuff this stupid hole. You have to plug it up. And you keep going even when you feel like you're gonna puke. And all you know is you gotta get rid of the temptation. Your mind is filled with the want and, when you momentarily suppress the wanting, you feel flat because you don't know what to want next.

Then came the shame. The self loathing. And the pity. I'd turn the shower on, lock the bathroom door, quietly weeping at the reflection as I clawed at the clumps of fat on my thighs, butt and gut. This is what my mother was warning me about when she said, "Watch what you eat!". I wanted to cry out loud but that was against some unspoken rule that my mother and me had invented. The *ABC After School Special* starring Jennifer Jason Leigh about anorexia explained I over-ate to compensate for the lack of love. I told my Mom this and she said, "Oh, really. I suppose that's what happened to me, you'll grow out of it, it's just baby fat".

Now that me and my mom lived on our own, somedays I'd sit on the cool floor tiles with the fridge door wide open and wade through buffet leftovers for hours. There was no-one there to say, "Wait till dinner" or "You'll spoil your appetite" like in *Happy Days*. All I could think of was Leo and his favourite saying when I was left sitting at the table with a slab of liver, "Waste not, want not, think of the starving Ethiopians!"

Waste not, want not.Waste not, want not. I guess my fucked-up obsession for food developed in Santa Cruz in First Grade when I started hanging' out with the Burrito Butt family. For a while my Mom was working at a bank so she could save up extra money for when she left Leo. Mrs. Gonzalas baby-sat me before and after school, Monday through Friday.

Rosie Gonzalas had eight children and was even poorer than us. The whole family were fat. Fat. Fat. Fat. The entire house smelt of fat. God knows how many burritos they got through a day. The house stank of gas bombs. At first, I felt timid and out of place, but we broke the ice after I won my first farting contest.

The first day I got dropped off there, I was tiny. After a year I was looking like one of her kids. Brown and chubby. Mrs. Gonzalas had boobs like Hiawatha and I loved them equally. The floppy jugs came together and rested on her belly button. I could never work out how she balanced all that weight on her little feet.

Before dinner I would help her make chilli by chopping the onions and grating the cheese. The whole family were amazed I could chop onions without crying. Every Friday night we made home-made, spicy French fries. I peeled the potatoes and watched as she dropped them into the boiling fat.

The Burrito Butts' eating was a sight to see. We all gathered in the backyard around a stolen picnic table. We always ate off paper plates and drank vanilla pop out of plastic cups. Each cup had our names written in nail polish, which we had to keep track of and put on the shelf at the end of the day. After saying grace we chowed down like pigs in the farm yard. Sour cream, guacamole, diced tomatoes, hot sauce, tomollies and tacos, melted cheese and stacks of tortillas. You had to eat fast in that family. From the minute we got in from school we were constantly vacuuming up tortillas. The more I fought for my food the less shy I became.

Food shopping with the Gonzalases was a hilarious event. Everybody wanted to go, so they could choose their favourite brand of beans and chips. By the time all those beefy thighs piled in the station wagon there was barely enough room for me. I used to sit in the very back with the groceries and the dog's tail in my face. But they always made me feel at home, like I was a Burrito Butt too. We'd all sit around that picnic table, everyone making jokes at once, passing this and that, doing the dishes together, having water fights in the bathtub.

When we moved to Las Vegas the pigging-out escalated. The difference was most of the time I would eat alone. In my room or by the pool. Like a secretary typing, it was my job and it was a job I hated. The fact that I was in my bikini most of the time didn't help matters. Nor did the mirrored walls help. I'd bend over to pick up a cookie I'd dropped and little rolls of flesh was always staring back at me. In every thigh or bicep I saw a vision that was three times as big as it really was.

I sighed with relief when I heard my mom pull up in the driveway. It meant she would temporarily take my mind off food. Even when I was full, I was starving. To her credit she did make dinner every night and in return I would gobble up every boring carrot and string of spinach lovingly. As we ate at the dining room table she asked me if I did my homework and I'd tell her Henry VIII was an asshole.

My greediness for my mother got worse as I saw her less and less and, when I did see her, I didn't want to share her with anyone. She wasn't workin' at the weekend but she was gone school nights. Most weekends I'd get conned into spending at my cousins' house. This was about the time she started sneakin' in dates. It was all planned by Aunt Erica. She set Mom up with some hairy-faced man and they'd all go out gambling together while us kids watched Bruce's pornos. These casino jaunts never led to anything regular though. She was allowed one or two brief dates but when they came sniffin' at the front door, I would kick them in the balls, spit and hang the phone up on them.

Although I didn't have her as much as I wanted, I treasured our time together at the weekend. These were the rare occasions I didn't act like a brat. Some Saturdays, after cleaning, we'd drive outta Vegas, to Spring Mountain Ranch that held horseback riding expeditions into the desert up near Sleeping Indian Mountain. The desert just went on for miles and miles and as I sat on my horse my mind just emptied. I didn't worry about snakes, or hunger or thirst, I just enjoyed the sensation between my legs like a true cowgirl.

One Sunday every month we putted up to Mt Charleston in our VW. From our backyard, Mt Charleston looked like a garden island poking out of a dirt sea. You never would have known the mountains could be so green and rich with waterfalls and creeks when the valley below was so brown and lifeless.

In just a half an hour the desert disappeared and gave way to green Joshua trees and jagged cliffs. The temperature dropped as our ears popped. Every single time we'd hit the Pine Tree Junction Mom-teacher would say, "You know Jess, what Betsy just climbed is the same as driving from Mexico to Alaska, we're as high up as airplanes".

Once we parked the car we'd strap on backpacks and hike Mt Charleston, two miles up and two miles down the mountain. As we passed signs warning of cougars and bears, Mom would try to interest me in reading by retelling chapters from Stephen King's *Four Seasons* and *Fire Starter*. I listened with sick fascination as she answered my questions about the Nazis. They were her speciality at school. Tilting my head back, I watched the sun dancing in the tall pine trees as she recapped Hitler's childhood. From the top you could see The Sleeping Indian mountains, Lake Mead, and the Strip.

"Las Vegas looks so small... did L.A. used to look like this?"

She took a breath of the crisp mountain air and exhaled.

"When I was a little girl, parts of L.A. were just desert, other parts were lush with palm trees. Actually L.A. was a lot like Vegas is now - not too big, not too small... but it grew so fast, by the time I was 18 it was overflowing with weirdos."

" Umm. Do you think Mt Charleston is gonna look like Beverly Hills does now - you know, like with mansions everywhere and all?"

"Well, it would be a shame... but if they did, I would build a house right on this rock."

My mom would always sit down and eat her apple and cheese in the same exact spot.

"I'll buy it for you," I said proudly like every other kid promise. She'd just inhale on her roach and hold the smoke in until I made her laugh.

On week-nights, when we were all alone with the dog and cat, I'd lay on her bed, watching her change out of her work clothes, wash her face and then roll a joint. I studied her body and face looking for signs of sadness. I was a spy looking for clues as to what she might be hiding. She no longer exuded that innocent child-playing-in-the-waves woman thing Marilyn Monroe had in *How to Marry a Millionaire*. She acted like the teacher she finally was. Just enough make-up and sensible clothes to project that Jane Fonda or Annie Hall look of intelligence and fragility. I tried to imagine what it must be like to work all day, and then sell underwear at night.

I started to copy my mother in order to be with her more. This was when I really got into practicing my Method acting skills. If I could become her, maybe I wouldn't crave her so much.

I tried smoking cigarettes but settled for doobies. The first time I got high, me and Kat stole some grass outta Aunt Erica's pot tray, and went out by her Jacuzzi to roll it into a doobie. What we ended up with were two candy wrapped puff balls of weed. Once we climbed into the Jacuzzi and smoked the candies we got what we soon found out to be the dreaded munchies. We ran into the house dripping wet and pigged out on a dozen, triple-layered, peanut butter and jelly sandwiches. We could not stop eating even as we rolled around giggling on the kitchen floor, dribbling peanut butter globs.

After my first attack of the munchies they never seemed to go away.

Since Santa Cruz I had admired my mother's ever-improving control over her life and weight. I started to diet at the age of 10. Every other commercial was for a weight loss plan with a Before and After person. Even though I was only like ten pounds over weight I begged my Mom to let me join the famous Jenny Creig Centre but it was a "rip off".

Through my cousin Kat's extensive Junior High knowledge we worked out what the pills in the freezer were for. They were speed tablets to control Mom's hunger. With them and her cigarettes, she kept her skinny little figure. I stole them from behind the ice cube trays and replaced the diamonds with aspirin. At school I made a few more friends in the bathroom by cracking open the capsules and distributing the powder like Flintstone vitamins. The dieting thing was a shared hobby that almost every girl was caught up in. We thought being thin equalled being strong and beautiful.

While the boys were skateboarding and learning how to be macho, us girls trudged through the desert to K-Mart spending hours in the magazine section looking at all the models. We'd spend afternoons out by the pool cutting and pasting pictures of Nastassja Kinski and Brooke Shields in scrap book collages. I learnt from the TV that Dextrin curbed your appetite like speed did so every Monday after school we stole a packet from K-Mart.

The pills didn't work. Even though I wasn't hungry I couldn't sit still to watch the bloody TV. As far as I was concerned it was like smoking a cigarette, the effect was not worth the effort. My stomach felt sick so I had to fill it with some more food.

Kat not only gave lessons in cheerleading, she'd also demonstrate how to make yourself sick by shoving a finger down the throat. One Saturday afternoon Kat and I had just pigged out and both decided we were so full we had to "upchuck". I cleaned the toilet bowl first. As I leaned over, gripping onto either side of the crapper, the floortiles pressed into my knee caps. I gazed into my reflection on the inner walls of the bowl. The water was clear but I would have preferred throwing up in my own toilet. Still I was grateful to Kat for finally showing me the ropes. I'd been trying for weeks on my own but all I got was a sore throat and a spotless toilet.

"O.K., on the count of three." Kat ordered. Just as she was making that horrible retching sound I slapped her on the back of the thigh.

"Wait Kat! I can't do it. Can I watch how you do it?"

"No, that's gross! That's like watching me pluck my bikini line... it's private."

"Please. I don't don't know how far to stick my finger down."

"All right, you little brat, but don't make me laugh. This is serious shit."

Holding the shower curtain open, I balanced on the rim of the bathtub. Kat's entire fist disappeared. Then it happened. Once her hand pulled out, the vomit sprang from her mouth like a Slinky. It sounded as if her guts were being ripped out. Velcro. With the shower hose, Kat rinsed away the Technicolor neapolitan ice cream and Cheetoes. I was ready to puke. I rubbed my queasy tummy and positioned myself over the bowl.

"Kat, does it hurt?" When Kat turned around her face was a mixture of green and purple.

"Don't be such a chicken shit - no pain no gain. This is womanhood!"

And with that statement she grabbed the back of my hair, tilted my head back, shoved her fist past my tonsils and jiggled her index fingers deep into my throat and wrenched it out. Puke came all over the rim of the toilet bowl.

I never attempted that kind of self-inflicting pain again. There were other ways I could hate myself.

Now that I was officially a woman, I went on a rollercoaster ride of dieting for nearly a year until the up and down pattern of bingeing, dieting, bingeing, dieting kept me at the same exact weight. I was glad I finally knew how I felt about myself. Before, I seesawed between thinking I was special and thinking I was a monster brat.

Hate was a gritty solid state so when I looked into the bathroom mirror there was no Judy Garland wonderment, no Jodie Foster cheekiness, just a snarling lip and a sunburnt nose. This was when I turned myself into a submarine. I tightened the hatches, painted the windows black and turned to devil music. I stopped listening to Michael Jackson's *Off the Wall* and turned to Ozzy Osbourne and The Scorpions. I redecorated my room with Heavy Metal posters.

Airplane. ✈

Another five hours to go. My hand hurts from writing so much crap.

I think it was the warts on my face that made me start acting like Jack Nicholson outta *The Shining*.

"OK, now just lay back and I'm gonna give you a dry ice peel. All we have to do is keep this treatment up for a few weeks and they'll scab up and drop off."

"Will there be scars?"

"There'll be a small amount of scar tissue but after a few months the little rascals will look no uglier than freckles."

Next thing I knew the nurse goes to the refrigerator and carefully hands the famous Dr Landlow this icicle-like cylinder. The freak pulls this smokin' ice popsicle from the cylinder.

"What's that? Is it gonna hurt?"

"It's sodium nitrate, it'll freeze those suckers off!"

By this stage in my life I had developed an addiction not only to food but to scabs and scars. After I discovered my rare wart disorder, I made my Mom buy me a whole book on skin diseases. I had two scab boxes. One for me and one for Sam.

BENNY BIGBALLS AND HIS BUICK

There is a man in my Mom's bed. His name is Benjamin Goodman. Not the famous jazz dude, but a baseball-capped, jolly green giant, Nazi look-a-like, ex-Mormon math teacher at my Mom's school.

I'm gonna be like Harry Houdini. I'm gonna escape through the bottom of my closet. Submerge into my own dirt sea. Dig past the septic tank underneath our house. I'll pass seahorses and sharks, fossils and coal steeped in deadly gases. It'll get darker and this world will look for me. I'm gonna take a look around using my spotlight lamps and my fingerprint kit.

Fuck Houdini, I'm never gonna rise to the surface again! I'll crawl into an underwater cave and soothe my skin cancer. Mommy Dearest will finally cry out: "It's all my fault" as she peers down the tunnel I've dug in my bedroom closet.

IT happened. The bed squeaking and grunting brought back Leo memories all over again. This time the sound of sex was twice as bad cos I had seen so many pornos, I could picture it. No matter how high I turned Ozzy up on the stereo, I could hear 'em going at it all night.

"Stop fucking that stranger!" I shouted over guitar solos, throwing myself against the floor howling, "666! The number of the beast!" and punching my prison walls. Each knuckle scrape gave me satisfaction. *Give me more scabs!* I let the snot drip and tears flow out loud for the first time in four years. I moved the chest of drawers, the bed, the bean bag and everything else against the door, as if to protect myself from what was on the other side. The only protection I needed was from myself.

I barricaded myself in my room for a three-day fast in protest.

Day 1. 11:00 a.m.

It's Saturday and I'm dying for my Lucky Charms cereal to go with The Smurfs *and* School House Rock *but I've made a pact to stay put. I set up my TV so I can see it from the bed I made myself in the closet. I pick mucus from the corner of my eyes as a way of pullin' out dead brain tissue. I hook the string of gunk to my fingernail so it creeps over my lower eyelash. It itches real good.*

Whenever I do this Aunt Erica goes,

"You'll get worms, they'll slime in and chew at your sockets and you won't even know you're going blind.."

"Good! Bring on the pain."

Sammy Cat swooped in the window gap like a tiger flying through a flamin' hoop of fire. He wanted feedin'... nothin' else. The little shit was too busy being King of the Cats in his new neighbourhood to pay me any lovin' attention. As he tried to bite me, I held him down at the neck like a snake charmer. If I was only gonna to be his human feeder, he was only gonna be my labratory experiment.

I didn't use my fingernails, I used Mom's tweezers. Sam hated me pickin' the buggers out of his eyes. When I finished with his eyes I examine his scabs. My cat squirmed as I separated the white fur and re-opened the scab on his neck, peeling it off like a bandaid. He growled and took a bite outta my upper lip. The bloody lip felt as good as it tasted. He meowed to go back out in the night. I watched enviously as he leapt over the rose bush and disappeared beneath the street lamps, his curved belly swaying close to the pavement. He was free.

Day 2 of the Benny Goodman Siege. 10:00 a.m.

I'm starving...
I'm growin' weak...
need food... can't take it anymore...
HELP ME HELP ME

Thanksgiving morning. Mom knocked on my door and asked me if I was gonna help with the buffet. I leaned against the furniture heaped against the door as if I was holding back a huge gust of wind. For once I fought against my devilish Greedy Mouth, muzzling it.

I listened for a small note of distress in her voice but all she said was,

"Well, when you get a whiff of that gravy and turkey and those pumpkin pies you'll never be able to stand it in your room. I know you, Jesusa, your food is more important then anything, including that cat. You'll both come crawling with your tails between your legs".

I hurled a chair at the door and punched a hole through the wall.

3:00 p.m.

I crawled out my window and skateboarded to Smiths' Food King. I knew I wouldn't be able to survive without food. On the way back I had trouble balancing with two brown paper bags full of cold turkey slices, canned cranberry sauce, yams, carrots, peas, gravy and frozen cheesecake. Just as I was climbing back in the window, my cousins pulled up in Bruce's van. Kat and Dona saw my Ditto Butt dangling above the rose bush. They jumped out of Uncle Bruce's van and skipped over to my window.

"Let's see your new TV set." Kat demanded.

But I just closed my tinted window in their faces.

4:00 p.m.

My favourite feast of the year - sabotaged. While the rest of my family tucked into Thanksgiving dinner, Benny Goodman entertained with sexist jokes. I couldn't make out the punchlines but I could tell by their dumb laughter they had fallen in love with the impostor.

I could barely hear Lauren Bacall's voice smouldering from the black and white movie. Envy. Envy. Envy. TV-stoned, I ate my way through cans of cold yams and pumpkin pie mix.

5:00 p.m.

Tomorrow they will be exploding nuclear bombs underneath the ground at the Nevada Test Site, about twenty miles outside town. If anything goes wrong, the newsman assures us, Las Vegas will be evacuated before the deadly clouds reached the town. Nobody gives a shit when the earth moves. They trust their government. My dad Max says, don't ever trust the government.

In the 50s, bomb testing was a tourist attraction. They'd all sit out in their deck chairs at sunrise waiting for the explosion. Casinos served Atomic Bomb cocktails, tacky motels and diners sold Atomic Bomb ash... that's fucked up.

6:00 p.m.

I love my TV set. He is like the sober grandfather I never had. So grey and wise. He's seen and done everything. He answers all my questions. He tells me about Gorbachev. He has time for me. His many voices replace my own. He's my Santa Claus ambulance. At night after the stations go off air, the static buzz sends me to sleep as good as Nyquil.

11:00 p.m.

They are doing it again. I'm gonna crawl out my window and sleep in the car.

Day 3. 9:00 a.m.

Benny Goodman is cooking bacon, eggs and waffles.

My TV programme for the day will be:

10:30 *Flipper*
11:00 *Laverne and Shirley*
11:30 *Happy Days*
12:00 *All My Children*
1:00 *Days of Our Lives*
2:00 *General Hospital* or *Phil Donahue*
3:00 *The After School Special - Angel, the Diary of a Prostitute*
4:00 *Partridge Family*
5:00 *M*A*S*H*
6:00 *The News*
7:00 *Cagney and Lacey*
8:00 *Three's Company*
9.00 *Paper Dolls*
11:00 *The Johnny Carson Show*

3:00 p.m.

I wish a cloud would cover the sun. The news update says the testing was successful. Whatever that means... Sometimes I forget that there are 1000's of tourists just a few miles away having the time of their lives casino-hopping and screwing the local prostitutes.

9:00 p.m.

Mom and Benny go out for dinner. Through the window I watch them leave. He is wearing a chequered suit from the 70s. She's got her disco dress on - the one I ripped at Charm School. He opens the passenger door of his red Buick and closes it after my Mom. He pats her on the butt. His car is nearly as long as our pool. I pull the furniture out from the doorway and run to the fridge gawking at the packed shelves. I take an old can of Ravioli rather than the booby-trap plate of leftovers she has wrapped for me to microwave. As I walk down the mirrored hallway, I contemplate entering Mom's sex room to smell the dishevelled sheets or unscrew the bedposts but I can't even turn the door knob.

Later that night.

I had a dream as I lay curled up on the closet floor bathed in TV light.

I'm kneeling at the sex room door, just about to peek through the keyhole. With my right eye closed, I position the left against the cold metal. My mother is being humped by a huge tarantula. There are mini sharks riding on a 1000 red rollercoaster cars. Instead of tracks, they're riding waves like surfboards. The tarantula's hairy front legs are wrapped around the bedpost, its two back legs are rocking on the carpet. It's side legs are spread across the whole room.

I woke up in a cold sweat to discover bleeding between my legs and an acidic taste in my mouth as if I needed to spew. Half awake, I peeled the door open and blasted across the hallway to my mother's room. Before I realized what I was doing I flung her door open and out of my mouth came a stream of venomous words,

Do you suck your thumb while he's lying next to you?
Do you go to bed with your make-up on, now?
Do his feet hang off the bottom of the bed?
Do you wash his clothes in our washing machine?
Do you clean his piss from the rim of the toilet?

A few seconds of smug satisfaction followed.

But my one last attempt at control was defeated. To my shock and disgust this man, who I had never even been introduced to before, jumped out of bed and came towards me. NAKED! I couldn't take my eyes off of his balls as they swung en route. I don't think I had seen a real man nude before.

Still trembling from my nightmare, I backtracked. I didn't notice if his eyes were angry or what my mother was doing, I just saw the hairy tarantula balls coming at me. What the hell did men keep in those sacks? I didn't even notice the penis! I got my kicking leg ready in case he attempted contact. I wasn't looking forward to putting my toe near those sacks, but I would if I had to. And just as I was ready to defend, all he did was shut my mother's bedroom door in my face. He won without even fighting.

I stood there in the dark hallway surrounded by useless mirrors. Shut out. Even though I knew it was making me worse I had to go blank like the TV. Numb, like lying in a pool of ice cubes. The way I learnt how to do with James Sprinkler-head.

I went back into my bedroom and curled up in the closet. Crushed like a can, I watched the white fuzz on the TV. I looked on the positive side of my defeat - at least they had stopped fucking.

10:00 p.m.

Benny's left the house. I knew he wouldn't be back again that day cos my Mom gave him a big long kiss in the driveway before he clanked away in his rusty '74 Buick.

I went into my Mom's bedroom and watched her strip the sheets.

"Who the hell was that guy with the big balls?"

"He's a teacher and you better get used to him because you're not going to get rid of him like the others." She spoke like an experienced school teacher.

"I hate you." I sulked.

"That's your problem. Get over it and get on with it. By the way, you're going to England as soon as I can book the flight."

"Goody goody gum drops!"

I ran for the refrigerator.

Airplane. ✈

When the freaky girl returns from the bathroom for the hundreth time, she bulldozes into another conversation.

"Is this the first time you've been to England?"

"Nooo. I've been flyin' back and forth since I was 5. My dad's in England and I grew up with my mom on planet Vegas."

Since she gave me her pudding I felt like I had to be a little nice.

"So, Gaaad, what was it liiike growin' up in Laaas Veeegaaas?"

"I'll tell you one thing, right now, it feels like I finally escaped. From *Fantasy Island*. The dirt sea where someone else's dream always comes true, but like, yours never do. The fuckin' promised land trailed through by pioneers who got lost and ate each other. The land that was sucked up and spat out by silver diggers and Nuclear Power Plants -"

"- you know whaaat? You have a reeeal poetic way of talkin'."

Drunk as a skunk, she slurs her words like a Valley Girl who's just had her wisdom teeth pulled out.

"I do? Thanks."

I lean over my food tray and continue writing my retarded life story, which by now, is getting real monotonous. ...the land that was soiled with dead Indians and serial killer victims. The land that still has the neon sign flashing The American Dream Available 24 hours a day, all you can eat. The land I left behind in a hurry...

Just then, the freaky girl's head falls on my shoulder. I push her back to her own head rest as if I'm lifting an injured lady bug off my skin.

ATLANTIC OCEAN

Aged 10.

We drove all night to avoid the desert heat. Sittin' in the back of Benny's non-airconditioned Buick, I realized the BALLS of this ex-detective, ex-Mormon, math-teaching, basketball jock from back East were too big to kick outta my Mom's bed. The only dudes who could do that were the Mafia and I didn't know any of them guys... yet.

We reached glamorous L.A. before morning rush hour. I lay down in the back seat so nobody could see me in Benny's poor excuse for a convertible. Every other car inching along Hollywood Boulevard was a convertible Porche or Mercedes. I wished they'd just drop me off on the corner and let me be an under-aged porno star.

Instead Mom took us on the same tour I'd been on every year, past her house, pointing out the palm tree she picked leaves from, when she was fat 14, to stop her rubbing inner thighs from bleeding. Benny laughed at every goddam thing she said and vice-versa. She was giddy as hell about goin' the beach after they got rid of me. Two's company, three's a crowd.

Before headin' for the airport, the three of us stopped off at the House of Pancakes. To the lovebirds' amusement, I sat at a different booth to show my anger. In six months I had not yet spoken one word to the Mom stealer. I couldn't believe Benny Big Balls and his Buick had to break our annual breakfast tradition with his presence.

We arrived at L.A.X. with the top stuck halfway down. Benny was puttin' the top up for when we had to drive through the dangerous part of L.A. and I *accidently* jammed a few of my lipsticks down the crack where the lever was.

The sun was shining down on the Buick's chrome and laser-beamed off everybody's sunglasses. Instead of the normal airport routine, check-in and boarding were outside near the parking lot, which added to the unwanted child brush off.

Holding back feel-sorry-for-me tears was like trying not to pee my pants so I walked away without saying goodbye. Mom twirled me back and dipped me, covering me with blonde hair. I took one last sniff of the Gee-Your-Hair-Smells-Terrific shampoo as she covered my face in lipstick and pushed me towards the smiling ticket lady.

I never ever could look back as I walked towards the plane. As the warm Californian wind rocked me side to side, I kept my head down, afraid to turn and see that Mom-Barbie had already roared off to the beach with Benny-Ken.

"In a hundred years, little girls will be travelling to different planets to visit their alien fathers." My mumbled words got swept away in the wind as Janice the stewardess led me up the steps to the plane holding on to my hand like a piece of luggage. "If we were to crash, the people in First Class would die first, that's not very good value for money is it?" I was Marilyn Monroe, ignored and misunderstood.

As the Jumbo Jet headed straight for the sun, out the window I could see Benny waving his baseball cap as if he'd just hit a home run. By the age of 10 I was a professional jet-setter. For ear popping, I knew just when and how hard to chew gum. My Pan Am flight bag held Hello Kitty coloured markers and paper; my Charm/Scab Box was full of nail polish and tampons. For luck, my Amelia Earhart picture book was tucked into the magazine pouch as usual.

I reclined in my seat before it was allowed and wondered what adventures my dad, the Sperm Giver, had in store for me that summer. The year before, my cousin Kat came over with me and we hippied around the South of France in a caravan eatin' goats cheese. We sat on those topless beaches reading *Little Darlings* in our long L.A. Raiders football jerseys and tube socks, dying of embarrassment cos everyone was staring at us as if we were nuts for keeping our boobies covered.

Although I screamed blue murder every year when my Mom showed me the airplane ticket, I enjoyed 20% of my English "holiday". The other 80% I suffered from culture shock and paranoia. Ever since my dad made me watch *International Velvet* starring Tatum O'Neal I was sooo afraid of English kids. I thought they would try and give me a box with a finger in it. Anyways, the first week in England always scared the shit out of me and the first week arriving back in Las Vegas always fucked me up too. Creepy smiles and whacked out climate change.

On this British Airways flight I was stuck in between the two fattest passengers on the plane: one English and one American. Both cancer stick suckers. Not only did my Mom abandon me, she also put me in a non-window smoking section! To make things worse, the English lady, who kept stealing my arm rest, started up a typical airplane conversation.

"So, young lady, you're travelling on your own, oh, I say, how brave!" I liked English ol' ladies but they always got overexcited about the tiniest thing, like a cup of tea or a scoop of ice cream.

"Ya, they call me Amelia Earhart back home. To answer your next question, I'm going to visit my dad in Manchester." I was givin' it my Jodie Foster from *Taxi Driver*.

"Are you from Los Angeles, love?"

"No, I'm from Leeds, bloody England." I replied in a rusty *Coronation Street* accent, trying to keep my fake Bette Davis smile goin'.

"I have a sister who lives just outside Leeds."

Whoopie doo I thought.

"It's a dump, huh?"

"Oh, I don't know, I suppose compared to Los Angeles..." She was already gettin' offended by my brash manner.

"I *wish* I was from L.A., I'm from bloody Las Vegas." I stared past her, out the window, trying to think of a way to end the conversation.

"You wouldn't think anybody would live there."

"Yah, I hear that all the time in England. My Mom's a showgirl at Caesars Palace *and* I've got my own pool."

"Oh I say, it sounds so glamorous!"

"Ya, for her, not for me. You'll probably think I'm a spoilt brat cos you lived through the war and never had chocolate as a kid. Well, for your information, I got too much chocolate, if you get my drift. It's like bein' a parcel neatly wrapped with a waterproof cagoule and a shopping list attached for Earl Grey tea bags. And me toting Grandma's Pan Am free flight bag full of gifts for grandparents: dice keyrings, poker cards, tortillas and refried beans - it's totally retarded."

I knew I was losing patience when I nudged her fat forearm off *my* arm rest. I buzzed for the air hostess and prepared to charm. Taken aback, the fat lady said nothing for a few seconds.

Just as she opened her mouth I cut her off.

"I don't know what's worse, rainy England or hell hole Nevada. Scorpions or grass snakes. Sitting in a Moss side pub watching social workers get drunk or getting sun cancer out by the lonely pool. The Lake District or Hoover Dam tours. Pissin' in a casino parking lot, waitin' for the gambling grown ups or bein' dragged on Stuff the Royal Wedding Party protest marches. Watching *The Story of O* and *Deep Throat* at my cousin's pool or channel flippin' between *Playschool* and *Wimbledon*.

By the time I finished my speech my mouth was havin' claustrophobic fits. The ulcers began to bleed. When I stuck my blood-bathed tongue out, the fat lady looked away in disgust. I smeared the blood underneath my nose. Janice earnestly rubbed her thighs down the aisle towards me. I liked air hostesses cos they felt sorry for me. They understood passangers' needs. And, if they were just like whores pretending, I admired their acting ability.

Breathlessly lying, I told her I felt faint and couldn't find my asthma inhaler.

"One moment." She smiled sweetly through her red lipstick and capped teeth. Janice probably knew I'd been shipped back and forth between a hippy hell broken marriage for years. These flat-butted airhostesses with perfect calves and ankles were the best moms a girl could ask for.

Good news came from Janice. As I grabbed my shit, I said to the British lady,

"I'm sooo sorry we can't continue our boring conversation. Look on the bright side, I'll die faster than you in First Class if we crash."

I was living up to my reputation as a fully fledged brat from hell.

I was just in time for First Class feeding. Aside from the air hostesses, my favourite part about flying was the perfectly sectioned food, unwrapped and served with loving care by the goddesses of the heavens. If I had that kind of service at home, I'd have had no weight *or* brat problem.

In my comfy leather chair I could swing my feet and spread my thighs. I put my headphones on and rested my head on the cool plastic window and imagined falling through the blue sky. I may have hated leaving my Mom but I didn't mind travelling. It made me feel important. Everybody looked at me. Sometimes I got to go up and meet the pilot with other transatlantic misfit kids. It was better than sitting in front of that fucking TV all day. Of course I couldn't tell my Mother that. I had to make her feel as guilty as I could, even if it was in vain.

Dear Mom,

You know what History teacher? Emelia Earheart was an escape route expert. Just like battleship Grandma, she spent her whole life flyin' away. Bet you never knew that.

It's like a tub of bubble gum ice cream waiting for me on the other side of this airplane window. My mouth waters to be boncing on the cream clouds. This is where I want to live, up here where the light stays the same, no Jonathan Seagull, no sun, just blue and white, silence, peace and space. I want more room in my head. Do you think Max will help me find more room in my head?

I'm turnin' into an escape route expert. I wish I was brave enough to pull the emergency lever and jump through the sky. Twenty seconds to say "I do believe in God! I do believe in God!" I'd probably just drop to the ocean, with its foaming white caps and its blood thirsty sharks.

I dream of sharks. Ever since you took me to see Jaws at the drive in with Leo. Do you

know that? Every single dream I'm chomped into pieces. Then another shark takes the top half and eats it in half. I'm not dead yet. I can feel every torn slab of me floating on the water underneath the white sun. I am Mexican minced meat.

In my dreams I never die. I just watch myself get eaten over and over again.

Mom, why can I only talk to you on paper? Mom, where do feeling come from and where do they go when they are gone? Where does all that poo from the airplane toilet go? Into the sea or into thin air? Why do I only think of gross things? Why don't I think of normal things? Do you think I could become famous for bein' the biggest brat in the world... do you think they have that catagory in the Guiness Book of World Records ? Mom, do you understand what I'm saying?

P.S. Breathe in and count to ten. I will always miss you even when you're sitting right next to me.

Atlantic Ocean
Flying home First Class six weeks later.

Max did it again. I looked like an English kid, spikey hair, ten pounds lighter, two-tone pipe cleaner trousers and my *Never Mind the Bollocks* ripped t-shirt. I felt special again, like I was sitting on the top hill of the Santa Cruz rollercoaster. I'd been love-bombed during my six-week British holiday. Most of it was spent staring at my dad's butt on the back of his damn tandem bike.

First we cycled to my English grandparents up in Leeds and had teatime with crumpets and Hob Nobs, played Pass the Parcel and ate rhubarb pie. I felt like Jimmy Carter's daughter on an official visit to spread a little American charm. As we walked down the Leeds High Street, English Grandma introduced me as "Jesse James from Las Vegas."

The best part of the holiday was me and Max cycling around the Lake District in the pouring rain and camping in his little tent for a week. Sperm Giver, the culture-vulture, dragged me to see the poet William Wordsworth's house. On the way we stopped off at this pub next to a stream.

For once, it was sunny and warm, the air was dewy. Max was tossing me Kendal Mintcake - pure sugar set in the shape of a chocolate bar.

"Hey, I'm the Statue of Liberty."

I was posing on stone in the middle of the stream.

Outta the blue Max goes,

“Don’t expect too much from your Mom. She loves you but she has to have her own life.”

He’d always come out with shit like this. She’d probably written him a letter begging him to dissect my head. He was training to be a social worker so he loved talkin’.

I changed the subject.

“Max, if you don’t believe in God, what do you believe in?”

He finished off his pint of Guinness, let out a small burp and came over to the edge of the water and began tossing rocks over the surface of the water so they skipped three or four times. “I believe in the soul,” he said proudly, as if he were the first man to ever say it.

“You are such a hippy hypocrite. Man, I thought havin’ a soul had to do with Heaven and Hell, the devil and God and all that crap.” I opened a pack of salt and vinegar crisps and hopped to another mossy rock.

“Well, it’s not my favourite word... and I bet William Wordsworth didn’t use it very often but having a soul....” He inhaled heavily, as if thinkin’ was the hardest thing in the world to do. “Having a soul is just simply exercising the brain.”

His sing-song, Manchester accent made his words sound comical.

I stood quietly on my tiny island in the middle of the stream, concentrating very hard on what he had just said, saying it over and over again in my mind in his accent.

“Max, I don’t think I have a soul.”

“Well, that’s what I’m here for! I may not be the dad of your dreams but I can exercise your brain for six weeks. Right, we better get going. Wordsworth will have all the answers.”

We climbed back on the tandem, and on his count of three, peddled.

“Mom says parents aren’t supposed to be good.”

“Oh, well,” he heaved as we continued uphill the country lane, “I don’t know about that, lass.”

And then he farted in my face.

Just as I was dreaming about an airhostess beauty contest I awoke to my favourite song,

Happy birthday to you.
Happy birthday to you.
Happy birthday, dear Jesusa
Happy birthday to you.

When I looked up I saw all these First Class passengers leaning towards me with smiles on their faces.

“Make a wish” said a dribbling rich kid. And to my delight, the stewardess pulled out my tray and set down a birthday cake for one with eleven candles burning out the top of German chocolate frosting - my favourite.

"What d'ya wish?" said the kid in front, thinking he was going to get some of my cake. I wished Benny Goodman and his Buick were outta my life! I blew the candles out and wolfed down every dangerous crumb.

My English uncle was the head of British Airways air hostesses, so I figured he set it up, knowing full well it wasn't my birthday. *I am special. Special. Special.*

I felt like Dorothy, all happy at the end of the movie when she's goin' up in the balloon. It didn't last long.

That summer, my mom met me *alone* at L.A.X. and we had dinner in the tower lounge before catching a flight back to Vegas. We usually drove back to Vegas but Grandma got us a cheap flight an account of her bein' a travel agent. I couldn't pretend I wasn't happy to see her, alone.

As we descended into Las Vegas I looked out the window of the airplane to see puffs of dust all over the city as if there was an air raid and a bunch of bombs had been dropped. But it was just the earth being moved around. Big ol' tractors looked like ants pickin' up crumbs and settin' them down somewhere else.

SHOPLIFTING AT K-MART

Aged nearly 11.

With stealing you got somethin' for nothin'... an easy way to win friends and influence people. It was a cure for kid boredom is all. Stealin' was a mixture of acting and being a magician. A mixture of Lauren Bacall, Siegfried and Roy, Houdini and Charlie's Angels. You had be real deadpan. Whatever kinda technique you wanna use, the main rule was you can't look around at people.

Apart from lyin' and cheatin', stealin' was the closest I ever came to Houdini expertise. Apart from piggin' out and makin' myself barf, these cheap shot stunts were the only escape routes I could perform skillfully.

Lyin' and cheatin' wasn't as much of a head rush as stealin', just a method of finding out more about myself - how smart, convincing and imaginative I could be without a hint of a smile. All acting, with no hope of an Oscar.

Mom says I started stealing when I was a 2. Sittin' in the shopping cart I'd stuff peanut butter jars down my diapers. At 6, I started stealin' from non-family members.

I made friends with rich kids so I could go to their houses, and look through their things while they ate with their parents. Bathrooms. Lock the door. Go through their drawers. It could be a safety pin or a hair clip but I always wanted something that looked special, like a great-grandma's brooch. I liked flipping through photo albums and stealing happy pictures just to rip 'em up. Sometimes I didn't care if it was a piece of ham out of the refrigerator. Or a box of tissues. Bad. Bad. Bad.

I stole my cousin's Barbie doll head and flushed it down her toilet.

At 8, I started stealing from my mother. I'd take her cap and tampax and just hide them somewhere else. I hid things she hid herself, stuff she'd never ask if I'd seen, like her pills in the freezer, then I'd put them in her panties drawer a few weeks later. Or my aunt's cigarette case underneath her dog's water bowl. Keys were fun when my mom was late for a date with Benny.

When my cousin Timmy stayed with us for a while, I would steal weed from the pot tray he kept under his stereo unit. He tried to hide it in different places everyday, but I'd get my ex-police dog, Blacky, to sniff it out.

At 9, I was sick of chasing ice cream vans, goin' round in circles at skating rinks and zoomin' down razor blade water slides. I graduated to cold, hard cash. Mom would hide her $$$$ in secret compartments of her purse but then my sneaky hand slipped into the white fake leather wallet as she'd be in the bathroom plucking her eyebrows singin' along to Neil Diamond. Out came a few scrunched-up dollar bills as I yelled,

"What's for dinner, Mom?"

I found some letters from my father one day after school during a commercial. I stole them along with my mother's high school diary. I stole a desk from school and dumped it in the golf course. When I was forced to go, I'd steal Bibles and plastic statues from church. Things I didn't really want, like flowers from a garden, the Yellow Pages, the neighbour's newspaper, or a teacher's favourite pen.

It got real real boring cos I wasn't gettin' good enough reactions. I decided to steal to hurt. I stole my mother's brand new, never-worn silk blouse for school photos. A drop of Kool-Aid stained the breast pleat for life. My mother nearly cried when she saw it.

At 10, I turned into the Devil's Daughter. I got into stealing good moods. Most of the time, I succeeded in making them as miserable as I was. Give me just one minute and I could practically ruin a person's day. All I had to do was pick up on one of their personality faults like a trained pick-pocket mood-grabber. I'd snarl and then sneak into their hearts like a tittie-twister.

"You are zeitgeber, you have a tendency to take over the emotional state of another person." No duh. I just stared out of his fancy glass wall. I could see Circus Circus and the Dunes Hotel but no Howard Hughes. For $50, he told my mother to ignore my "zeitgeber attacks".

The counselling worked cos I decided to steal from someone who cared. Those giant villains who made me want so much. Stores – department, convenience, grocery and, my favourite, K-Mart. We'd plan our attack route real careful. Probably a little too carefully. In the scorching heat, me and my boob-tubed cousins would stock up at Dairy Queen, cross the freeway, weave through patches of desert and stumble through the Meadows Mall door.

The first time I got caught was from J.C.Penney's. I wanted a pair of Dove shorts like my cousins were wearing, more than anything in the world - that day. Mom could have offered me a six-month Jenny Creig weightloss plan and I would have chosen the $10 shorts. They have black on the left cheek and white on the right, with a cute little dove perched on the corner of your thigh. If you were slightly overweight, then your butt cheek showed and you had to keep pulling them down every other minute, which drove male drivers wild. Honks was what we were after.

I slipped them on under my Levi cut-offs. I thought I had made it out of Penney's scot-free until a security guard stopped me in front of Hot Dog on a Stick. My cousins had nothing on them so they weren't charged like I was. I didn't mind getting caught cos they actually read you your rights.

After that I was a known shoplifter at the mall. I had to go down market to K-Mart. The security was crap.

I finally convinced my cousins to do their local K-Mart. I was too well-known at mine. K-Mart was the biggest, cheapest rip-off store in America. I started out on lipstick and eye shadows, shoe laces and Sun-In. The best place to hid your lipstick was in the folds of your bandanna strung through Levi's belt hoops. When they strip searched, they never looked there.

Little objects were easy. It was when I moved on to clothing that my luck changed... but, like I said, I was looking forward to gettin' caught.

Us ol' Dove Butt Angels wanted new bathing suits for a Jacuzzi make-out party that night. We decided to put them on underneath our old bathing suits so, even if we got strip-searched, the stolen suit would be hidden by our own. Our first mistake was spending an hour in the ladies' changing rooms, which was not a pleasant thing to do cos the walls were smeared with bougers. None of us could find bottoms to fit our tops so we kept having to run out, swapping garments.

Sadly, my cousins weren't Method actresses like I was. It was all that Catholic school that made them look guilty as hell.

Once we made it out of the store, we skipped to the back of the building buzzin' on our scam. All of a sudden, Aunt Erica came screechin' around the corner in her new Trans-Am. She'd been spyin' on us the whole time. Like a Nazi, she got out of the car and lined us all against the huge K-Mart dumpster for interrogation. She stood there, hands on bulging hips.

"So, Jesusa, I suppose this was all your idea. Your mom may let you get away with murder but I know how to discipline! I don't think my daughters should hang out with you, if you're gonna lead them into temptation. We all know you don't know the difference between right and wrong but I spend a lot of money on my girls' Catholic upbringing and I don't want them to end up in hell with the likes of Commies like you."

She paused to light a cancer stick from her car lighter. As she bent through the window, her crochet bikini top released even more of her left boob. When she scrunched towards us in her sweaty flip flops, I could see the edges of her large brown nipple. I couldn't take my eyes off it. Not that I hadn't seen Erica naked before - she was always goin' skinny-dippin'.

"You think I wanna be following you brats around on my Saturday afternoon off?"

My mouth started bleeding on account of chewing it too hard. We knew not to answer. She was pissed.

" Take. Them. Off. We're gonna march right back in and hand in everything you stole - so start stripping, girls."

I was so scared of gettin' another scar on my face from her rings I swallowed my blood rather than spit it out. As we stripped to our bare butts, we looked at each other, trying not to laugh. I still had three lipglosses hidden in my bandanna. After we got dressed, we held our stolen bikinis and walked like prisoners into K-Mart to turn ourselves in. Jesse James had been caught.

I had finally succeeded in reducing Mom to tears. It didn't feel as good as I thought it was gonna. It was like peeling a scab from my cat's skin. It felt like heaven while I was doin' it. But then, when the bleeding wound got infected and oozed with pus, I felt guilty as a Vietnam Vet.

There she was sittin in Juvenile Court, in between Aunt Erica and Benny Goodman, as the Dove Butt Angels stood in front of the Mormon, grey-haired judge swearing to "tell the truth and nothing but the truth so help us God". Crying in unison, Kat and Dona promised they'd never steal again. I couldn't understand why kids thought cryin' would make adults feel sorry for them. I remember thinkin' *most grown ups like watchin' kid tears cos they can't cry themselves*.

The judge noticed I was giving him the Charlie Manson eye and the Elvis lip curl.

"What have you got to say for yourself, young lady?" The Mormon Santa Claus raised his silver eyebrow.

O.K., I could have done some Method actin', beggin' for forgiveness like my sorry ass cousins, that would have been the "right" thing to do. But I just got back from England and I was feelin' all rebellious and special again. The Greedy Mouth devil in me had to wipe that God-salesman smirk off his face.

I said the first thing I thought Sperm Giver would say,

"I'm a socialist! People shouldn't have to pay for that poor quality stuff they get in K-Mart. They get the Mexicans to make it for no money, you white men are the ones who steal!"

My TV mind half anticipated a standing ovation.

"Your insubordination leads me to believe you have no remorse, and that you need to be taught a lesson young lady. I take that back. "Young lady" is the wrong term to use for you. Do you know what it's like being locked up?"

The judge was practically havin' orgasms.

Blah Blah Blah. To cut the story short, I had to spend the night in Juvie.

Swear to God.

I ate with these other big butt girls in the cafeteria. Then they made us watch *Scared Straight,* a juvenile crime prevention TV documentary where small-time offenders like me were taken to grown-up prisons where prisoners would supposedly scare them with stories about homosexual rape.

As I sat in Juvie all night, I decided I didn't want to steal anymore, not cos I was scared of going to jail and being gang-raped by a bunch of girls with a broom handle - it couldn't be any worse than James Sprinkler-head. It was seein' my mother break down and cry in court . I could think of more exciting things to steal... like boys' hearts, or friends' personalities.

I moved on to the ice cream shelf in the freezer.

SUGARFOOT

Aged 11.

Sugarfoot wasn't just a street. It was a short cut. A bridge to teenage torture. And I wish I hadn't Red Rovered over so quickly. Forever the outsider, saying everything I could to be liked, worrying if my smile was right, wondering if my style of walking could be sexier. Hankering for cooldom.

Apart from facial warts and premature breast lumps, my biggest problem at the time was excessive body hair. I had to trim my pubic hair every day so the girls in the locker room wouldn't notice how abnormally long it was. I thought it was the worst thing that could happen to me. It wasn't.

Each problem I faced quickly got replaced by an even larger one. My head became so full of equations, it started to cure my boredom sickness. But even when I was in a thick forest of adolescent pain, I always saw the funny side. It was all really serious shit, but also really ridiculous. Everything that was occurring seemed to be just another TV cliché. Each new trauma I faced with an almost knowing smile, like I had already seen this episode on last week's *Facts of Life* or *Go ask Alice,* that TV movie about that teenage girl who gets addicted to drugs after getting mixed up with the "wrong crowd".

Just a block from my house, opposite what we named Sugarfoot desert, stood a four-foot concrete wall. Underneath the Sugarfoot street sign, nearly twenty drop-outs, virgins, drug addicts and unloved losers would sit in a row throwing rocks at cars, spending sweltering hours capping on each other and getting far too stoned. At dusk boys stole their long-lost dad's guns and played target practice off a Sugarfoot wall.

Ever since they arrested Mrs Swartz for putting razor blades in her Halloween candy, cop cars would drive up and down every hour, which added to the excitement. Kids from a five-mile radius met there every day after school and stayed until single moms put TV dinner on the coffee table.

Sugarfoot Street was off limits after my mom found out I was stealing a bottle of whiskey from Grandma's house during our weekly visits. I'd take Grandma's bottle of whiskey and hand it over to Marco, the Mexican Matt Dillon, with a lizard's tongue and scorpion sting. Under the pre-teen influence of dudes, drugs and stealing, sneaking out windows and hiding behind streetlamps became a daily routine.

I had no choice: back at the ranch, everything turned Little House on the Prairie when Benny started givin' his opinion about how I should be restricted from Sugarfoot. For the first few months of knowin' Benny Big Balls, I managed to give him the silent treatment but when he started doin' somersaults into *my* pool and blowin' his nose on *my* water I had to Houdini.

As far as those two church-lovin' teachers were concerned, the Sugarfoot sign spelt "corruption zone". My mom and Benny would drive by in the Buick with the top down calling out my name. Cos Benny was a basketball coach, his voice was like five Ozzy Osbournes in one. Since he saw my mom cry in Juvie Court, he was determined to scare me straight.

I couldn't stand staying in our house at night, especially when I found out my mother was planning on getting hitched to him. He was practically livin' with us and, worst of all, he started making me go to church again and he wasn't even Catholic. He was a jock and all stoners hated jocks! He was obsessed with betting on football and basketball games so he'd have like three TVs on and portable radios blaring out of the bathroom.

He drove me nuts, so me and my cat went crawling out the window over the rose bush at 11:00 p.m. almost every night. Sammy Cat would go off in one direction and me in the other. We were on HEAT.

The Sugarfoot ghetto blaster boomed Ozzy Osbourne.

First time I ever saw Berto, he was sitting on *the* wall with a bottle of Bud in one hand and a joint in the other. This Zorro badseed had a wicked, crooked gringo grin, no shirt and faded, ripped Levi's with his boxer shorts showin' through. Him and the other drop-outs whistled at us virgin eighth-graders to come on over and spit a while.

Me and my new itty-bitty-tittie committee - Caitlin, Stacy, Julia, Laura and Lisa - gave the guys some beer money, and they lifted us on to their wall.

"Do you want a tortilla? Do you want some acid?"

I took a sniff of poppers and fell off the wall but Berto caught me and I melted into him like cheese. He invited me into his rec room to see his pet tarantula. While the other guys worked on popping cherries in the heat, Berto showed me his waterbong. On top of the pool table, he showed me his tongue. That was the first day I started washin' my own underwear.

All the guys ask us embarrassing questions about our holes.
How hairy is it?
How big is it?
Has it been popped?

I looked away shy for the first time in my life and whispered "Shut up!" like a wimpy little girl. I had found my Manson family. I trusted none of the backstabbers. To get away from Aunt Erica, my cousins had abandoned me to live with their dad in Seattle. My new leaders took me in and fried my brain. Within weeks my personality took a nose dive. I was performing amazin' Houdini escape stunts. I was better than Robert De Niro at Method acting. I could fly away further than Amelia Earhart ever could.

The safe country-lane adventures of England seemed planets away. Physically I had gained ten pounds within three months of being back from England, but mentally I shrunk to the dot of an ink pen.

The Sugarfoot guys didn't bother with shooting animals or young boys. They got off on picking on girls, probably as a way of getting back at their moms. These dudes were like a bitter margarita, a dash of Cheech and Chong and 90% James Sprinkler-head proof.

Howie, the balding, 18-year-old doobie dealer was the "home grown man who can." Three knocks on the shed door and you're in. Ten bucks for a healthy dime bag. We would ditch school to hang out with all these Sugarfoot losers, following them into the desert watchin' them dirt bike-riding or doin' BMX jumps. Us girls never took part in anything except for lying down on the desert rocks and lettin' them do Evel Knievel jumps over us. Otherwise we'd just talk about who liked who, leaning against lowriders and peeing behind tumbleweeds.

Sugarfoot nearly destroyed what little "oomph" Judy Garland taught me. When I first showed my smart ass at Sugarfoot I was a jet-settin' cheeky chops lookin' to steal boys hearts. I'd been to Juvie and survived *Scared Straight*. Of course, I was still havin' zeitgeber attacks and black days, but I was tryin' to fight my soul monsters with memorised Sperm Giver sayings and smiling stoner style.

Marco put the icing on my microwaved man-hating cake. Like Berto, he was three years older than me and ended up raggin' on me for the next five years. Marco was the "King of the Cuts". That peckerhead put me in my boy-worshipping place on the first day of Sugarfoot hell. He could shrink-wrap anyone with cuts. He always said the things he knew would hurt the most. Like when he wanted free weed from Howie, he'd just go something like,

"Come on dude. . . take your hat off and show us your balding, scabby ol' head, we all know you're a 30 year-old faggot living in your mama's shed."

Before I met him I thought I knew how to reduce people to tears. Once he shot his water pistol at me, I never wanted to induce tears again. Marco's favourite trick was making me laugh at the insults he threw at me. His words were like a 1000 sprinkler-heads fuckin' with my crotch. He'd rag on my name, the size of my thighs, the wart scars on my face - every part of my body was dissected and spat out on to the sidewalk. It was one thing to sit there and disappear mentally until he moved on to the next victim but to have to smile and giggle at the most hurtful things anyone could possibly to you was worse than feeling the dermatologist burning warts off your face.

After a while I got used to it and just tried to sit at the very end of the wall. I never let him see me cry but when I got home to that bowl of ice cream and locked myself in the bathroom it was like the sinking of the Titanic.

So I became quiet, paranoid and non-stop stoned. One good thing about bein' such a hardcore stoner was that my facial twitches mellowed out. I just walked around with droopy eyes and cotton mouth. The bad side of gettin' so fried all the time was that I could feel my brain cells disappearing. Every time I hit the big waterbong in Howie's shed and held it in to the count of thirty, I could hear them bursting like tiny balloons.

When I woke up in the morning, I lit a roach and before I went to sleep I lit a roach. After I'd snuck back in my window, I'd lie there for hours listening to Ozzy on my new Walkman to block out the sound of sex. While the black room got furry with linty particles and spun around, I acted out in my mind the day I would heroically "cut" Marco with my memorised list of insults, then everyone would cheer at the end and I'd be the new Fonz.

The itty-bitty-tittie committee wanted to be girlfriends so we'd wait patiently to be pulled off the wall and dragged up to the Sugarfoot bombed-out car. At 4:00 p.m. everyday you'd see some guy carrying a young, sun-spotted girl up there into desert to try and de-virginize her. I thought if I could only be someone's girlfriend then I would belong to someone, somewhere. Caitlin would go,

"You don't gotta even worry about speakin' if you're somebody's giiirlfrieeend."

Finally I was Berto's girlfriend cos he'd already gone down the line of girls on the wall. It was my turn for finger fuckin'. Two weeks was the normal run. It had only been a week when he whispered in my ear, "I love you baby." I knew he would say anything to get near my pubic hair.

I should have known he was crazy, due to his fondness for tarantulas, but he convinced me to let him and the Sugarfoot posse invade my house one school day.

When we first got to my house and stripped down to bikinis and boxers there were about five couples lounging in and around my pool. Poor Howie was rolling joints on his own on the diving board. Of course I was sure everybody would pee in the pool cos they secretly hated me. Every now and then a girl got carted off to the bathroom.

"Give her another joint. Maybe that will loosen her up." Marco called from inside my mom's bedroom window. Me and my new boyfriend were lying on my personalised mail order raft. I remember he took off his gold chain with Jesus on the cross and lassoed it around my neck. As usual it was hot as hell and I was trying to keep one eye on Berto's hand and the other on the look-out for my neighbour Mr. Hensen. Since Benny had started golfing with him, he was like their spy. My bedroom window faced his so he'd keep an ear out for any sneaking around at night.

I barely heard Benny come out of the sliding glass door cause Berto was jamming his slimy tongue in and out of my ear. Bathing suits were riding up and just as Berto was about to slip his worm in, Benny's voice jilted Berto's butt off the raft. I slipped to the bottom of the pool and stayed there as long as I could. When I came up for air, beer bottles had been tipped over, boys went scattering like cockroaches and Benny had captured Marco and Berto by the back of their greasy necks. Berto was trying to get his jeans back on over his soaking hard-on.

For the first time I saw Bejamin act like the almighty teacher-detective he truly was. He looked pretty scary as he lined us all up against the backyard wall.

"I want to know what your names are and where you live?"

Silence.

"NOW!" He had his pad of betting paper and a pencil in his hand. The girls gave their names and when it got to Marco and Berto they both muttered,

"Fuck you, man!"

Benny's face turned red as he lunged at the two Mexican jumpin' beans. Marco's skinny ass bounced over the wall but Berto got slam-dunked against the cement wall.

"YOUR. MOTHER. NEVER. TAUGHT. YOU. ANY. MANNERS." Each word accompanied a punch. Then, by the belt-loops of his Levi's, Benny picked up Berto and threw him over our five-foot concrete wall.

My Zorro landed in a bed of tumbleweeds and spiders. Berto's Vans were still carefully set against the base of my palm tree where he had placed them. My now ex-boyfriend was so mad his brown skin turned plum-coloured as he swore in broken Spanish and pulled glass from his bare feet.

Then the rocks came flyin' over our wall like golfballs. I peeked through the wall and watched as Benny chased those losers all the way back to the corner of Sugarfoot. I knew Berto and Marco would plan their revenge swiftly.

Under strict orders from Benny, Mom put me on restriction forever and goes,

"If you ever step one foot on Sugarfoot Street again, you'll be sent to England for good."

Locks were put on my bedroom window and I was forced to go to accordion lessons again. None of the Sugarfoot girls were speaking to me, except for one day when Caitlin came knockin' on my door askin' for Berto's necklace back. I kept his Vans though and cried over them every night for a week. Between peeling off toilet-papered trees and hosing down Benny's egged Buick, I watched *Endless Love* over and over again, convinced someday Berto would take me back.

Killer's playground.

Aged 12.

It was six years ago today when I first got turned on by the enemy. Sometimes I think I just made the whole thing up, a stoner chick's hallucination, the latest attention-seeking stunt. Or like it coulda just been one of those TV memories. But, if it didn't happen, where did the fear come from?

There ain't no words to describe terror when it electrocutes you in a split second. Maybe it's different when you have time to live with it, like if you're on a sinking ship or bein' slowly lowered into a pool of sharks. All I know is that I courted the fear, prick teased it, like my dad says, "narcissistically."

Sugarfoot desert was a mile long and wide. It was a rugged short cut home from school. Usually I walked through Sugarfoot with friends but they all hated me that hot April day. Nobody was walkin' through Sugarfoot these days: it was temporarily off limits cos two girls had been found murdered there in the past three weeks. Before Julia Busha and Nancy Baldero were killed, I was allowed to walk through Sugarfoot all the time.

After the murders, I really did plan on avoiding the desert. But, on this particular day, I had no choice. The Sugarfoot bitches at school were coming down on me real heavy. At lunch the word was out - I was gonna get my ass kicked behind Spanish Trails apartment complex. It's not like they hadn't tortured me enough - toilet papering our house, egging Benny's Buick, and spreading rumours about my non-existent sex life.

And my ass. I had the most famous butt at school thanks to them. Actually it originated with Berto, the ex-boyfriend. He had said that there were twelve purple worm-like stretch marks running down my butt cheeks. When I found that out, I burnt his Vans.

After I came out of 7-Eleven, there were all these brats right outta River's Edge waitin' for me. I knew it was gonna to be a bad childhood memory the day after I got expelled for beating up this black boy. It happened in fourth period P.E. class. All the guys were fighting to line up behind me when we were about to do toe-touches. They were hoping for a glimpse of the purple worms.

Since I hadn't been hangin' out with the Sugarfoot losers, I was kinda back to my sassy self. I swooped over and touched my nose to knee cap, placing the palms of my hands on the sizzling gravel. I just hung there, having a good stretch in a kiss-my-ass kinda way. All of a sudden this little shit grabbed a chunk of my ass and squeezed it so hard I wailed out at the top of my lungs, "FUCKER!" For that I had to go to the Dean's office.

So I'm standin' there quenching' my thirst with my Big Gulp Slushy in front of 7-Eleven, tryin' to plan an escape route. Buying time Clint Eastwood style, I took a big looong suck on the straw. Just as I was about to do the cowardly lion thing and hide in the 7-Eleven bathroom, I heard Stacie shout,

"Hey, we're gonna cut your hair, slutface!"

This was a fate worse than death. My hair was the last part of me that held any hope at specialness in the future. What was left of my 12-year-old instincts told me to run. Run. Run. My Big Gulp went flyin'.

I high-tailed my juicy ass so fast to that desert. I looked back to see these hee-hawin', Aqua-Net girls waving cigarettes, as they galloped after me. They were gaining on me but, just in the nick of time, I did my best Charlie's Angels stunt roll underneath the barbed wire fence.

There they all were, lined up against the fence like barking chihuahuas hungry for a bite of humiliation but not enough guts to enter the candy-coated land of Sugarfoot where I don't know how many corroded feet laid buried beneath the lizards, rattlesnakes, scorpions, Black Widows and tarantulas.

I kept running for another three hundred yards. I was gonna sprint the whole mile. But not only was I the most hated girl at school, with the biggest tits and ass you've ever seen on a white 12-year-old, but I also suffered from asthma. I had to sit down and catch my breath. I slumped over my favourite look-out rock and loosened my grip around my notebook. It was filled with sex stories I wanted to send to Penthouse.

Sittin' on that rock, I couldn't believe just two years before, me and my cousins used to play with Barbie dolls in an alcove of big, white boulders I named *Jessie's Lookout*. If you stood tippy toe on top on the highest crag you could get a view of the Strip and Sleeping Indian Mountain.

Inside was a secret cave we cleaned out and made into our club den. When I first crawled in, I found all these Penthouse magazines full of nasty, naked chicks, legs spread-eagled with hairy tarantula crotches. Some of the pages were stuck together with cum. We had great fun pullin' each page apart with my mother's rubber gloves, screaming and giggling, as we shoved the centrefold into each other's faces. Crusty particles sprinkled their Catholic school uniforms with sin. The photos made me sick but the stories at the back kinda turned me on. Readers' wives would write their sexual fantasies where the plumber comes to fix the toilet and instead fixes the horny wife over the sink.

Before it dawned on me that I was sittin' in an uncaught serial killer's playground, I thought it would be a good idea to smoke this roach I'd been saving for lying by the pool. It was my mom's Maui Wowie, the best Hawaiian weed you could get. It was left over from before she started hangin' out with the ex-Mormon school teacher.

Getting stoned was a bad idea. My breathing was under control but the actual actuality of the reality not only dawned on me but knocked me off my rock.

I remembered that ol' story Howie told us in his shed, about how Sugarfoot desert was where a famous Indian tribe was massacred by white settlers a hundred years ago. The fear and paranoia set in and I burst into tears. One 12-year-old's perception of hell. Half the school chasing me down the street and now I'm in the middle of Sugarfoot, an Indian haunting ground.

I wiped the tears from my eyes with my t-shirt. I was a tuff chick: I handled Juvie and finger-fucking, I knew I could handle this. I took a few deep yoga breaths and counted to ten as I exhaled. I scanned the desert landscape and wiped the sweat from my brow.

I picked up my books, checked my house key around my neck, and started along the path at a slow, steady pace. It was too damn quiet. There were no vultures cackling, no drills pounding at the earth, no dirt bikes, no sound of money-counting machines. Just a few hallucinated heads popping out from behind rocks... John Wayne and Clint Eastwood-looking types but no Lone Rangers.

Sugarfoot is my rocky playground - it belongs to me, not to those fucking men with their dick problems. There's no way any murderers would be hangin' around here, they'd be in the next state looking for their next victim. Sugarfoot was just the dumping ground for bodies, used condoms, tortured cats and unwanted couches. No freakshow could be campin' out here in this heat waiting for a tight-assed 12-year-old fox to be skippin' along like Little Red Riding Hood. This was government property sealed off by the F.B.I. O.K. O.K. O.K. Breathe deeply, tuff chick. 10-4 Big Buddy.

It was weird cos I started thinkin' about those girls who'd been murdered. I began to imagine the emotions, the sound of the shrieks, how much pain was involved. Did the shock and fear numb any physical torture? Why did I think these things? Why?

Then the tears came again, not sobbing, just slow and steady like my walking. I could just about see the edge of the desert. I was at the halfway point now. The heat in the distance was rippling above the dirt.

I pick up the pace. Neck ache. Paranoia. Watch your back. Keep skipping little girl. Three blind mice, three blind mice, see how they run, see how they run. Brushing past the famous "make-out couch", I hummed my favourite clapping game:

take a peach, take a pear, take a piece of underwear,
caught you with your boyfriend last night - nosy
ate a box of candy, greedy-so-oo ba-ba-baleeny

My heart beats faster-faster-bumpety-bump-slap-thump-pumpy-pump-bang. And then heart stop! Just as I was starting to see the edge of the desert, there he was. The faceless man. The evil man I have dreamt about since I was 5. Heart stop and then the beating, the heart beats so fast, beats so fast, you're sure it will explode. And the lightning bolt terror.

He was about forty feet to the left of me. I giggled nervously. I thought it might have been someone from Sugarfoot Street. Maybe Marco. But I wasn't going to stick around to find out. I dropped my notebook and began to sprint. Another chase. I had about a hundred yards to go to the edge of Sugarfoot, where a big beautiful cement wall would be waiting for me, holding a pool to dive into. All I could think of was Mommy. I knew I should have been concentrating on how to hurdle the next tumbleweed or dodge the next rattlesnake but my head was just Mommy. MOMMY.

He was going to try to cut me off at the fence. I felt like bloody Nancy Drew. I turned my head once. I wanted to see the look on his face but all I got were his shoes. Would you believe it? He had Nikes on, too. The edge of the desert was so close now, but so was he.

Luckily, I knew exactly where the fence curled up so I dived, like I'd done so many times before, into my turquoise pool. I tore my skin right open on a strand of barbed wire. I was now on the other side of the fence but my hair was caught in the wire. He was there. Upon me. He couldn't get to me from under the wire, so he attempted to pull me through by knotting my hair around his fist. The wire was scraping at my face. He didn't have my neck yet but that's what he was going for. Then I saw the switchblade, and that was it. I wasn't worried about my hair anymore. I dug my shoes into the earth and bolted my body away from the wire.

I tumbled back down the slope of dirt which descended to the gravel a few yards below. I didn't feel the pain of the strands being ripped from their sockets. I just remember the sound, the sound was like the worst tree-splicing thunder I ever heard. I staggered across the street with the last morsel of energy I had, then crumpled up against my street sign pole.

My sweet, safe, lower middle-class street paved with neighbourhood watchdogs. I knew he wasn't going to come out from Sugarfoot desert. There were too many cars going by and I could see Mr Goober mowing his lawn.

I couldn't move. My muscles had turned to mush. My stomach and face were bleeding and there were clumps of hair falling all over me. A car stopped. I just slumped in the gutter, shaking like a run-over dog. I couldn't take my eyes off him standing there at the edge of the desert. He had my notebook, my notebook which had all my sex stories I'd been trying to write, like the ones in porno mags. Would he make it sticky?

I still couldn't really see his face, he just looked like any other Las Vegas man or tourist ; a baseball cap and mirrored sunglasses.

And then he disappeared back into the desert.

That's what gets me the most. I knew this freakshow had or still has my most personal writing. Or maybe he doesn't, maybe he's dead, maybe he's in prison, maybe he works at the International House of Pancakes, or maybe I just made him up - I don't know. But it makes the edges of my mouth curl. Although I hated the terror somehow... somehow I got turned on by the enemy.

They never found the killer of those two poor girls. They never found the guy who spooked me. Something bigger replaced the news headlines. A couple of weeks after the chase, they started doin' construction work on Sugarfoot. The land was smoothed out and rows of cement walls holding swimming pools were slapped down. Whatever ghosts that may have lurked through that patch of desert would be long gone by now.

After the Sugarfoot bitches at school found out what had happened they thought I was really cool, fighting off a serial killer and all. So, after a few weeks of not going to school, I went back a heroine. I think they were just happy because my hair looked like shit. At least I was allowed to walk home with the Sugarfoot girls again. I didn't like them much, but at least I was safe... apart from the occasional kerb-crawler.

I never went into Sugarfoot desert again, but my little secret is - I did sit on the kerb, underneath the street sign in the following weeks, hoping, just hoping to get a glimpse, but I never did. In the following years, sometimes I thought I saw him at the airport, or at the 7-Eleven counter, or cleaning my neighbour's pool, or delivering a pizza, or at the traffic lights, sitting in the car next to me... He's always there.

Airplane. ✈

The freaky girl sittin' next to me is still zonked out... so is everyone else. It's just me and my little spotlight.

On to the next memory...

BEHIND 7-ELEVEN

Aged 12.

Laura Ray was the most beautiful and scary girly girl in the eighth grade. By girly girl I mean a Nevada bobcat tuff chick with a Barbie Doll exterior. This Pinky Tuskadero used her hair like a weapon. In class, Laura Ray'd be sittin' in the front row and, when she got mad at the teacher for makin' her spit her gum out, she would flip her hair so hard and fast she'd knock out the five kids sitting directly behind her.

Laura Ray had the coolest hairdo for miles. Unlike every other girl, it wasn't even layered or Aqua Netted. Most stoner girls only styled the front of their 'do. The back would be a scraggly, chlorine perm, but her hair was sculpted all around like a Santa Cruz wave. It was as blonde as the sun-bleached baby hairs on her arms. She had sapphire Hawaiian eyes and a butt made for shrink-to-fit Levi's. She reminded me of my mom. When she walked down the street, cars would slow down to check if her face was as nice as her hair and ass and then honk approvingly.

You could say I was obsessed with my cool clone leader... maybe even in love. Laura's quiet arrogance was intriguing as hell. She wouldn't pretend at anything for anyone. At 13 years old, she made Farrah Fawcett look like an ageing Diana Dors. She had that wide-eyed panther edginess Nastassja Kinski oozed from her dewy pores.

Laura had a vent brush that doubled up as a hairspray bottle. She always had vodka in it and sprayed it in to her mouth between classes. Of course, I got a vent brush just like hers and filled it with whiskey. Nobody gave a shit.

Us girly girl stoners used to walk home together through the golf course. We stayed about fifty yards behind the Sugarfoot guys who hadn't been kicked out of school yet. It was like walkin' through Vietnam or somethin', you never knew when an attack would break out. Everyone at school feared us cos we were the Sugarfoot cool clones.

We looked and talked exactly the same. I replaced my own unique vocabulary with generic sayings. "That's so retarded", "You're soooo gay", "I'm buzzin' dude", "Hey, girlfriend". We had big hair, the matching tan, Le Sport Sac under-the-arm purse, shared blue eyeliner, cut-off t-shirts, Dr Pepper Lip Smackers and white Nikes.

Laura Ray's throne was the sidewalk and my big aspiration was to walk next to her. When I tried, she'd bump me into the gutter with the swing of her tight hip. She never said why she didn't like me, but she hardly said anything to anyone.

I studied her outta the corner of my sunglasses the way I used to study my mom. If I could just get her mannerisms down pat I might soak up some of that specialness.

When we laid out by the pool I counted all her beauty marks. The two on the edge of her earlobe were perfect, I can still see them now. I don't know what's so appealing about beauty marks - they're really just sun spots. For some reason, particular girls' beauty spots looked better than others. When she closed her eyes, Laura's long eyelashes touched her cheeks. Occasionally, I'd get this urge to lean over her and lick them...but I never did.

Her fingers were as delicate as spiders' legs, thin and precise. Bein' a Method actress, I copied everything she did, and practised in front of the mirror at home. I even tried finger exercises to get my hands thinner.

The way she twirled her gum; the Jean Naté perfume she wore; the 'Foxy' gold necklace charms she fingered all the time. If she had a roach clip hanging out of her hair, I did too. Every day I'd stick a joint into her locker. That's probably the only reason I was allowed to hang around with the Sugarfoot chicks - I was practically the Junior High drug dealer since my cousin Timmy moved in with us. I had a full stash to steal from daily.

The Sugarfoot Gang was still going strong, but nobody hung out on that street corner cos of all the Pigs. Berto was in Juvie for stealing a bike, so the pain of our two-week love scab had healed. After school, we assembled around 7-Eleven and at Beth's house. She had a pool and both her parents worked nightshift. When someone wanted to screw, they'd go over to the golf course or use one of Beth's bathrooms. The running joke was girls always ended up with sore heads from skull-banging on the base of the toilet while humping.

I didn't like my Manson family much, but it was better than sittin' at home watching *Hill Street Blues* with the lovebird teachers. One week, I was hated by the Sugarfoot Gang and the next, I was tolerated. It was cos of my zeitgeber mood swing attacks. On Monday I'd be an obedient, cool clone, smoking away, hand on hip, and then the next day I'd insult them all.

"You're not feminists - you follow the guys like zombies... there's a difference between acting like Marilyn Monroe and acting like Amelia Earhart." When I talked like that they'd just go,

"Dude, you're sooo gaaay".

After school this particular day, while we were walkin' towards 7-Eleven, I waited for the lighter to be passed to me so I could light my Clove ciggy. I hated smoking, but I had to.

Laura Ray was up at the front, doin' that Laura Ray walk I had nearly perfected. I was bringin' up the rear with my identical, mirror cop sunglasses. I had to keep pushin' 'em up with my cigarette hand cos my nose was so small. The Queen kept lookin' at me over the top of her sunglasses and then exhaling perfect 'O's. She could always do the best smoke rings.

She was still mad at me because I wouldn't take the blame at recess when we both got caught sneakin' to the golf course ditch. The Sugarfoot girls did this every day, at lunch time, to get high. Seven girls in skin tight jeans, running across the baseball field. I was never any good at short distance running. I was way at the back with Laura Ray cos she was too cool to run.

All the other girls were in the ditch when the security guard blew his whistle at us to come back. Of course, Laura Ray had all the weed on her. We had to turn back otherwise the other girls would have been busted too. She grabbed my arm and ordered me to take it. I said "no way". She couldn't drop it because he had his binoculars on us. We got dragged off to the Dean's office, as the others watched from the ditch. Laura Ray got searched and kicked out of school for a week. Because my mom taught the Dean's kid at her school, I just got detention for two weeks.

So anyways, when we were in 7-Eleven filling our Big Gulps, Caitlin whispered to me that there was gonna be a fight between Laura Ray and this girl called Susy. I was feelin' paranoid and I wasn't in anyone's good books.

"Let's go to my house for a joint and a swim." I said.

She went,

"You knooow we haaave to waaatch. That's the ruuules, honey!"

So I got my Diet Coke and a packet of Watermelon Bubblicious and headed out into the 110-degree heat.

There were always fights at our school. Mainly between the black kids and the white kids. I hated fights, hated watching them and hated gettin' into 'em. Lately, I'd been gettin' into lots of fist fights, most of them were with boys.

One day when we were playing tag football this kid tackled me and pushed his fist against my crotch. I never reacted to verbal insults but when he touched me, I just beat the shit out of him. I just got a hold of his Afro with one hand, got out my fingernails and scratched his face up good. My throbbing body was covered with white fist marks, but he didn't make me bleed so I reckoned I'd won. Blood was always the score keeper.

So we were all standin' behind 7-Eleven waitin' for somethin' to happen, sippin' on our drinks, smokin' our fags and sweatin'. Then, a few evil kids started chanting "Fight! Fight! Fight!" More than fifty kids came running around the corner of the store. Laura and Susy kicked off the ceremony with the standard name-calling ritual.

The big stand-off seemed to last forever. Who would attack first? I turned to walk away. I wanted to go home, eat and curl up with my snacks and my Grandad TV. Way better entertainment. Then I heard someone shout,

"You're soo gaay".

It came from Laura Ray.

I felt a hand on my shoulder. As I swung round Laura nailed me right on the sweaty nose. Her thin fingers held no force though, as her hand slipped off. The Sugarfoot bitches knew I was gonna be jumped. More punishment. I dropped my cigarette but I didn't have time to take my glasses off. I tried to defend myself all the while pleading,

"Laura, I don't want to fight you..." over and over again.

"Fuck off and die!" was her reply.

It was like bein' hit by someone you really love, a combination of pleasure and pain. *This is my Story of O.*

I knew she was as nervous as I was cos she started slappin' at the air, not even really aiming at me, all haphazard and girly. I figured I had to end it as quickly as possible so I grabbed that long, luscious, blonde hair, twisted it round my hand, like a yo-yo, got the claws out and started doin' a Jack the Ripper on her arms as she punched me. Greasy boys were pushing to get to the front line.

I wanted to cry, but of course I didn't.

She made the mistake of homin' in on my hair. Unfortunate for her, since half of it got ripped out by the serial killer. She lost precious seconds that she needed to keep on her feet. Because her jeans were so tight, her perfect legs gave out from underneath. The hair that was formerly attached to her head was now dangling from my fist. She fell, as if in slow motion. With not even an elbow to break the fall, Laura Ray landed right on her bronzed forehead. The crowd gulped hot air and exhaled, "Riiight Ooon!"

I couldn't stop clobberin' her.

I lost control. I hit her over and over again. Her gold charm necklace fell to the ground. Hatred or anger didn't even come into it, just this physical release. I felt like a man. The surge of adrenaline snaked around my muscles. Once the rush came, I couldn't stop pounding. My fists seemed to grow into these jumbo-sized burritos, fleshy white knuckles meeting head on with Laura bone.

All of a sudden, my brain put the brakes on my limbs. Like a sock to the stomach. Having lost control of my body once again, I contracted and fell directly on top of my opponent. The Sugarfoot girls greedily scrambled for Laura's gold trinkets. It didn't look good, Laura, the girl of my dreams, locked beneath my pelvis in missionary position.

Exhausted, I sprawled out like a pancake cooking in the heat. We flopped there for a minute, while everyone laughed. Because I was about fifteen pounds heavier than Laura, there was no way she could budge. Laura was still flailing her arms above the gravel like a lady bug tryin' to turn over on its feet. I waited patiently to catch my breath and for my throbbing body to stop aching. Everyone was chanting,

"The witch is dead, the witch is dead".

I never knew everyone hated her so much. I thought they all worshipped her.

I sat up on her back, spluttering,

"I didn't want to fight, I didn't want to fight".

Then the 7-Eleven guy, Gus, came out.

"I'm gonna call the cops if you don't beat it."

Silence fell like miracle rain as Laura slowly rose to her feet. I wanted to go over and help her up, the way I helped my mommy,when Leo beat the shit out of her.

I almost cried when I saw Laura's perfect blonde eyebrow clotted in blood and gravel. More shocking was the bald patch, smack in the middle of her scalp, just above her lovely widow's peak. With her hand around her bare neck, she took one last look at me before she hobbled off in one direction and I, triumphant, in the other.

For the first time I led the Sugarfoot Gang along the sidewalk to Beth's house for my victory celebration. The girls were passing me cigarettes, gum and a comb for my hair. I was also handed Laura's "# 1" gold charm. As I pushed my sunglasses up on to the bridge of my nose, I didn't feel like the big shot I thought I would.

Why is it the minute you get what you want you don't want it no more?

All the guys re-enacted the fight. "Girl fights are way cooler than dudes, way more blood". New names were appointed to call Laura in the hallway, the way they had done for me. The girls called her on the phone and told her she was out of the gang. I was nicknamed "Jessie Duke" from then on.

The Sugarfoot Gang were supposed to be so rebellious, but they were still sticking to the rules more than any Lionel Richie, lounging-by-the-pool loser. We all had to follow suit like a shoal of fish. The minute someone was brave enough to change the direction, the rest would follow. For a few weeks I became the coolest chick in the neighbourhood. Marco stopped saying "No fat chicks". He even started passin' me the doobie. I think he was worried I might go crazy on him.

Poor Laura Ray, on the other hand, suffered a big-time change in status. She disappeared from school for a week and rumours flew round that I had broken her nose, put her in the hospital and that now she needed plastic surgery. The following week she was back at school with scabs all down her face. Once again I felt like a thief. I may not have had any luck with stealing boys' hearts but I sure fucked up a 13-year-old's beauty.

I felt sorry for her because nobody liked her anymore and I knew what that was like. All she had to do was swallow her pride as I had done many times with the crowd, supply cigarettes and walk in the gutter for a while. But now that she couldn't wear her "# 1" charm around her neck with pride, I guess she thought there was no point in hangin' out with us. She had to be either the best or nothin' to do with the rest.

She had more guts than I ever did. Maybe she'd thank me now for beating all that stuck-up pride out of her.

Over the following years she became almost invisible, a real hermit. The famous hair went strawy and limp. She grew into her eyelashes and her face seemed leathery-sad and unapproachable. In high school, she'd always walk with her head right down. Instead of spending her days partying, word was she studied her ass off because she was gonna be a doctor.

I was heartbroken over Laura Ray. At first all I wanted was to be her, near her and, now that I had taken her place, it was the worst place to be. I had gobbled up the Sugarfoot Manson dream and spat out the bones. I was ready for my next feed.

LAKE MEAD

Aged 13.

The salmon sunrise tickled my outstretched tongue as I snake-danced it into the zillions of air pockets that made up Nevada space. The gust waves slapped my face and titillated the peach fuzz on my jawline as I hollered a big "Yahoooo!"

Death coulda taken us any second. But I needed to feel that blast I felt the first time I stuck my head out the VW window when I said goodbye to California. Adventure, turbulence, escape, tear up that lake. I was gonna drive that baby through the danger zone.

I had to steal Timmy's boat, I couldn't stand being a part of the stillness of that July morning one second longer, with all those sleeping bodies. When the sun reached its peak, it would bake families of bathing-suited, fatty flesh, turning stretch marks hamburger colour.

But for a while it was just me, Jessie Duke horsepower slicing through the glorious hundred-mile, man-made swimming pool. Me, James Bond, driving the coolest hot-rod of a speedboat I ever did see. Chrome pipes shootin' out my ass, givin' the speedometer a work-out. I tightly gripped the furry, tan steering wheel cover. I put on Timmy's mirrored sunglasses and tilted my head back like Jack Nicholson, ready to take on the world.

I was an Easy Rider girl racer skimming the glassy water, swooping and skimming, carving and curving the smooth surface of the water at fifty miles an hour. I pretended there was a helicopter movie camera filming me looking yummy in my white bikini with my caramel tresses rippling above the speed boat.

Aunt Erica, Uncle Bruce, the Ditto Butt cousins, Timmy and the two teachers of Las Vegas were all sleeping in our private alcove on lawn chairs and rafts in mosquito-proof sleeping bags. The ants would be rumbling and working away under the dirt, piling up leftover beef jerky and string cheese strips. The flies were getting ready for a busy day of pestering. Soon, the dreaded sun would stretch its rays, grumpy as hell.

I floored the gas pedal and went over in my mind how I was going to explain "borrowing" my cousin's speedboat. *Sleepdriving. I took off in the boat when I was asleep.*

I sensed movement in the back seat. Kat was wipin' the sleep from her eyes.

"Hey, Farrah Fawcett, we're headin' for the Hoover Dam. I'm gonna find my soul. Yee Haw! We're finger-fucking free!"

Still half asleep, Kat pulled her blanket up around her head, shielding herself from the whiplash wind.

I lit one of Timmy's roaches from the sexy ashtray. The silver roach clip was in the shape of a Playboy Bunny. In the half light not even a fish was stirring. No sign of life anywhere. Just me and Kat left on the Unforbidden Planet, everybody else musta got rescued by Captain Kirk and Doctor Spock. There may have been a few other fortunate Las Vegans with hot rod boats campin' on these islands and alcoves, but not many.

Where else could you just get in a boat and claim your very own island for the weekend? The tourists hadn't discovered its beauty yet. They always headed straight for the Grand Canyon. Lake Mead was twenty times more magical than the English Lake District.

Timmy Cousin taught me how to drive his small four-seater boat the year before. It wasn't as big as Uncle Bruce's but it was his pride and joy. It's one thing stealing his weed but his speedboat was like an extension of his penis. That and his van which pulled the chrome beauty to the lake every weekend. Yep, it would be worth the few thumps and bumps he'd give me.

"Hey Kat, when we grow up - we could set up our own tourist scam. Like, maybe take out-of-town folks on tours of the lake and Hoover Dam. It'd be like the *Loveboat* mixed with *Fantasy Island* with a hot-rod taxi. We'd give 'em a picnic, skiing, inner tubing, doobies and ice chests full of booze. We'd have a portable margarita machine and even do weddings-on-your-own-island type of deal."

I glanced round to see Kat screaming. I couldn't hear a word she said with the wind.

"WHAT?" I barked and rocked my foot off and on the gas pedal, making her jolt on the back seat. She finally shut up, and enjoyed the ride. It was impossible to feel anything but pure joy when you were jettin' through the air on something the size of a Jacuzzi. There's nothing like the feel of the wind beating against your face. To scream and not even be heard by the person sittin' next to you is pure stoner heaven.

Lookin' back, I'd say Lake Mead weekends were the closest I'd ever get to havin' a normal childhood. Every Saturday morning during the spring and summer, half of our dysfunctional family would pile in Uncle Bruce's van and the other big-bottom crew into Timmy's, with the speedboats rigged to the vans. On average there would be about fifteen of us.

Friday night food shopping was the beginning of the buzz. I was in junk food heaven. I'd throw at least five family-size bags of everything in the cart: Oreo cookies, Chips Ahoy, two 24-packs of Diet Coke and Sasha's Cream Soda, eight packs of Reese's Peanut Butter Cups, fifty Popsicle Sticks, ten bags of giant size Dorritos and Lay's sour cream and chives potato chips, frozen hamburger patties and hot dogs, mustard, mayonnaise and buckets of bananas. And, when Grandma was dragged along, a case of whiskey.

In order to get a good island, we all had to meet at my Aunt Erica's house by 7:00 a.m. and load up the drinks, towels, rafts, skis, deck chairs, dogs and kids. The drive to Lake Mead took an hour and I could barely wait to feel the lake beating the belly of the boat, vibrating my toes.

Sometimes on the drive home, after the boats were reattached to the vans, I'd sneak into Timmy's boat and illegally ride alone in the windy sunset. I finally got to see the Vegas skyline.

Just as the van crept over Sleeping Indian mountain pass into town, you could see this island of lights in the middle of a sea of blackness set against jagged mountains. The black desert with a bit of light at its vortex...

Kat crawled over into the front seat, her blonde mane thrashing round her crabbed face. The gigantic mountains looked spooky, like we were being swallowed up by them. Timmy's speedboat cruised beneath, weaving in and out of the shadows and sun. The lake narrowed as we got closer to Hoover Dam.

We had done about three miles and had another five to go. Within a half hour the sun was in full form, radiating through my hair, on to my pink scalp. The blue sky had turned white. I glared upwards through my sunglasses.

"Come on sun, just try and give me cancer you motha-fuckin', tittie-suckin', two-ball bitch!"

The mean ol' sun was like a monstrous 150,000,000-watt lightbulb, nine trillion gallons of Colorado water bein' sucked up by its vapour rays.

"Gas it, dude!" Fully awake now, Kat came up front and co-piloted. "If you can't beat 'em, join 'em."

"Not far to go now, Kitty Kat."

She handed me a Diet Coke and started chompin' on some Cheetos. Kat reached out and let her fingers skim the white frothy water hitting the side of the boat. Her Seattle

New Wave haircut waved round like whipped cream. She threw off her Duran Duran night shirt, exposing her fully developed breasts.

"Watch out for piranhas" I shouted. I noticed the gas level was on empty but like Amelia Earhart I kept going... searching for a soul... searching for a soul...

I'd been on restriction for nearly a month, ever since I stole Benny's Buick. In a way I was glad for it, like a dryin'-out period from the Sugarfoot Gang. Time to work on the tan and stick to the Slim Fast plan. My cousins were down from Seattle for the summer and I was happy hangin' out at their pool every day, coatin' our bodies in Criso oil and holding mirrors to our faces so we could bounce even more sun on to our burning skin.

"Do you wanna drive, Kat?"

"As far as I'm concerned, I've been kidnapped. I'm not getting the blame for this one! Slow down while you're at it." I eased my foot off the accelerator. She was referrin' to the time we stole Benny's car.

I could barely reach the gas pedal when I eased Benny's Buick outta the driveway. We were supposed to be waxing it but instead I steered it down Sugarfoot. Sugarfoot was like a ghost town, not a loser stoner in sight. That Buick was so goddam long it took up half the street. After we got around the block, we switched seats.

As Kat turned on to our street, I could see Benny standin' in the middle of the road, squeezin' his baseball cap. The top of his head looked as if it was gonna blow off. As Benny dragged her across the lawn into the house, Kat tried to put the blame on me. But Benny's voice was like a fog horn.

He was so mad he had to jump in the pool to cool his temper off. Not that I saw any of it. My juicy butt was halfway way down the street.

The lake narrowed as we entered the final stretch of our destination. Time passed. Not too fast, not too slow, right outside of ticking time. No sound but the motor spraying chunks of water. Kat and I tilting together as the boat swooped in and out of rock caves. Amelia Earhart and her co-pilot.

"Hey, look at those cables up there. I wonder if we'd get electrocuted if one fell into the water."

They loomed over our heads, stretching like rubber bands from cliff to opposite cliff.

The water was so deep it was pitch black. I thought of Houdini plummeting to the bottom of oceans in chains and locks.

"Can you believe there used to be a town underneath us?"

"What?" Kat interrupted my dark thoughts.

"Yep, when they built that dam it got washed away."

"I bet if we dove to the bottom we'd find a bunch of souls locked in trunks."

"What are you talkin' about? You're soooo gaay... Gawd, remember when your mom gave us that stupid history lesson about Hoover Dam when you just moved to Vegas?"

Three cousins guzzling grape sodas in the back seat of a smoke-infested Pinto with no air-conditioning. There was this tour you could do where you went inside the dam and an elevator took you into the base of it. Luckily it was too expensive, so we walked around on top, leaning over the ledge, daring each other to jump.

"Be careful and listen up, kiddos," Mom had instructed in her teacher voice, that day. As she dragged on her cigarette and pulled up her boob tube, tourists gathered round to listen to the beautiful blonde. "Hoover Dam was built back in the 1930's. It holds back the Colorado water, and it pipes water through, when needed, to California and New Mexico."

When her baby powder voice got goin', us numbskulls were transfixed.

"A lot of men died building the Hoover dam. Can you imagine all that concrete put into place with thousands of starving gold diggers, who had come out West, during the Depression, thinkin' they could strike it rich . Life was cheap back then.They would simply put their foot in the wrong place, lose their balance, and go plummeting down into the history books."

Kat interrupted my memory of a Bennyless mother.

"Can you believe all those dare-devil idiots tightrope-walkin' over the dam just to get famous. That's crazy shit, man."

Almost every other week you'd read about some stunt or suicide taking place at Hoover Dam.

"Do you wanna be famous when you grow up?" Kat asked.

"Duh! Whoo the hellll don't?"

Kat munched on a second bag of Dorritoes and thought hard for two seconds.

"I don't know, Jessie Duke. But did you ever think about *why* you wanna be famous?"

"Kat, you sound just like my Sperm Giver."

We were nearly there and all I wanted was silence from my co-pilot.

"I think people want to be famous to feel more special, you know, like be better than everybody else. Well when, you're like *famous,* everybody totally adores you and does whatever you tell them to - it's like total power, dude."

"Ya, but Marilyn Monroe was famous and she was fucked up. It didn't do her any good."

"Ya, but look at her now, she'll be famous forever."

"Duuuh. She's as dead as a doornail, what good is bein' famous if you're not around to enjoy it?"

Our boob-tube kid conversations went nowhere but circles.

"Wow, man, we're here!" I shouted.

Once I turned off the engine, we drifted in the dissolving wake of the boat. I sat back and stretched out my legs over the side of the boat.

"What a beautiful view."

The buzz of silence was eerie as the boat's nose did a slow circle giving us a full sweeping panoramic view. Because we were on top of the dam, I was unable to see the face of great white wall. I closed my eyes and imagined flying over the ledge.

All of a sudden, Kat went berserk. She leapt to her feet, jiggling up and down, tits bouncin', arms flappin', doin' the typical girly thing.

"What's the matter with you, girl?" My voice echoed. Outta the corner of my eye, I saw a tourist on the dam's bridge-road.

With one hand, Kat pointed towards the water while her other muzzled her mouth.

Fish. Hundreds of small dead fish surrounded the boat. They were floatin' on their sides, chalk white. Their eyes were wide open, encased in fluorescent beams of yellow mucus.

And then there it was. A Great White Shark. The words look so matter-of-fact on paper. A fucking shark was in Lake Mead? For miles, our teeny bopper screams ricocheted through the canyon walls.

All of a sudden we heard this man's voice,

"Get away from the dam. Move your boat from the dam now. You have five seconds to get away from the dam."

The silver shark body was about five foot long, nearly the length of the boat. Its eyes were black. The shark appeared to be dead, cos its fin was floating sideways on the water like a surfboard.

Our boat was drifting closer and closer to the top wall of the dam. Tour buses were travelling over and people started takin' pictures of us. Kat jumped up and down, tipping the boat this way and that.

What happened next is almost too ridiculous to be plausible.

Kat fell overboard. Just like in some terrible piranha movie.My cousin grabbed at the side of the boat. My knees gave out underneath me and I flopped back into the driver's seat. I was in a silent film with the speed going too fast. The boat was turning in circles and I just sat there.

With no help from me, Kat clambered back into the boat, water splashed over the sides of the boat, wetting Timmy's furry carpet.

"Let's get out of here, Jess!"

I turned the key and started to rev the engine. But just as I was about to gas it, the lake policeman, who owned the voice of authority, sidled up in a huge white speed boat.

"There's a shark trying to kill us. Rescue us, please. Pleeeze." I was half expecting him to lasso us like the Lone Ranger. He turned off his engine and shouted through a megaphone,

"Just stay where you are. I'm going to come closer."

"Are we in trouble?"

"This is a restricted area. Didn't you see the signs back there?"

I had to think fast.

"You're lucky the suction wasn't on. You would've been dragged under in seconds - like a whirlpool."

Kat helped me stall for thinking time,

"Look at the shark," she gurgled hysterically.

The ranger lifted his baseball hat off and took a closer look.

"Oh, I'll be damned, it's a shark all righty. Jesu cranberries, you wouldn't believe some of the stuff we find at filter point. Looks like they've been electrocuted, usually the fish go right through to the other side. There must be another damn block-up. Well I'll be... Still that's beside the point, girls, I'm gonna have to fine you unless you have some good explanation."

I took a deep breath and launched into one,

"I know it sounds crazy, sir, but somehow the shark musta' got tangled up in the boat's propeller or somethin'. Of course we thought it was attacking us so I just gassed it. I was trying to ditch the pecker for miles and I knew I'd run into some lake policeman eventually. It's not every day you see a shark!"

The ranger didn't even suspect we were underage, nor did he ask us for I.D. He assumed the boat was ours. For once we got away with it. He hauled the shark into his boat as the tourists standing on the road waved and snapped cameras. Sunglasses on, bikinis and this shark hangin' off a rod.

"Somebody must have dumped the shark in the lake." He prodded it, took pictures of it, measured it. "We find all kinds of thing out here - cows, dogs, I didn't see it myself, but one of the rangers pulled up a dead body with cement boots. The Mafia sure do love Lake Mead."

When we got back to our private alcove, Timmy pulled me out of the boat and strangled me underneath the murky water. As I held my breath and waited for the punishment to end, I looked through the dirty water. I couldn't see no Houdinis or Amelia Earharts or souls chained in trunks... I saw desert covered in water.

Escape.

Escape.

Escape.

SPEAK NOW OR FOREVER HOLD YOUR PEACE

Aged 13.

Jessie, would you like to be bridesmaid?

Yes please, and while you're at it could you slash my wrists and slit my itty bitty titty right down the nipple. Reach in and pull my silly, spoilt heart out and when you throw the bouquet can I catch it? And wish that one day I will fuck up as badly as you and marry a jock with a name like Benny Goodman,who has a gambling addiction. Gee, Mom, that would be just swell. Yah, sure you can stuff me in that little pink bridesmaid dress but I'll tear out the seams and chew my mouth so it bleeds and when he asks,

"Does anyone see any reason why this couple should not be brought together in holy matrimony", I'll stick my finger down my throat and puke up blood and guts.

and I step. pause. step. pause. step. pause.

I've never seen so much pink. Pink bow-ties, corsets, ribbons, nail polish, shoes, cushions, streamers, flowers, banners, toilet paper, plates, cakes, tablecloths, carpets and underwear. I am my mother's bridesmaid, but I haven't spoken to her since she met the goofy man. "Now you hold those flowers pretty for the camera," she says as she applies a little blue eyeshadow to my lids. Fake. Fake. Fake.

and I step. pause. step. pause. step. pause.

The pink flower combs are scraping at my scalp. I feel like I'm going up to the operation table to have my brain fixed. As if they finally discovered what was wrong with me. But I am too far gone for saving. As I walk down the aisle towards the altar, I peel back my top lip and stare demonically at the priest. I'm smiling a fake, American smile like Minnie Mouse with piranha teeth.

Walkin' down this aisle I finally get the message. I've lost the battle for Mom control. Forget it, I'm burnt out. My long lost dad, Max, patronised over the crackly long distance line, "Your mom needs love in a grown-up way. A way you can't give her. You're a young lady now, you have to let go."

Duhh! Fucking Freud social worker. I hung up on him.

With all the marriage classes the church makes my Mom and Benny attend, the ol' priest couldn't teach them how to get the sickness out of me. It was either, do the St. Francis family counselling classes or get shipped off to England for the whole summer. England wasn't an escape option anymore cos my dad had remarried too.

and I step. pause. step. pause. step. pause.

The phoney priest churns out rules and regulations like the grandfather I never had: "to have and to hold till death do you part". Will I ever marry? No way in hell. Will I ever have kids? No way in hell. We are now standing in our rehearsed places on the curved carpeted alter. I had to help Grandma up on to the step. Me in between Grandma and Aunt Erica. Aunt Erica looks ready to pounce on me if I try anything,

"This is the happiest day of your mother's life, don't blow it kid, otherwise I'll tie you to the freeway and drive over you myself." She pinches my lacy armpit and twists the fat.

Both their hands are covered in tourist diamonds and gold. Grandma is swaying ever so slightly. Her eyes look like they're sliding off her face. I'm thirsting for a drink as much as she is. I've taken a real liking to whiskey. Now the Goodmans have to hide the whiskey bottles from me the way I did with Grandma. If she falls, I suppose I'd have to catch her and then we'd knock each other over like a row of dominoes. Last time I was on this altar I was screaming,"I am a bloody Atheist". I'm surprised the priest let my fat ass back in. But, of course, you are always forgiven for your sins. The choir boys are grinning like Bette Davis piranhas. Deja vu in a wash of pastel crayon smiles.

No siree, this ain't the Hollywood wedding I hoped for, this isn't even a cheesy, down Las Vegas motel wedding, it's more like a Utah Mormon wedding or a Brady Bunch wedding. Everybody is pretending to be so perfect.

I ain't no beggin' dog salivatin' for a Heaven Biscuit. And you up there. You won't get my pity or faith staring down at me with raised eyebrows from your boring cross like some pathetic pigeon trapped in a telephone line. What sign did you ever give me? All you know how to show is suffering in the form of sprinkler heads, granola bars and Mexican fingerfuckers. Suffer, have faith and you will have a soul. Yah, right. God doesn't see you or me, in this concrete bungalow, out here in the desert.

The church still smells like a carbon copy imitation of the real thing I used to see in England. I bet if I scream all that I have to scream, I could crack these stained-glass windows made in some factory in California. This House of God can't fool me with its hogwashin' plastic water fountains, cheap, ceramic statues and Spanish tiles made in Taiwan.

The sharks are bulging from my skin as the hippy choir sing my Mom's list of requested songs, Emmy Lou Harris, Joni Mitchell, Linda Ronstant and Neil Diamond. With their folksy guitars and jangling tambourines, the Sunshine Choir wail as sweetly as the Partridge Family.

The priest addresses the audience,

"Speak now or forever hold your peace."

Now's your chance Greedy Mouth! Everybody is wondering if you're gonna do something crazy. I look at my powdery Mom as if I were 6 all over again. She looks so happy and cleansed of pain as if she's just come out of the Santa Cruz ocean. The lifted veil reveals her sun-blotched face. Pretty. Pretty. Pretty. I can't ruin her Barbie Doll day.

I tried my best to get rid of him, but he won fair and square with his sexist jokes, morals and pool cleaning technique. The wedding ceremony was over in fifteen minutes. Another anticlimax. It was a miracle, no money basket was passed around.

Time for photographs. As my Mom put her arm around me, I stiffened into a mannequin. *It has nothing to do with me.* Grown-ups spend so much time trying to capture special moments on camera, the Kodak moment finishes before anybody experiences it. I snarled my Elvis lip.

Next, we all followed the bride and groom out of the swinging glass doors. Everything happened in slow motion. *It has nothing to do with me.* My new stepdad's white polyester suit sparked like aluminium in the midday light. He looked like a cross between Abraham Lincoln and a car salesman from Heaven. He opened the passenger door to the Buick.

The chrome shone in my eyes. Furry focus. Benny put his fake Ray Ban sunglasses on and revved the Buick as confetti fell over my mom. Beer cans and papier maché flowers dangled off the back of the Buick as it rolled away. Mom's white, overflowing wedding dress was caught in the door and her veil blew in the scorching breeze. Grandma, me and the rest of the two hundred guests staggered across the street. Some were skipping in anticipation of buffets and the free bar. Drive-by Las Vegans honked horns like it was the 4th of July. Everybody loves a wedding. It was a funeral for me.

The Buick didn't go too far, just across the street to the newly built Sugarfoot

Reception Hall. The construction workers built right over the fence I dived underneath a year before. There were now at least twenty houses surrounding the glitzy reception hall.

I was blown away when I entered the gigantic, stained glass doors. It looked like a Beverly Hills mansion - balconies, high rise ceiling, wooden floors, winding staircases, big band playing music, chandeliers, two pools with four surrounding Jacuzzis and a steam room. It has all kinds of secret passages leading down below to more Jacuzzis and steam rooms.

As I approached the bar, another video camera swung in front of my face. Benny's school teaching buddy.

"Hey Jessie, you want to give a well-wishing for the new couple?"

I pushed my face up into the lens and spelt the word D.I.E. As I strutted away in full brat stride, I overheared him say to some other teacher,

"Home run, Benny boy sure hit a home run. Shame about the kid, she's gonna be a real handful."

Benny's friends had all hooked up with women with kids too. I guess divorcee chicks was all they had to choose from. These beer-swigging guys gambled on the same sports games, played golf every Sunday and met at the tittie bar every month, on pay day. What I hated most about them was their predictable fucking jokes, most of them racist and sexist, tossed back and forth in the locker room.

I order a Whiskey Sour and a Tom Collins.

"It's for my mom!" I replied dryly as the bartender hassled me for the first and last time. I sat on the balcony that faced what was left of Sugarfoot desert. I ignored all the commotion on the other side of the sliding glass door as the sad band sang *Uptown Girl* by Billy Joel. I was waiting for the Sugarfoot chicks to come and hang out with me. They weren't officially invited, but I was gonna let them in through the back gate, when I saw them flash their mirrors from Jessie's Look-out Rock.

More photographs and kisses as Mom cut the cake.

Grandma was holdin' up the bar and cryin' into her snot rag. Aunt Erica was bitchin' at Uncle Bruce. My cousins Kat and Dona were present, but they'd changed since they started living in Seattle. They had gone a gross mixture of New Wave and Preppie, with asymmetrical haircuts and Izod shirts. They had a bunch of their own friends down from Seattle who were all on diets and hated buffets. No fun.

The flash of a back pocket mirror from the desert caught my eye. I stood up in my frilly pink dress, went to the balcony railings, like Juliet, and waved them over. There seemed to be a whole Sugarfoot crowd of brown legs. I went to the bar again and ordered a tray of drinks and headed down the spiral staircases. My Mom rushed up,

"Let's show these cowboys how to dance."

"No, Mom, leave me alone. My feet hurt."

Luckily I had a change of clothes waiting in the downstairs bathroom. I felt much better once I had my bikini top and cut-offs on. There were already people getting changed into their bathing suits. Swimming at a wedding reception - only in Vegas. I downed a few more Whiskey Sours and headed outside.

When I opened the side gate, I was horrified to see Julia, Caitlin, Stacie, Marco, Berto, Howie,... even James Sprinkler-head pushed past me.

"You guys can't come in here. If Benny sees you, Berto, he'll call the pigs."

As usual they ignored me. I didn't know what to do. There were three hundred people there so I thought maybe the burrito boys might go unnoticed.

No such luck. They cannonballed into the pool. Not giving a shit. The girls were on drinks duty. I nervously led them into the basement door. We opened door after door. Behind the sauna door I found my cousin Timmy makin' out with some blonde showgirl he'd been fuckin'.

"Score, dude!"

Behind door number 8 was a storage room full of extra food and booze. Julia handed each of us a bottle. By now I was too caught up in the excitement of stealing to think sensibly about what I was doing to my mother on her wedding day.

I was sent back upstairs to get a few bottles of coke from the bartender. On my way back down the spiral stairs, the Billy Joel guy announced the throwing of the bouquet. All the women gathered up awkwardly, like a herd of cattle, to the centre of the ballroom. In the middle of the staircase, my mother held up her not-so-white wedding dress, showing the room full of teachers her Jane Fonda legs. She threw her bouquet of flowers and I, arms full of coke bottles, raised my eyebrow unamused. Some sad chick caught it desperately and I continued on down to the basement to join my 'friends'.

We Sugarfoot girls shuffled back out to the pool. The Sugarfoot dudes were obnoxiously surfboarding down the water slide. It wobbled, ready to break. The other guests in the pool were shouting at them already. James Sprinkler-head started throwing the rocks from the planters. I looked up at the balcony to see Benny.

The familiar thunder of his voice cackled,

"Get the hell outta here!"

He started down the outside steps. The girls ran for the gate and the guys followed, leaving their shoes behind once again. I stood there, rooted to the pool deck, in shock. Benny was literally sprinting after them.

"I'm gonna catch you this time, you little shits." His tuxedo was a lightning bolt.

To make matters worse, just after he leaped over the pool bridge, his white patent leather shoes skidded across the wet pool deck. First, his butt hit the deck, and then his head. I can still imagine the pain of that concrete thump. Benny lay there flat out, swearing.

The Sugarfoot cockroaches got away again. While the guests gathered around Benny in their dripping bathing suits, I tossed my bottle of whiskey in this sand pit behind me and snuck back through the basement door of the reception hall.

Hiding in one of the saunas, I could hear my mother calling my name in that high shrill she used on cleaning days. *Boiling hot. A sauna is the scariest place to be on your own.* I sat there thinking of that *Charlie's Angels* episode where Cheryl Ladd got trapped in the steam room by the bad guy and he turned up the heat.

All of a sudden, Kat came bulldozing in,

"Jess, everybody's looking for you, they think you ran away with the rest of your stupid friends. Get upstairs!"

Her palmtree hairdo wilted within seconds and I laughed uncontrollably. All I could see was Benny - some detective he musta made - fallin' on his ass like Benny Hill. Ha Ha Ha.

I stop laughing when the worst possible person could enter the sauna. Aunt Erica. She steamrolled her daughter into the wooden panel where the coals were kept. She pulled me up the stairs by the hair.

"I found her, I found the attention-seeking brat!"

"Mom, I swear to God I didn't invite them, they knew about the party but I didn't let them in, they musta jumped the fence. It's not my fault."

A silence fell over the ballroom like they were watchin' a nuclear bomb test.

Bitchin' the whole way, Aunt Erica drove me back home in her Trans-Am. Her boobs were practically hanging out of her bridesmaid dress and her pink lipstick was running into her peachy pores.

"Why do you do this to your Mom? God! If your Mom doesn't send you to England this summer, I will. That Commie father of yours needs to knock some sense into you. I tell you one thing, if I was your mother I'd send you to England forever."

I wanted to say, "Well, you drove your kids away, why not?" But I had enough scars on my face.

The Trans-Am passed the corner of Sugarfoot. They were all sittin' there, drinkin' the stolen whiskey. Oblivious, Aunt Erica sped right past them. I ended up having to stay with my neighbour, ol' golf-club-swingin', window-spy himself, Mr. Hensen.

That night my Mom stayed at the MGM honeymoon suite, compliments of Grandma.

The next morning a wedding shower buffet was held at our house for opening presents. I was sittin' in my room watching TV, still sulkin' for havin' to stay at Mr. Hensen's all night. I heard Benny call me. I dragged my heels into the living room stacked full of wedding presents.

"Well, you've succeeded in ruining our wedding." His voice was very calm, which was unusual.

"I told you it wasn't my..."

"Shut up and listen, you little smart-ass brat," As far as I was concerned, he had just paid me a compliment.

"Last night the reception hall was broken into and vandalised. Walls were kicked in, the pool slide was demolished to pieces and the stock room was emptied out. Twenty bottles of booze! Now *we* have to pay for damages because it was still under our care."

I was stunned. He then raised his voice to the more familiar lion's roar,

"For all we know, you were there. You're so damn good at sneakin' out windows. At any rate, we know who was involved, and we all know whose friends they were. And whether or not you were there, you *will* take the blame and apologize and tell the police exactly where every one of those scumbags lives so we can match fingerprints. Do you understand?"

I nodded my head. "Yes."

"That's not an answer. You answer me when I ask you a question."

"Yes!" I snapped a little. I wanted to put my hands to my ears to shut him out. But I stood there with clenched white knuckles.

"We are not having any more of your behaviour. Things are gonna be reeeal different when we move into the new house."

I looked to my Mom for some support, but she was busy trying to stay happy with a half unwrapped toaster on her lap, wiping tears from her mascara-stained eyes. Then I said it for the second time in my life,

"I'm sorry." I felt like throwing up.

After a lecture and warning of what was to come, my mom came up to me and said,

"Thanks for ruining my wedding," I'll never forget her saying those words. It was like her saying, "Thanks for bein' born." I broke down into tears and then she finished me off. "And, by the way, you are going to England as soon as I can get you on a plane."

She said it in such a deadpan manner, as cold as Bette Davis. I no longer knew this woman. The swinging on her hip. The brushing of her hair. The sleeping in her bed. The endless drives through the desert. That mother-daughter Hallmark card thing was all history.

MUTATED STEPFATHERS

The first time you hit me I felt like Joan of Arc taking all the pain for a nation of victim kids. It was a new tingling sensation I'd never felt. Better than finger fucking. I'm not a real victim victim... more like a TV actress victim. If I could show the real ones how to hold out, it would give them hope. I could be a role model. My great Houdini disappearing act. Stand your ground and go numb with each smack.

"I am a victim! I am a victim! Call 911!" I shouted at the top of my lungs in time with each blow.

How could I call myself a victim? A victim doesn't have her own pool and champagne brunches and her own personalised raft that says "I love Jesusa". A victim doesn't have a fridge full of frozen burritos, and three flavours of ice cream to choose from. A victim doesn't fly across the world in First Class with birthday cakes or ride a speedboat to Hoover Dam. Feeling sorry for myself was the only way to keep my feet rooted to the pool deck.

It was a week after they got back from their Hawaii Honeymoon. When the neighbours heard Benny shouting, "You're gonna pay. You're gonna pay.", they slid their beer bellies off their rafts, drinks in hand, and spied through the holes in the cement walls.

"Mommy, Mommy." I was on the far side of the pool and Benny was on the other. He was trying to catch me. My mom was shouting at Benny, as if she were calling her dog off attack. When he headed for the deep end I'd sprint for the shallow. Then we'd retrack as if we were playing tennis. It was like something outta Monty Python or Inspector

Clouseau. Four steps to the left. Four steps to the right. Playin' pool tag only made Benny turn into the Incredible Hulk.

The police had found my fingerprints all over the storage room at the reception hall. Now I'm never gonna confess to whether I was there when the place got trashed or not. It's my secret. But even if I had explained I was in the storage room during the day, before they broke in that night, Benny had all the proof he wanted. I was booked along with the rest of the Sugarfoot crowd. My second criminal offence.

Real drama out by the pool. I centred myself, crouching, as if holding barbells above my head. The iced tea jar fell into the pool. My mother flailed her arms like a cheerleader as she tried to break up the battle with her teenager voice. And it never really hurt cos I thought each strike would be a blow against Benny.

Self-control intact. Piranha teeth clenched. I will not fall. I will not fall. I am strapped into my First Class kid seat. I am an escape route expert. I am the best goddam taste tester of pain in the world. You just gotta look at as if it were a heavy duty massage, or a football tackle, or hitting your head while doing a cartwheel into the pool. No pain no gain. Hello Sammy Cat, I am on TV. Is my make-up all right? Is this a basketball dribbling lesson? Where's the referee? Your team of knuckles and God-fearing joints knock the ball right outta my hand. Confidence drifts out my ears and nose. It's working, Benny, your discipline is working. Every insubordinate kid needs a good smack up the forehead to shake the TV out of their peanut brain.

I was pounded into the ground like a tent peg. It felt like an experiment blowing up in my face. At first I fought back, like all women should. I got in a few good hits, otherwise he wouldn't have hit so hard. I took pleasure in knowing I had the power to push him over the point of no return. He thumped me ten times. I counted every one out loud, like you do when you get your birthday spanks. This only made him more angry.

It was the eardrum slam dunk that floored me. His huge basketball hand covered my entire head. A tranquillised tiger laid out by the pool. A dead Mafia man.

Getting hit didn't give the results I hoped it might. I got into even more trouble because Benny had to drain the pool to clean out the broken glass. My mom didn't see Benny as an evi,l stepdaughter-beater. She had faith in his discipline techniques.

Off to England, I went.

Airplane. ✈

The hippy chick next to me all of a sudden jumps up and runs to the bathroom. The cabin is dark and quietly noisy with the hum of engines. After five gin and tonics, I follow her lead. She's there waiting in the line. Now that she's standing, I can see how grotesquely skinny she is. I get a rare flash of compassion.

"So, what's the book you're reading?"

"Ah... it's about... um... how to love yourself... by becoming at one with yourself..."

"Ohhhh, one of those self-help books?" I was right, she was an *I'm O.K. You're O.K.* fruitloop.

"Judging by the cover, I thought it was about the soul or something. My dad says havin' a soul is just havin a brain."

"Oh no, it's so much more than that... I don't... oh, you know what I mean."

"The bathroom's free now. Go ahead."

As I stand waiting for the next free door to open, I peek out of the emergency exit window. The bottom half of the sky is black and the top is red.

She's throwing up. I can hear her retching. She doesn't seem *too* at one with herself now.

Learning How to Dance

Aged 14.

Picture this. I have a stepfather who walks around the house in his underwear force-feeding me morals in the shape of blueberry waffles. Along with his waffle-iron Benny Bigballs has just purchased a Weedeater and a Creepy Crawler from J.C.Penney's.

The kid-beater uses his Weedeater to trim the edges of the grass and sprinkler-heads, reaching corners the lawn mower can't. The Creepy Crawler slinks along the bottom of the pool, with a long serpentine hose, sucking up dirt, palm tree leaves, lizards and spiders into the filter.

When I got back from England, I discovered the Goodmans had moved into a new two-storey house on the other side of the golf course, five miles from Sugarfoot. On every TV and radio except for mine, there was some sort of sports games blaring scores and touch downs.

Weekends, Benny went to the Bingo Palace to place $50 bets on sports games. I could always tell when he'd lost because he wore his baseball cap back to front. It was the grandma scenario all over again pretending to tolerate each other only for the benefit of others. If my Mom wasn't around, we could go for hours ignoring each other.

Unfortunately the Goodman house was decorated in the same 70s browns and oranges as the others I'd lived in. It wasn't a mansion by any means but it was a step up from the Chason house. This new house had a bigger, kidney-shaped pool with a diving board *and* a slide. In the front courtyard water sputtered and trickled from a naked girl's mouth, mounted on a two-level stucco fountain. Ivy grew all along the side of the house and surrounding walls. We were right on the outskirts of town again with lots of glorious brown desert. From my top floor bedroom window, I could see the drive-in movie screen and Sleeping Indian Mountain.

Siegfried and Roy, who performed a white tiger magic show on the Strip, had bought six houses in a row down the road from us and at night I could hear their tigers roaring.

Every time I passed their house, all you could see were twenty-foot white walls, all smooth and zoo-like with lions' heads impaled on to spikes attached to two big, black iron gates. And inside those stuccoed lions' roaring mouths, video surveillance cameras kept an eye on the street.

Our gay next-door neighbour to the left worked for Siegfried and Roy at their place cleaning the cages out. George was hardly home since the Siegfried and Roy Tiger Show was becoming so popular downtown. He allowed me to use his hand-built, pink-tiled Jacuzzi whenever I wanted to. One time me and Caitlin were in his Jacuzzi and he brought us pink popsicles and pink lemonade in pink plastic champagne glasses.

Now he never came out and said "I'm gay". But with that much pink he had to be. The inside of his pink house was covered in Liberace memorabilia and pictures of white tigers. Everything in his backyard was pink... the landscaped rocks, the pool furniture and deck, the barbecue station. He even had a pink Creepy Crawler pool vacuum.

I copied George and wallpapered my huge bedroom pink. A wall separating two rooms had been knocked down. It was down the hallway from the Goodmans so there'd be no chance of hearing them making babies. I'd built a walk-in closet. I threw away the posters of sharks, tigers and Ozzy Ozbourne and replaced them with pictures of oceans and ballerinas.

Once I'd sterilised it all, I moved all Benny's white plastic bachelor furniture into my boudoir. His spaceship white stereo sat beneath my three-panel mirror, while the white plastic swivel chair in the shape of a hand sat caddie-corner next to the walk-in closet. Playboy-bunny-printed beanbags littered the floor like magazines.

All of a sudden we were pretending to be the perfect family unit. My mom got pregnant and started havin' orgasms over wallpaper.

One hot bloody day, me and Mom were on our way to the wallpaper store. I was walkin' around Thrifty's, up and down the aisles, checkin' out the latest cosmetic invention, while Mom filled her prescription. I had three minutes to find a new lipstick and get back to the checkout before she paid for her hair bleach.

It was such a hard decision to make as L'Oreal kept comin' out with new shades of frosty pink lipstick. I had to try them all on and, by the time I'd tried them all, I forgot what the first looked like. As I was practising my Hollywood pout, I heard the most beautiful piano tinkling from the back of the store. Without thinking, I followed the music and it led me to a door which carried on into a corridor.

The door was ajar so I took a peek through and found a dozen girls dancing in pink and black. Their hair was scraped back and their clear complexions glittered in the peach light. Their tight little butts squeezed as a dozen torsos arched in unison and military precision legs swung high over tilting heads. It was a room full of Bambis. Where did these girls hide? They were so pale and delicate, nothin' looked like that in Las Vegas.

To my embarrassment, the dance teacher swung the door open, pounded her stick three times and invited me in. I was standing there in my OZZY RULES Vans. These bright-eyed Bambi girls couldn't take their eyes off my forearms which had boys' names carved into bold scars. I had just gotten out of the pool and was still wearing my fluorescent pink bathing suit top. The teacher handed me a leaflet and told me to come in and do a class, finishing with, "But don't *ever* interrupt my class, honey!"

First ballet class.

As I pas de deux into 3rd position my left knee cracks. It's the best pain I've ever felt. Better than sliding down rusty nails or horseback riding sprinkler-heads or having my basket ball head slam-dunked into the pool patio. It's self inflicted. The story of Jesusa.

When I start to turn, my body kinda explodes from the inside out. Warm jets of electricity tweaking and throbbing. Anguish bolts ricochet off my ribs and kidneys like a pinball machine. How can such an elementary action as turning spark such a water bong headrush? My dumpy body balances gracefully on the tiny ball of my left foot like a jewellery box ballerina. My heavy arms somehow find the correct position.

I'm not beating the shit out of some girl behind 7-Eleven. I'm photocopying the pretty, tight-assed girl in front. The smile on my face isn't forced or crooked. I haven't smiled like this since the Santa Cruz red rollercoaster ride.

Beneath my skin, something like gas was bubbling, pronging, spiking, trying to bust out. With each new movement I executed, these... inner body bullets hammered at the stretching skin making more marks. I wanted them out.

For once every part of me was working effortlessly. The sensation was better than my other new found hobby – masturbation.

Like a parachuter landing, I staggered out of my first sloppy pirouette. And then it happened on my twentieth turn. Two spasms dashed out like rays of light, one through my mouth and the other between my thighs. I went weak at the knees and gasped out loud as if I'd finally discovered how to give myself a multiple orgasm. Perfect swan heads whipped round to watch the lumpish weirdo at the back of the class with the wrong attire. I felt a wet patch through the crotch of my mother's Jazzercise leotard.

"Imagine there is a rope coming out the top of your head, girls."

I was momentarily pulled back to reality by Sherry Lee, our buxom Texan dance teacher. I turned again and again and again around this imaginary rope. It was a shock to find that I was kinda good at something apart from lying, stealing and snarling. I stopped and started quicker than any of the other 8-year olds standing next to me, who were doing triple and quadruple pirouettes. On my thirtieth turn I tumbled to the ground, but diligently got right back up and tried again. Each tiny sweat pool on the floor was a vessel of hatred droppin' from my body.

We moved on to combinations.

"Three grand jetés, turn, turn, turn, balance in attitude." The dance teacher ordered. I could do the attitude part no problem. As we waddled to the corner, I xeroxed and memorized every tiny detail from those talented Bambi swans. My eye muscles strained to reject the new contact lenses I was wearing. I mentally mimicked the swan waddle, toes turned outwards, butts tucked under; the way they rested one dainty hand on the neck while the other delicately wiped the sweat from their arched eyebrows as if it was a choreographed movement.

I homed in like the Bionic Woman, mouth gaping at the prettiest girl as she straddled the electric fan, stopping it from turning. She owned the room with her presence, oozing self-confidence, while I dripped embarrassment.

As the statuesque prima ballerina rotated her hair in slow motion, her cut-up sweatshirt slipped down from her right shoulder. So cool. Jennifer Beals, eat your heart out. I thought I was watching the Playboy channel. Everything went soft focus as she licked her lips like a girl who knows she's bein' watched. My eyes followed her luscious body as she strutted, like a prize horse to the front of the line to take her position as teacher's protégée. The other girls stepped out of her way. It was just like *Fame*, the TV series. But I was in the wrong show, I was Miss Piggy transported from *The Muppet Show*.

5. 6. 7. 8. - go!

5. 6. 7. 8. - go!

It was like lining up to jump off a cliff.The experienced girls went ahead in pairs, as I clung to the bar attached to the mirrored wall. The Thrifty's door was just feet away. I could have run.

"Just focus on the ceiling corner and go for it," whispered Sherry Lee in my ear.

I'm in love. She likes me, we have the same thighs. I'm ready for a new pain game... competition, self control and more bruises. This could be my new religion, my new Manson family. Upgraded to First Class. I watch the swans glide across the floor like an ugly duckling.

"5, 6, 7, 8, and 1 and 2!" Sherry Lee banged her stick on the linoleum dance floor. Plucky pug noses tilted toward the sky like planes taking off. The sound of neck muscles tweaking, collar bones jutting, feet flicking and stretching high above the ground turned me on. Arms and hands like butterflies zipping through the Vegas air. Through the glass window, moms watch their little girls proudly. Even if my mom wasn't busy wallpapering, I wouldn't have let her come.

I had no partner to dance across the floor with. I didn't even have ballet shoes. I took a deep Mom-inspired breath and tagged along with the pissed off 8-year olds. I lost track of counting, and smashed into one of their toes. The second time around I nearly landed on top of the record player.

Giggles and screwy eye signals clawed me in the back. Class clown. At the opposite corner of the studio, the star pupil doesn't even bother making fun of me. She's too busy checking her face hasn't altered in the last minute. She leans on the bar staring in the mirror, which has loved her since the day she was born.

I was a glutton for self-punishment.

"5. 6. 7. 8. Jesusa you're late! Concentrate, girly, you're not watching the TV now... think about the next movement while you're doing the last, on your toes. 5. 6. 7. 8." Ohh, I love it when she yells at me. She wants me to be good. She's better than the air hostess moms.

After I got through my first class I sat in the gutter waiting for my Mom ride. As the other ballerinas skipped to their Cadillacs while adoring mothers stroked their buns, I did some painful, serious thinkin'.

I was depressed and elated at the very same time. After spending a month with my Freudian father and his vegetarian new wife, Sugarfoot and sprinkler-heads crammed up my crotch seemed light years behind me. My revelation was that I had to stop feeling sorry for myself. Pain and self-punishment was the norm. It didn't matter if I hung out with the Sugarfoot losers or the prissy dancers or the crooked smiling church congregation, there would always be rules of humiliation, pain and losing.

I had to stop letting things just *happen* to me. I wasn't watching a movie that was already scripted and beyond my control. I didn't have to play the victim forever. I didn't wan't to do my Marilyn Monroe act, I wanted to play heroine, like Bette Davis or Judy Garland.

Instead of gettin' sucked in by those big-ass waves I had to learn to dive underneath them mothafuckers. It was so easy to see how TV people worked their problems out but when you had to apply it to real life it was retarded.

I missed my dad. He was so good at making me understand why people do the things they do. I used to moan and groan when I'd have to sit on the back of the tandem with him farting in my face, singing songs about Karl Marx, Margaret Thatcher and the First World War but he was a good explainer, unlike these Las Vegas aliens. They didn't give a shit about explanations. They wanted to use their bodies, not their minds. Drive their boats, swim in their pools, pull the slot machine handle, but not sit around discussing it.

I was proud and also disgusted with myself. A new feeling. I knew there would be more personality beatings, fisting the mirror and yanking on fat pockets. But I was learning to enjoy correction and humiliation.The prospect of a challenge was all of a sudden exciting. I was just about good enough at dancing to make me want to do it more.

Sherry Lee shouting, "Be the Best" meant somethin'. My new mom's voice sent me to sleep at night, "Sashay, sashay, grand jeté, attitude... and balance, imagine the rope, hold it, hold it!!!!!!"

When me and my birth giver were fixing dinner after my third class I couldn't stop talking about pirouettes. I cut the cucumber and demonstrated my improving pirouette. Sippin' her Californian Chardonnay, Mom was mildly amused at my enthusiasm But she didn't appreciate the "poetic quality", as my Sperm Giver would say.

"Mommy dearest, I swear on your life - I will never be bad again if you pay for the dance school."

"I want one promise before I agree to pay for the lessons."

"What?"

"Be nicer to your stepfather..."

"Don't call him that."

"...without him we wouldn't have been able to move into this nice house and you wouldn't be able to have the lessons."

"Mom, I'll iron his underwear, just give me the money," I said, starving, perched in grand plié, holding on to the refrigerator door for balance with a carrot hanging out of my mouth.

From then on, my nights were spent eating Lean Cuisine 350 Calorie Lasagne and then practising my dance moves in front of the mirror. I went to the Sunset Dance School at the back of Thrifty's almost every day for the next year. I was given a partial scholarship.

No more experimenting with soft drugs and heavy metal boys for me, never mind glue or acid, ballet and jazz were the best buzz yet. Orgasms were fucking excellent but only for a few seconds and then came that lonely feeling of withdrawing whatever you were using.

With spinning around, the pleasure lasted a little longer, especially when I finally got something right. Physical pain had taken the place of mental pain. The first thing we did before class was stretch our hip joints to increase our turn out. We lay for half an hour, listening to Bach, backs to the floor, crotches to wall and spread our legs as wide as we could. Sherry Lee would then place weights on each ankle and I would gasp in pain-pleasure. It was like a torture chamber made in heaven. My face twisted in agony. But it was good pain. It was correct pain. My toes were an inch from the floor which meant I was practically doing centre splits nearly as wide as Miss Flash Dance protegée.

As Mom filled in the cheque, Sherry Lee said I was progressing real fast. "She's got talent. I wish you had got her in here when she was younger." After a few months I went on pointed ballet shoes, which were the ultimate pain test: after half an hour it was like tiptoeing on glass.

I had a goal and it was to be as good as the others. I had lost fifteen pounds with only another ten to go. Then I would look like the Bambi swans. Sheryl Lee gave my mother diets to put me on. Iced milk, vanilla ice cream, beetroots and two bananas for two weeks.

I am weighed in front of the other girls. There is a chart on the wall. They clap when I lose a pound. I have a new family. No longer last in line, I am fourth from the front. I can do triple pirouettes and split my legs in the air. At night I dream of my teacher massaging each vertebra and then cracking my arched back so that my toe nearly touches my head in arabesque. I love the sound of ligaments tearing and bones cracking crack crack cracking.

I lived for her approval. Not my mom's. My dance teacher. Every time she gave me a compliment it made my heart race and it kept me motivated for days. The best reward was when I could actually look in the mirror with pride. I had all the dance gear and I even could pass for one of them. I had been accepted into a new gang of swans and Bambis. We did recital shows at the mall. I was so busy with dancing I had no time to think about boys or my stepdad's invasion or a new baby on its way. It felt great to have a place to go everyday, to have a schedule which didn't revolve around the TV and the refrigerator.

THE HEAT OF TOBY'S BREATH

Aged 14.

There are some kid memories that stay in your mouth forever. The worst tasting one I have is the moist panting of Toby's breath. I remember the temperature of that day. The way the light coloured my hair and the trees blowing in the cottony, nuclear breeze. I can still recall the salmon glow of the sun reflecting off the surface of the pool and how it took all my ballet muscles to turn over gracefully on the silver raft without capsizing into the 80-degree water.

All the insects in our new yard came to drink from the pool as I lay there like a cancer stick. I was waiting for my best friend Caitlin to come over. Her gross brother was dropping her off in his clanker. Apart from the dancing Bambis, Caitlin was my only friend now. After Caitlin's fingerprints were found in the storage room at the reception hall, her mom made her go to the school where she taught. We had escaped Sugarfoot together, but where she ended up was even worse.

Caitlin had just moved to the west side, which was the poor black side of town across from Lorenzi Park. The only thing that separated our neighbourhoods was the huge golf course. One minute you could be in the sleaziest part of Vegas and just by driving a mile you suddenly found yourself in Brady-Bunch-land with weed-eaten lawns and Creepy Crawler pools. Her neighbourhood reminded me of Leo and Santa Cruz. But in Santa Cruz at least we had orange trees and sunflowers. Hers was just dirt coloured.

My mind switches back so easily.

This raft is like my hospital death bed. The sun has made me too weak to swim and it's poisoning my skin intravenously. I'm Marilyn Monroe, in the last hours of her life. Flesh and water fighting for survival. Daddy-longlegs, wasps and other unidentified flying objects crash land on my upturned wrists. The wasps and flies are attracted to my cocoa -butter suntan cream. I have to clean the insects out of the pool filter on the hour. Apart from poolside soap operas, poop-scooping and Kool Aid, this is my only other task of the day.

Some of the insects are on the verge of death. Others are still alive and kicking because the chlorine hasn't vaporised their guts yet. I hate insects more than I hate my stepfather. I hate insects more than the right-hand neighbour Jason, who watches me with his droopy, teenage eyes as I dump dead insects into his yard.

Benny comes outta the sliding glass door and puts the Creepy Crawler in the pool. He does it on purpose cos he knows I hate it.

"Jess, I'm not gonna tell you again. You gotta pick up the dog poop before Caitlin comes over."

Next door, through his bedroom window, I know Jason's beatin' his meat, watching my bikini ass as I bend over to pick up my dog's shit with the Pooper Scooper. Even though I can't see him through his tinted window, I know he's there.

I glance up, point to him and then point the shovel of shit in my hand. Fucking pervert. If it's not him it's my stepfather and his sports buddies stealing glances while watching the Super Bowl on the TV.

I finish my job, spray some more Sun In on my hair and dive off the board. I climb back on my raft and watch the ants commit suicide and turn over every ten minutes. And over. And over. A barbecued chicken leg cooking evenly on both sides. For the perfect tan, I sweat it out, bouncing against the edges of the pool, watching jumbo airplanes lower themselves into McCarran Airport. Ten an hour.

I swab the water over the surface of the azure pool tiles. They are oh so pretty and smooth even though the chemicals are fading their Tijuana pigment. My painted big toe dangles beneath the surface of the water. Shark bait boredom. My fingertip makes a wake in the turquoise fluid. I feel clean and have nothing in the world to do but bake. The radio blares out grand openings and special offers. I love the smell of chlorine and burning flesh. Stuck somewhere between consciousness and dreaming.

My thoughts drifted back to Caitlin. She said I was changing, especially since I'd been back from England and started doing dance classes and had a new house. She said I was prettier and thinner and had more money than her. I had done just what my mom did when she was 14, what do they call it, I'd blossomed from ugly duckling to average swan. Caitlin was jealous, and I knew what it felt like to be envious so I tried to be extra nice to her.

I feel like I've started a new life. It's true the sharks only swim in my head a few times a month. I'm learning how to control my zeitgeber attacks with the aid of stepfather discipline. It's still only just Spring but the sun is scorching and the water on my skin dries in seconds. The kind of heat you get in Vegas is a blowdryer heat. Mean heat. White heat.

The heat hates itself as much as its victims. It makes a buzzing sound and stings itself. ZZZZZZah. There's always a buzzing sound in Vegas. The noise bounces off the walls of the encasing mountains. Construction workers operating forklifts and drills. Nuclear bombs going off at the test site. Nickels and quarters clanking into slot machines. The heat burns metal and cooks eggs on the pavement. I'm living in hell. But it's a hell I've grown accustomed to. I could have stayed in England but my Evil Master, the sun, ordered me back. Even at night with the fans blowing I sweat in twisted, wet sheets and the buzzing of the black sun seeps between the blinds all through the night.

The insects never give me a moment's peace as I drift on this silver raft like a held-up movie star. They invade my thoughts of Hollywood and my acceptance speech. They try and hitch a ride to the steps but a wasp lands on my back and sends me sinking to the bottom of the pool. I stay at the floor of the deep end for five minutes. I still can't cool down. The buzzing heat comes to me in sound waves.

I reapply my oil and position myself on the raft. I drift off to sleep as I practise my movie star lines. I dream of Toby, the most disgusting teenager I know. I see his face and the way he looks at me through his bifocals. He is obviously in love with me but at the same time he looks like he wants to kill me. He hates lovin' me.

He reminded me of that guy who chased me in Sugarfoot. He was a pervert like my next-door neighbour Jason. You could hardly see his face for all the acne, and he never popped them. He would just let them sit on the surface of his lips, nose and eyes. Little hills of pus volcanoes just about to erupt. One continuous eyebrow crossed his forehead and his monstrous metal mouth never smiled. I couldn't keep my eyes off him when he ate. When they came over for barbecues I could always smell his breath across the patio table. There was this wall of chalky rot around his braces.

I don't remember how long I had been dozing or, in fact, if I had been dozing but I'm pretty sure I awoke to this hot sensation on my face. It was Toby leaning inches from my lips. I blinked my eyes open and then shut them in disgust and horror. The flashing whites of his eyes were like the shiny glowing eyeballs on my stuffed animals. He looked so different without glasses. I pretended to be sleeping. To this day I don't know if I dreamt it or if it really happened. I wanted to open my eyelids but I was too afraid. I should have just screamed, but I was too embarrassed for him... and me.

Maybe if James Sprinkler-head never happened, I would have kicked Toby's ass right then and there. I can't explain it. I didn't want his sister to tease him, he had enough pain in his life. He wasn't touching me, he just was leaning really close. I laid there, barely breathing for about ten minutes, as if I didn't know he was there, inhaling and exhaling on my waterproof mascara. It was the worst smell ever, a mixture of dog farts and Brussels sprouts, but, in a sick way that was all my own, I endured it as another test of pain. I think I was paralysed from dehydration, stuck somewhere between consciousness and dreaming.

I tried to think about something else. I remember my mind switched to a moment earlier that day. I was walking my dog in the desert opposite our house, where this poor excuse for a tree was hiding out, looking for shelter within its meek shrubbery. I looked down and there was this scorpion trying to kill a lizard. It stung the lizard's tail and ripped it right off with its clippers and the tailless lizard went scuttling away, but lookin' sorta self-righteous. They both won the fight in a way. The scorpion got a tail to chew on and the lizard only lost its tail which was gonna grow back in a few days anyways.

Just then Caitlin came out of my sliding glass door in her bathing suit and Toby swam away under the water before Caitlin saw. Toby didn't scare me...really. It was like I'd got past the stage of being frightened for myself. In the last few years I had gone through so many different states of fear and bravery, I wasn't experiencing it anymore.

Everything that was happening felt like it was outside my control. I had, at 14, already come to terms with pain and knew it was a feeling that was going to be around for the rest of my life. My childhood had gone. I had become this budding, sexual minx, who upset almost every male species I came into contact with.

Eddie's Ranch

Aged 15.

Benny won a huge bet on the L.A.Raiders at the Palace Station so he took us to Hawaii. The day after we got back I had my last physical fight with him. My Mom's gigantic Santa Cruz fern flew across the room and detonated all over the TV and Blacky Dog. I completely missed Benny. He didn't miss me though. After he scratched my cornea with his wedding ring, I had to wear contacts for the rest of my life. I never raised my hand to another man after that clobbering.

We'd been gettin' along fine, boogie-boardin' in the waves and playing baseball on the beach with coconuts. He even taught me how to swing a baseball bat. I mean our relationship was always up and down. I was never nice to him for more than an hour, and the only way we could speak to each other was if we were bein' sarcastic.

The one thing he'd say to me on a daily basis, when I was lookin' in the refrigerator, was, "Take a picture, it lasts longer."

One day I hated his guts and then the next day he brought me home chocolate peanut butter ice cream and I endured his presence while we watched *Cheers* in the same room. But then the next day I'd be angry for eating a whole gallon of ice cream and blame him for trying to make me fat. The reason I was grounded was because in Hawaii, Benny had decided to play detective and found me with two older guys sittin' in their car makin' out. He freaked out and started pounding his basketball fists on the window. If he had come one second earlier he woulda' seen this guy snorting coke outta my belly button.

The sun was just about to set and I was beggin' my mom to let me off my restriction one day earlier because there was this warehouse party that I really wanted to go to. Agent Orange and Black Flag were playing. Benny was in his Abraham Lincoln mode.

"Jesus Cranberries, honey, you gotta stop goin' back on your word, she's not supposed to go out for another week. You have to teach her boundaries otherwise she'll get away with murder." He'd say "Jesus Cranberries" in front of almost every sentence he said.

That's when I pitched the fern at him.

"Fuck off! Fuck off!"

For some reason "fuck" was the worst swear word a kid could throw at an ex-Mormon, basketball coach kinda guy. He slam-dunked my head three times as my pregnant mother fell back with a dizzy spell. While the priest attended to Rosemary and her baby I grabbed a bottle of whiskey out of the garage and ran down the street. Escape. Escape. Escape.

I ran down the street and used the phone at the local 7-Eleven. I called Caitlin, my partying buddy, and begged her to come get me. In Las Vegas if you didn't have a car you were stranded. I was only 15, so I had another year to go before I'd have my own wheels. No-one walked and if you did people assumed you were down and out or had just been released from prison.

I decided to never go back home. As we drove to the gig, I changed into some of Caitlin's clothes. I was dressed in a tight mini-skirt, neon green bobby socks, plastic high heel pumps and a Flash Dance cut-off t-shirt. I looked like a Madonna Wannabe compared to the serious punks but they liked having young, innocent girls there to mess with.

I always got drunk too fast at those keg parties. All you had to do was bring a cup, pay three bucks on the door and for the rest of the night you had free access to ten kegs of beer. There were always drinking games and beer bongs, slam dancing and scamming. When you went outside to pee behind some car it was impossible to find a spot without piles of throw-up.

As usual, I lost Caitlin. By 11:00 p.m. my head was swimmin' with sharks. Travis, the neighbourhood coke dealer, pulled me from the gutter and propped me up in his mom's Cadillac. He had his own car but it had been stolen a few days earlier. When I woke up we were out at this ranch with a few dozen cars parked skew-whiff. Travis shook me,

"Come on, dude, we got another party ."

I took my shoes off and leaned on him as we stumbled into the old shack. Twenty lines of coke on the glass coffee table. It was the most coke I'd ever seen until Travis placed an ice cream bowl baggy on the table.

"Hey Eddie, what's happenin', dude?"

"Hey Travis, how's it hanging? Is this your little sister?"

"No, I'm just a friend," I slurred like Lolita. I nudged Travis. "I can't believe you took me on a fuckin' drug run, you retard."

I took my line, it was the last thing I wanted but it was considered very rude not to accept it. I went out the front door again to comb my hair. I reapplied some more lipstick and threw up.

Las Vegas glittered down in the black valley like a thousand fireflies fucking. As I watched the Big Dipper swing back and forth, this huge, crude lumberjack of a man came out the shack door and said to me,

"Hey, honey pie, you look a little green," I looked up at this dark and handsome man. As I fought to keep my eyes open, he flirted like a bee looking for a juicy flower to stick his needle in. "Which high school do you go to?"

"I'm gonna be a sophomore at Sleepin' Indian."

"Ohhh, your first year at highschool. I can tell you're gonna be prom queen."

"I don't like any of that preppy shit, anyways I'm in heavy training to be a dancer."

"Show me your best move." Barefoot, I did a triple pirouette on the porch. He eyed me like a lion ready to attack.

"How old are you?" I said, stumbling.

"I'm 19 and horny as hell for you."

"More like 25 and desperate. What do you do apart from robbing the cradle?"

"You should watch how you talk to your elders... I'm a construction worker... workin' on The Lakes right now."

"The Lakes? Oh, those fancy houses that have their own personal lakes. Gaaad, where they getting all that water from? I need some water." All of a sudden I was real thirsty.

He was attractive in a Rob Lowe, cheesy kinda way. He had one of those church smiles that was so straight it was crooked. His forwardness was repulsive and enticing at the same time, one of those people you meet for the first time and you hate them but still feel uncontrollably attracted to them.

He was a MAN. His ass filled his Levi's and his thighs were bulging so that the jeans had faded into the shape of his contoured muscles. Like most construction workers I'd seen in Las Vegas, they were especially faded in the groin area around his buttons.

"Come with me little girl, I'll get you somethin' to drink."

"I can't drink no more booze."

He took me by the hand, down the carpeted hallway past all the coke snorters, bong smokers, jocks and big-haired college girls scooping coke up with their fake, pinky fingernails. He lured me into Eddie's bathroom to sample the punch he'd made earlier. I don't recall his name so let's name him Mr Levi's. The bathtub was filled with ruby red Hawaiian Punch with bits of browning apple, banana and oranges. There were no more cups so he took the toothbrush holder and scooped up some. He took a sip and then offered me some.

"Water! I need water." I twisted around and ducked under the sink's water tap. Just as I was ready to gulp some fresh Lake Mead water, Mr. Fuckin' Levi's pulled me around and shoved the toothpaste holder to my mouth. "Come on, little girl, back in one!"

We drank four minty cups. The tasteless rum helped wash the cocaine down. Even though I swore I'd never play victim again, I fell for Mr Levi's slimy seduction within seconds. The next thing I knew the fruit punch was forced into my mouth via his. As I swallowed, he snaked his way around my tonsils, plunging his octopus tentacle deep into my throat. Before I could react, he pushed me up against the bathroom wall and manoeuvred me off the ground with his bulging, denim hard-on. He was holding me up off the floor!

Jeeez Louise, if Caitlin could have seen me then, she would have peed her pants. He was slobbering all over my face, smothering me with his coarse tongue, licking and flickering up and down my neck. And then to top it all off he ran rings round my ears slurping and gulping as if to suck my brain out. He was the most vulgar and pushy pig since James Sprinkler-head.

I hate to admit it but I was oozing with wetness. I know I shouldn't make excuses, but, when you're 15 and stuck out in the middle of nowhere wasted as a dog, you tend to go along with situations because you're starvin' for fun. My toes were straining to reach the bathroom floor again. Then came the forkliftin' arms. His left bicep pinned my arms above my head and his right hand wheedled his way around Caitlin's little denim skirt. I'd had kisses by the truck loads but nothin' like this caveman kiss.

Luckily moose man pulled away when Travis pounded on the bathroom door.

"Jess, are you O.K?"

I gently bit Mr. Levi's tongue and shouted, "In here!" through the bathroom door. I managed to get past the brute, running out the house for the second time. Travis followed.

"What the hell are you doin' with that guy?"

"Will you roll a joint?" I was outta breath and my lipstick was smeared. As we walked along the desert dirt path immersed in hot moonlight, I tried to do my breathing exercises. "Travis, I don't know what I'm doing. I'm so..." I couldn't decide what I was.

I tried again fishing from my limited vocabulary. "I'm so fucking ANGRY!" I shouted the word at the top of my lungs but it didn't echo. "You know what Travis, I've spent the last like five years running from you guys."

"Hold your voice down! You wanna start an avalanche, girl?" He wasn't interested. I walked barefoot in self-absorbed silence.

"I need to sit down, Travis." We perched ourselves on a red rock the size of a car.

Travis passed me the joint. "Jessie, do you like me?"

"I like you as a friend."

"Most people only like me cos I'm a coke dealer. I know I'm ugly." He was ugly. Usually, I would have sympathised with him but he didn't want to listen to me so why should I massage his pain? I had my own problems and, anyways, he snorted too much coke so he was insecure about everything.

The head-spinning rollercoaster started up again. I laid back on the cool rock soothing my Hawaiian sunburn. Just when my panties were drying out, Travis jumped on me.

"Please, I just want a little kiss... just touch me!"

Poor Travis didn't get his advances reciprocated. As he wrestled me to the gravel and fought his way into my mouth, I vomited all over his face.

When I woke up I got very frightened and cold. I realised that Travis had left me there on that spooky path covered in cacti and Joshua trees. I followed the trail back to the ranch shack. Travis's car was gone. I made my way through the now sprawled bodies and locked myself in the bathroom to fix myself with make-up.

When I stepped out of the bathroom, Mr Super Bulge Levi's intercepted me.

"Where you been all my life, baby?" He was a total shark.

"Can you drive me back into town." I could barely stop myself from swaying.

"It's 4:00 a.m. I'm not driving *anywhere*, I'm too fucked up." Placing his forklifts either side of my head, he leaned into me like the Fonz would.

"I need to keep awake," I slurred.

He persuaded me to have a few more lines of coke. "It'll cancel out the alcohol."

Just as I was starting to enjoy a few compliments from other hunks, Mr Caveman picked me up and carried me to Eddie's bedroom. He tossed me on the bed. All of a sudden he was on top of me, tongue plunging and clothes rolling into balls of tissue. Head swimming with sharks. Before I knew what was happening he had pulled my halter top up around my neck. It all was happening so fast as he pushed on my crotch. He already had his pants down and he was trying to pull my underwear to the side. But I wouldn't let him in.

He tried poking his fingers around to moisten me up but I was too tense. He kept thrusting his dick up against me. I drifted away. There was laughter and knocking on the locked door. I kept fading in and out of consciousness and finally passed out. I still to this day don't know whether I lost my virginity to that cradle snatcher.

The next morning I awoke in the bed alone with my top twisted around my armpits but everything else seemed intact. I wasn't sore, so I figured nothing had happened.

When I walked out into the living room all the guys were watching some football game on the TV. You could tell by their faces that they assumed I had had my cherry popped. The cute little virgin. My head was too fried and hungover to say a word. Then, to add to the embarrassment, Berto the Burrito, my ex-boyfriend from hell, walked in the door to score some coke. I was petrified because I hadn't run into him for almost three years. He took one look at me and just laughed. I knew I had to get out of there. I felt so ashamed. There were like twenty guys and just me. I ran out of there so fast I forgot my make-up bag.

With cracked lips and bare feet on fire, I walked along the dirt road for a good two miles dodging ant hills. My pink, peeling shoulders were burning all over again. I felt like a sleazy piece of shit, a stupid little girl who had been eaten up and spat out. To crush the last bit of pride I had left, Berto drove up behind me and whacked me on the ass leaving me in a whirlwind of dust.

"Ha ha! Very funny, motherfucker! "I flipped him off. " I'll have the last laugh, you

Sugarfoot highschool drop-out loser mowing lawns for a living, burrito brain." He didn't even hear me raggin' on him.

I finally reached the main road and flagged down a highway patrol car. Maybe it was normal to find a girl walking barefoot on the highway, because he didn't ask for any answers. He dropped me off around the corner from my house.

My feet were blistering so bad. I crawled into the kitchen. The house was empty apart from the animals. A Post-It note was stuck to the refrigerator

"Jess. We are at the hospital. Your Mom's gone into labour. Sorry for hitting you. Benny. PS feed Sammy and Blacky."

Now that I'm a rampant teenager I don't get so hungry. A few years back I would have sat in front of that fridge and gorged myself to alleviate the blisters on my feet and mind. But today I grabbed a Diet Coke, slid the glass door open, crawled to the pool and flopped into the water. I took Caitlin's filthy, wet clothes off and flung them into the flowerbed.

I sank to the floor of the deep end and screamed, "SURVIVE! SURVIVE!" When all the air was gone I stayed at the bottom of the pool. When would the Nasa spaceship come to rescue me?

SATURDAY AJAX

Not only can I dance, I can perform aerodynamic acrobatics and disappearing acts with my aerosols. I'm a flash Houdini bartender mixin' Windex with Pledge, and shakin' Ajax with Liquid Drano. I'm an ant eater, vacuuming up carpet bugs.

With the exception of applying make-up, teaching me how to clean the house was either the best or worst habit or addiction Mom passed on to me yet. To tidy clutter away, neatly concealed, erased from view. Outta sight, outta mind. That's why the two of us liked wallpapering. Pasting over the peeling past so that faces and places fade away.

Saturday had turned into official mother daughter-bonding day, scrubbing away at the same tables, chairs and sinks for the two hundredth time. The big difference between our cleaning techniques was that she cleaned out the insides of cupboards. Automatic like a wife slave. For her, cleaning was another addiction, but at least she had thrown in the cigarettes and speed pills.

Me, I just wiped the surface, leaving the inside a mess. I knew if I cleaned out the cupboards in my head, I'd have to go through and throw things out. I'd have to get Mom guidance and I knew she didn't want to deal with my shit, she was too happy floating on Stepford Wife cloud nine, surpassing her dreams of *Little House on the Prairie* with her newly decorated home and cleansed family.

Weekends spent cruising Lake Mead were long gone since my cousins had moved up to Seattle and my Aunt Erica got a divorce from Bruce. Saturday Ajax started at 9:30 a.m., come hell or high water. Even if she was sick as a dog, Mom had to clean and that meant everybody else too. I'm guessin' a messy house reminded Mom of her kid home, a dump yard of travel brochures and receipts, browning in the stench of alcohol and smoke.

Pyjama sleeves rolled up over chapped elbows, veins throbbing with three MOM mugs of caffeine, she'd pick the lock on my door and burst into my bedroom,

"Come on honey - let's bond!"

She'd yank the blinds up and let that fuckin' sun pour in. A list attached to a clipboard would be thrown at me with a can of Diet Coke and a granola bar.

"You better be up and cleaning in ten minutes... and don't tell me you have a hang-over."

I lay there, contact lenses dissolving into my cornea. Not-so-luscious hair matted with gum and hairspray, my sunspotted pores steamin' with alcohol sweat.

Saturday Ajax was pay back time for Benny. He'd be right behind Mom, tossin' the dog's bone on the bed and shouting as if he were at a baseball game,

"Hey, Jess, you got any whites to wash?" There's something fishy about a stepdad putting his hands all over his stepdaughter's underwear. But that was his assigned job. Benny'd always go,

"Don't think I don't know your stealin' my Coors".

I got candelabras to polish, streamers to staple to palm trees, and Welcome banners to hang for the Buick and the Volkswagens. It's the 4th of July and we're having our 10th Anniversary memorial of my granddad's death. He didn't die on the 4th of July but Aunt Erica, who was always in charge of this kinda crap, decided to combine the two, an excuse for an even more excessive layout.

Plane loads of relatives from back east are flying in. As usual it's a dress-up party. This year's theme is "favourite American invention". I'm gonna throw a box over my head and say I'm a microwave. My Mom's gonna dress as Betty Crocker, Benny's Abraham Lincoln and the new born Jack will be Baby New Year. In two hours there will be 100 people eating barbecue burgers and hotdogs around the pool, pissing in my freshly cleaned toilets and marking my slick carpet with chlorine footprints.

The four of us were doin' individual chores to the beat of Madonna. My family couldn't stand her, but they preferred her to Billy Idol and The Clash.

Benny had his own portable radio taped to his baseball cap. He was dropping chemicals into the pool, and placin' gamblin' bets on his brand new cell phone. Baby Jack was cleaning his baby pen with his feather duster. And even though she was pregnant, Mom was moppin' the floor and waterin' the plants like an octopus. I was on my second bathroom and flyin' high on the fumes. I'd just finished Windexing the sliding glass door. My aim was to get it so spotless Benny would walk right into it.

As I deodorised, sterilised and savoured the flavour of the chemicals, I admired my reflection in the toilet bowl. It was clean enough to throw up in. Unfortunately on those drinking days, I never made it to the toilet.

Not every Saturday Ajax was as serious as this 1985 4th of July. During spring my Mom and I finished Saturday off with gardening at sunset, Bruce Springstein boomin' through the outdoor speakers. As she weeded, she talked intensely about all the new furniture she wanted to buy and which walls to knock out. All we talked about was domestic stuff. I couldn't complain because we had a lot more money to spend and she didn't have to work two jobs anymore. Ironically she was around the house a lot more now that I wasn't.

By 3:00 p.m. the biggest record-breaking buffet our family had ever seen was laid out like a multicoloured parachute. Duplicate mini buffets stood on reserve in every inside room. Even the bathrooms had Dorritos and bowls of peanuts. We didn't have fountains of champagne but our water fountain was spillin' over with icy cold bottles of Corona and kegs of Budweiser.

By 4:00p.m., cousins I'd never met before were belly floppin' and blowin' their nose in our pool. Water splashed into the flower beds as relatives jumped off the roof into the pool. Mom won the hula-hoop contest. Benny was doin' the Twist and the Alligator to Chubby Checker. My grandfather's brothers were sittin' in the shade playing poker and guzzlin' whiskey.

At the corner of this picturesque slice of American life, Grandma was in the living room on her own. Just out of Betty Ford rehab. Her second time out. She had a hole in her throat where they had cut away the cancer. A voice box had been installed. She never used it. I kept an eye on her as Uncle Frank, from New Jersey, taught me how to make margaritas in the kitchen.

I didn't drink everyday, not until my senior year. I still smoked doobies but drinking was a much better sort of high for socialising. Getting stoned was for when I was layin' out by the pool. It helped to endure the sun's needle pricks. Drinking made me say things I wouldn't normally and on this day I was coming' out with some real whoppers.

Nobody was payin' attention to Grandma, playin' solitaire on our cork coffee table. There was no ashtray or whiskey glass now.

"Would you like a drink?" I'm standin' there in my microwave box costume with a Big Gulp cup full of margarita juice. Grandma nodded yes.

"What would you like?" I could have said sarcastically "Whiskey?" I was a fucked-up little brat but I was not an asshole. I really did pity her. I kinda respected her for enduring all that pain. The two things she loved most in life had been taken away from her and yet she was still hangin' in there.

Grandma used her pad of paper and pencil hanging around her neck and spelt the words, "water please".

When I returned I sat down on the couch next to her.

"How's the solitaire goin'?" She scooped up the cards and hand signalled a cut across her neck.

"Do you wanna try a game of poker?" I'd learnt how to play poker during our last visit to the Betty Ford Centre. She nodded her head O.K.

Grandma shuffled the cards like a true professional.

"So, Grandma, it must be kinda weird to see all these people from the past? Most of them are from Grandpa's side of the family, huh?" I found it easier talking to her knowin' she wouldn't answer back. I wouldn't have been so forward if I was sober.

"Grandma, if you don't mind me asking, how did you meet Grandpa? I'll understand if you don't want to talk about it. It's just that I'm doin' a report for this English class. Getting anything out of my Mom to do with the past is impossible."

She ignored my question and dealt the first hand of the game.

"Oh, hang on, let me get my piggy bank so we can play for big bucks." I refilled my drink and returned with the same piggy bank I had made in Charm School all those years ago. I sat down on the carpet. She handed me the pad of paper. On it read:

I met your grandfather because he was my fiancé's best friend. They were stationed out in Japan together during the war.

I had to read it a few times. Grandma was waiting to play her hand as if it were her last. I proceeded with my investigation.

"So, like, you were gonna marry Grandpa's best friend? Why did you end up with Grandpa instead?"

She repeated the same slit throat gesture.

"Did your fiancé get killed in Japan?" Grandma nodded her head up and down three times and shuffled the cards, not once meeting my gaze. I took a large gulp of my margarita.

We carried on with the pathetic game of nickel poker for another half an hour. I tried to imagine how she must have felt marrying her sweetheart's best friend.

"Grandma. Umm, I'm sorry to be nosy and all, but, did you love Grandpa when you married him?"

She made no gesture of recognition. She put the cards down and wrote on the pad of paper, "I'm tired. I sleep now."

A great fat sadness swelled, piercing every joint, muscle and vein inside me. I wanted to hug my grandmother but she looked too frail with her neck wound all scabbed up. I wanted to cry the tears she hadn't in years. I wanted to tell her, *You're the real Hollywood heroine, not Bette Davis*.

"O. K. Grandma, would you like some more water?" She nodded her head yes.

When I returned she was leaning back on the couch cushions, eyes closed, seein' glasses restin' on a string above her indented chest, snot rags clasped tightly in her hand.

I set the glass down and looked at the pad of paper. The last page had been flipped over. On the fresh page “No” had been pencilled in lightly.

The party spilled out into the street. Neighbourhood cars honked and waved as we finished the three-legged race through the desert opposite our house. Where would we be without alcohol and food? Alcohol and food.

Airplane. ✈

Freak-show-hippy chick's back from the toilet. She's been in there for an hour. She has a handful of baby gin bottles and two plastic glasses of tonic.

"We got more booze to get through, soul mate."

"Great." Here we go again.

"God, you haven't stopped writing since we took off. It must be a reeeal mean letter to your mom."

"No, I'm not writing to her anymore. I don't know who I'm writing to really."

She gulps her drink down in one.

"Read me out your last sentence," she says through a mouthful of ice cubes.

"Excuse me?" I can't believe how pushy she is.

"Please! Pretty please with sugar on top!" Her eyes are glazed and desperate. So I read out what I had written.

"My dad always said "people spend most of their lives either running towards or away from something or someone. That was the fridge for me."

"Wow. I'm gonna get some more tonic water. I'll be back in a sec."

Another Shelf in the Fridge

15 WAYS TO BECOME A CHEERLEADER

1. Start orthodontist treatment early and exercise smile muscles.
2. Be a Charm School graduate with good colour co-ordination.
3. Be two-faced and a hypocrite.
4. Remind yourself that no-one is perfect even if you disagree. You must appear humble and sweet at all costs.
5. You will be adored and hated from afar, like a famous person. Boys will watch you through bedroom windows and girls will follow you into the bathroom to watch you comb your mane.
6. Remain a virgin as long as you can and, if not, keep the numbers low. When you do high kicks, football players will be looking at the size of your hole.
7. Practise school-yard hand-clapping chants like, "Say, say oh, Playmate".
8. Practise walking with head tilted to one side, toes pointed outwards.
9. Practise twirling gum and blowing bubbles with eyes shut and opening them when the bubble pops.
10. Study yourself in every angle of the mirror counting to eight over and over again, all routines are choreographed in cute sets of ten.
11. Practise sleeping in curlers and panty liners.
12. Study *How to Win Friends and Influence People* and make a list of Do's and Don'ts

next to your vanity table for your campaign to win Homecoming Queen
13. Grow hair long and one length. Study your old Barbie doll - that is the look you're going for.
14. Learn to "feel the burn" working out to Jane Fonda twice a day and get used to the bruises and slapped thighs. Do leg and butt lifts before going to bed at night.
15. Perfect different hair styles with ribbons and combs and pom poms. Remember practice makes perfect:

the palm tree or the water fountain - hair piled scrunchy on one side of your head or centre with luscious curls cascading down.

the stickshift - pony tail shoots out top of head, wrap scarf tightly around to create a four inch stick. French braiding is optional.

the whipper snapper - one large braid hanging down the side of your face used as a weapon against any guy who gets too close.

O.K. so a cheerleader is the stuck-up, made-up, fake, pretty girl, who is consumed with herself... and she always gets the boy. She is solid, oozing with compassion, spirit and self confidence. She's also the girl with the deep dark secret. The girl who cries herself to sleep over fears of varicose veins and cellulite.

But she gets the job done. She sees herself as Joan of Arc leading the battle on to the football field. She gets out there and flashes her ass at the horny teenagers so their hormones are revved up for that night's football game. That is her job.

And I wanted a job.

When I hit the big 15, I was tired of being known as a Sugarfoot, back-parking-lot, stoner, loser chick. It kinda ain't so cool in high school. I didn't want feathered hair anymore or to lie on the bed to zip my pussy pants up. I didn't want to hang out with drug dealers or get asked out by construction workers in Burger King.

I wanted to feel clean and look like the virgin I believed I was. I wanted to wear white shoes with pom-poms and bells, sport ribbons in my hair. I didn't want to wear black eyeliner on the insides of my pink eyes. I didn't want to be known as a big, fat slut. I wanted to check out some polite, virgin boys with moms and dads who lived in nice neighbourhoods. I didn't want to sit in sheds, or out in the desert on an old couch. I wanted to use some of my manipulation and Charm School tools to dig my way outta my loser hole once and for all.

For years I had hated these preppy, goodie-two-shoes, Mormon cheerleaders, wearing Izod T-shirts and Ralph Lauren. In junior high we mocked them and spat chewing gum in their hair. But secretly we envied the special treatment everybody gave them. They were the closest thing to a movie star we'd ever seen, show horses prancing through the school hallway and malls in clusters of matching uniforms and white teeth. They knew boys dreamt of either killing them, raping them or fingerfuckin' 'em. Whether you hated or adored them, you couldn't help staring, glued to their brash quest for perfection.

The try outs.

When I decided to try out for cheerleading, I did it as a dare from those ol' Sugarfoot sluts. I made poor Caitlin try out too. The Method actress in me wanted a new role to play. I worked my ass off even harder than I did with dance school.

Although I had made progress with the dancing swans, I was getting bored with that kind of regime. I wanted something new to feed on. I kept getting told off for not losing more weight and I started turning up to ballet class stoned. I didn't have the body to be a showgirl. And nobody seemed to be impressed with my triple pirouettes except for me, Sammy Cat and Jason, the next door pervert. Anyways, I wanted to feel good yesterday not in five years time.

I studied the Sleeping Indian cheerleaders the way I spied on the ballerinas, with a calculating coolness of Bette Davis. I slept in curlers every night like I learnt at Charm School and started praying to God all of a sudden.

Half the girls in the school bravely showed up on the first day of try-outs. There we were, sitting Indian style, 300 girls on the cafeteria floor blowin' bubbles trying not to let the odds psyche us out. The Mormon advisors and head cheerleader gave speeches about commitment, hard work and "soaring with the eagles". The following day at least a hundred kittens had fallen out of the race.

For those two weeks leading up to the try-outs, I nearly died of niceness shock. Not only was my throat sore from shouting, but my facial muscles ached from smiling so damn much. This was the biggest acting job of my life. Because of all those years of self inflicted zeitgeber attacks, I didn't know the first thing about acting sweet for more than two minutes. At first I was actin' like Grandma with the withdrawal shakes. Every now and again I'd have to dive into the bottom of the pool and scream my fucking head off.

The most sickly part was learning the "Sleeping Indian Warrior Spirit Chants". They were all about how great our school was and how we were gonna "scalp" the other team. Good ol' healthy competition stuff. Every cheer started with, "Are you ready! O.K." We had to act like we were on the verge of orgasmin' with happiness, like those beauty contests on TV. I was turning into the Stepford stepdaughter Benny had always fantasized about.

As I ticked off the days, I noticed my hair grew bigger. The make-up got thicker. The lipstick got pinker, as if I was changing into a stick of cotton candy. I went on a Slim Fast diet and practised each part of the routine until 1:00 in the morning. I was obsessed. I was looking the part, unlike my poor friend Caitlin who didn't have a chance in hell. It was pretty unheard of for stoner chicks who were known cocaine users to try out for cheerleading. I still had my Laura Ray reputation from junior high for being a fighter. In order to ruin my chances, some of those Mormon Varsity cheerleaders tried to spread bad rumours about me.

Luckily, I had taken all those dance classes so I could run circles around the competition. Not only could I do the jump splits without crotch bouncing, I could also do the Chinese splits and somersaults. Within days, girls were flocking around, askin' how I got my hair so full, just like Charm School days. I was in there with the preppies. For my sins I even started tying pink sweater around my shoulders and sporting pink Bobbie socks with yellow Reeboks.

Day of triumph.

It was Friday the 13th. My birthday. We all had to be given a try-out number. None of the girls wanted #13 pinned to her shirt. I jumped at it. "I'll have it if no-one else will"

It was my lucky number. Sure, I was a little nervous but not as bad as Caitlin who, at the last minute, ran out of the gym and into the bathroom with the runs. My white tennis shoes were as brand new as my padded bra. I had lost five pounds in two weeks and was looking clean and fresh as any of those "virgin" Mormons. My bangs were curled under and I had invented a new hair-do called the nuclear bomb mushroom cloud. Actually I adapted it from Chrissy on *Three's Company*, which Mormons weren't allowed to watch.

I had that crooked, fake smile down pat. My jump splits were to kill for. First of all, you place hands on hips and gleefully yell, "Ready! O.K!" Then you sashay sideways and shout, "Boogie, cross that line! Hey, it's touch down time!". By the time you say, "Time," you have shimmied, prepped and sprung three feet in the air landing smack on your crotch.

I finish perfectly, arms in a precise V-shape and smile concreted in rootbeet Lip Smack. Some girls landed in the most hilarious positions, you couldn't help giggling in the bleachers. Sometimes you could hear bones and ligaments snapping. That wasn't so funny.

This one girl jumped up into the air and when she landed on "time" she bounced like a penny settling on the floor. She couldn't quite reach the gym floor so she supported herself with her hands. To her credit, her smile never altered, even as she was being carried off on a stretcher.

I did a perfect somersault and my shouting was so loud, it set off rich kid car alarms. The judges looked a bit dubious about the size of my thighs but that was the only thing on the list they could fault me on. An hour after the try-out, the selected girls' names were listed and pinned to the principal's office window.

I was so relieved to see my name at the bottom of the list. "Jesusa Whitby." Some girls were crying, others screamed and stomped their feet. I just stood there, mouth 0-shaped. Caitlin congratulated me and then walked to the back parking lot. We both knew we wouldn't be seeing much of each other anymore. Those were the rules.

I feel a little stupid admitting it, but it was the happiest day of my life so far, mainly because I hadn't had that much loving attention from my mother in years. I was finally adored. She was a cheerleading advisor at Sunrise High so she knew what it meant to be a cheerleader. I had finally achieved something that was good and wholesome.

At the end of sixth period, the names of the new Sleeping Indian varsity cheerleaders were announced over the intercom. Nobody could believe an ex-Sugarfoot stoner, like me, had made cheerleader.

After school, in the front parking lot, seniors who had never spoken to me before came up inviting me to this party and that. All the big jock studs and chicks had welcomed me into the élite breed club handing me the traditional red, white and blue roses. Yuck. I was also presented with the Letterman's Coat all jocks sported. My very own nickname had been stitched onto the back -"Jessie Duke #1". My stoner history had been erased now that I had a First Class title. I held one of the highest positions in school, a heroine once again.

To top off the day of triumph, my mother and Benny took me out to Ricardo's Mexican restaurant and told me they would buy me a red Convertible VW Beetle

"I'm so proud of you, Jessie. I can't believe how much you've changed." She slurped away on her margarita while I sucked on my Diet Coke.

Benny gave his long-time-coming speech, "Well, Jesus Cranberries, it's amazing what a little discipline can do for a young person."

I loved the slaps on the back but at the same time I resented the fact that I was praised because I'd conformed, as if they'd finally taught the dog how to walk to heel.

Even Marco Rodriguez, the Sugarfoot King of Cuts, was all of a sudden respectful as if I had risen above them. But a person doesn't change all that quickly, those ol' scab picking habits don't just disappear miraculously. Miss Goodie-Two-Shoes was just a front. An *ABC After School Special*.

Virgin Gorge

Age 16

Marco Rodriguez, cousin to Berto the Burrito Brain, used to call me "The Grand Canyon". Now there was the Grand Canyon and then there was the Virgin Gorge. I preferred to think of my vagina as the Virgin Gorge. Virgin Gorge was a pass of mountains that crossed into Arizona. A highway had been chiselled in between the rocks as a quicker route to the Grand Canyon. There was a dirt turn-off that only trucks could tackle. It clambered up into breast of the mountain.

Bein' the cool clone I was, I lost my virginity up in the Virgin Gorge. It was supposed to be the good luck charm thing to do. Driving up the steep freeway we kept passing crying, de-virginized girls walking along the side of the highway. Used sperm trickled like lava down from the mountains.

He unfolded the back of his Chevy. There was a breeze that kissed my hungry hole underneath my miniskirt and lifted me onto the back of his Chevy. It was dying to be filled. Sparkle had been working towards this night for two months. I decided to relieve him because he said he wasn't playing good baseball. And my new cheerleading pals said it was long enough time to wait.

"Is this your first time, baby?" Sparkle pressed his body against mine, under the blanket.

"Yah, I'm pretty sure, baby," I replied kittenishly. I loved making Sparkle insanely jealous. One time I kissed a boy and watched excitedly as Sparkle pounded him to the ground.

"What do you mean, you're pretty sure, either you know or you don't!"

"Well, there was this one time I got kidnapped and dragged out to this place called Eddie's Ranch..."

Just as we're about to have sex, the angriest boy in school starts boxing with the midnight air.

"I know Eddie's Ranch - you didn't fuck that dude Eddie. Did you?"

"No, it was his friend, but I really don't think anything happened cos all my clothes were on when I woke up..."

The thought of me not bein' a virgin was obviously a turn-off. Sparkle jumped outta the truck and pushed his hard-on back down and threw rocks at the moon.

"There weren't no blood, baby. I remember him trying but the doors weren't open, honey pie. Get over here. I'm aching for ya." Watching Madonna singing *Like a Virgin* on MTV was making me horny as hell those days.

"I bet you were doing coke, that's all they do out there. God, I knew you were a coke head. Don't make me angry. You wouldn't like me when I'm angry." He said it reeeal serious, as if he didn't know he was quoting *The Incredible Hulk*.

When Sparkle finished listening to his voice reverb through the mountain crevices, he jumped on to the back of the truck like a surf-boarder and dived under the blanket. "I'll find out if you're a virgin!"

I lit another joint, getting more and more nervous.

"Slow down, man!" The grids of the truck were digging into my shoulder blades. At least I wasn't banging my head against a toilet bowl. "Look, there's Sleeping Indian Mountain... ain't it?" It was at least twenty miles away but the beak-like nose was so easy to spot, even with a sliver of a moon. Black against black against black. "They shoulda' called it Dead Indian Mountain, he don't look like he's sleeping." I inhaled. "Do you feel like an Indian?" I exhale. *Count to 10.*

Apart from his tan, you couldn't tell he was half Indian. He looked like Marlon Brando and acted like Charles Manson.

"Yah, sometimes I wanna kill white people, especially my coach, my dad and your stepdad, too. I'd like to scalp 'em all." His pecs flexed as he shook his fist. "I'd love to shoot the breeze but I'm horny as hell... so ... are you O.K? I mean are you ready to do it?"

"O. K, let's get it over with." I pulled him to me. His tiger's mouth clamped on to my neck. While Sparkle was doin' his thing on top, all these boys' faces Ferris-wheeled against the starry sky. The black sun seemed to be smirking at me as if to say I'd lost something more than my virginity. Maybe I'd forfeited the battle against man hating.

Even while I was fucking, it felt like I had already seen it on TV. Me, Brooke Shields in *Endless Love* with a lunatic boyfriend. I didn't want to feel like that. I waited and prayed for a mountain lion to pounce, or a vulture to swoop down, even a shooting star would have been O.K. But nothing except for Leo Brown. James Sprinkler-head. Berto the Mexican hood. Marco who made me cry... The sound of Sparkle's grunts freaked me out. I closed my eyes tight and the 1000 microscopic insects on the inside of my eyelids squirmed round like sperm eggs. Lizards shedding skin. I hated the sound of sex.

"Shut up!" I put my hand over his mouth just as he came.

It was cold, piercing and quickly out of there. I burst out laughing. He thought it was because he came so quickly. I was just glad it was over. I knew for sure it was my first time. I don't know why I held out so long anyway. I wanted to fuck him the first night I saw his glowin' green eyes but I played hard to get, giving it my best Lauren Bacall.

Afterwards, afterwards, afterwards... why does there always have to be an afterwards? We cuddled up together in the back of his truck and admired the view. I thought of my mother curled up in bed.

"Hey Sparkle, just imagine, like a 100 years ago pioneers were travelling through this pass with nothing but wagons and horses and just, like, sheer bravery. Did you learn about the Donner Party and how they had to eat each other and shit? That's so gross. Would you eat me if you had to, baby?" I'd eat him.

I looked down to see Sparkle sleeping. Just like the movies. I hadn't ended up with a Woody Allenesque dude or even a Howard Hughes type. I'd ended up with an angry brute jock as if the only way I could get turned on was by the enemy... by having raging fights in the middle of the desert.

Mom love had been replaced by crowd love, Sparkle was in the front row screaming "Yahoo! Go, Baby Boogie, cross that line". But it wasn't a love thing, it was a me me me thing.

Apart from fantasizing about being crowned Homecoming Queen, I'd spend every breathing second thinking of him and what he did for me in his truck underneath my cheerleading skirt. Off and on for the next two years of high school we'd spend countless nights fucking and fighting. Fucking and fighing up at Virgin Gorge or Sleeping Indian Mountain or sneaking into each other's bedroom windows, planning all kinds of escape routes together.

After about twenty-five fucks I let loose and it was him who had to muzzle me out of embarrassment. I was Nastassja Kinski in *Cat People*. Like everything else so far, I gobbled him up and eventually spat him out.

Sparkle's favourite thing to do was make me get out of the car and leave me standing in the scorpion-infested desert. He'd zoom off towards the highway and then do a big, dramatic, dusty U-turn as if he was coming back to run me over. He never did though. He'd just get out of the truck, howl at he moon, blame his dad and then beg for forgiveness. I loved to see him cry. He played victim as much as I did.

At first Benny and my Mom approved of him cause he was a front parking lot jock.

My Mom would go, "He reminds me of my first boyfriend".

That was until she started getting phone calls from my teachers complaining about Sparkle's temper. He'd sometimes strut into my classroom like a caveman and carry me out over his shoulder. We'd fight in the hallways and parking lot and then drive off somewhere and make up. He never hit me but he scared the shit out of me. Cos of Benny, all Sparkle had to do was raise his hand and I'd flinch and crouch in my grand plié position. Since I'd been loving' in a grown-up way, I understood a lot more about men. I no longer saw the world in black and white, good and evil. I understood why woman make such wild noises while fucking. And I could see why people hit each other.

OFF WITH THE HOMECOMING QUEEN'S HEAD

Aged 17.

When my scabs had nearly healed, I peeled them open again. I was doin' so damn good too, I even had chopped up vegetables in the fridge so, when I felt like filling my mouth, I would bypass the peanut butter for the Tupperware of peeled carrots. But it didn't feel right to be living my life so tidy and all. Miss Apple Pie Cheerleader wasn't getting me high enough.

Being awarded Scalp 'Em Warrior Cheerleader was another all-consuming dream to swallow up and hope to be swallowed up by. My high school days were like a three-year free pass at Magic Mountain Theme Park. With cotton candy and ice cream smeared down my uniform, I ran from one ride to the next, mowin' down adults and kids in order to get front row car on the upside down rollercoaster. As the crooked-smiled crowds spun manically around, my Greedy Mouth gulped and hollered out at the distorted world, my wild, long mane dressed in feathers swingin' dangerously close to the rails.

Ever since that Santa Cruz rollercoaster, I'd been inching up that first hill. But the car always reversed back down the slope to where the zitty operator toyed with the stick shift. Now, it was on automatic pilot of high and low orgasms. Whether it was on the sidelines of a football pitch, zoomin down a ski slope in a biking top, or running through casinos messin' with the Mafia dudes, I was on a perpetual ride. And, even though it was exhilarating, I wouldn't say it was fun. I had my contact lenses glued shut the whole time, missing every single Kodak Moment. Even on the night of my prom, I passed out drunk before we got there.

I remember the first September day I had to model the uniform through the school. I was terrified someone would pull up my skirt. I had my new, green contact lenses in and my Autumn Green Estée Lauder eyeshadow. I was shittin' myself because I knew everyone wanted to see my ass, to see the alleged purple worms of junior high. All kinds of stories had been building up over the years and, as the monstrous little boys got older, the stories got weirder. The best one was every night my stepfather turned me over on his lap and scraped the back of my thighs with hot knives as punishment.

After second period, I had to walk up these steps to get to my algebra class. I turned around to a sea of faces studying the backs of my legs. The purple worms were not worms at all, just plain ol' stretch marks. But the sun had decided to tan them with its laser rays. I felt better when I saw the head cheerleader had them running along the back of her knees.

That's the kind of crap a cheerleader worries about, that and clean knickerbockers. Our knickerbockers were stretchy Wonder Woman numbers with red, white and blue tomahawks printed on the butt. What would Steve the Turkey Farmer think of me pretending to be a warrior?

Knickerbockers were my favourite article. Easy access. Sex in between classes was as drive-thru as 1, 2, 3. All I had to do was jump on Sparkle's lap, pull the knickers to one side and *wham, bam, thank you, mam*. The humpin' was covered by the skirt so, if the security guard knocked on the truck window, things were cool.

Strutting' the cheerleading uniform was not only stressful from an exposure point of view, it was torturous in the 115-degree Las Vegas heat. The red, white and blue skirts and sweaters were all wool so, in the summer, you sweated and itched in your desk chair and, in the winter, you froze to death in nylons and legwarmers.

Every year the new cheerleaders had to fork out $500 to pay for the annual cheerleading camp and uniform. If you were lucky you could prance into a casino and get the boss to donate a few $100 bills.

I was back to the selling cookies routine, but this time it was in the hallways at school to guys wanting to touch my flesh. Sellin' hot dogs downtown was O.K. but the car wash fund raisers were just retarded. Us girls would dress in our uniforms and rotate from attracting attention on intersection islands to cleaning the cars. Basically our clientele was perverted husbands, wanting to watch us bend over while they stood there with their Big Gulps chatting to other perverts in baseball hats and mirrored glasses.

A cheerleader's life wasn't the easy ride I thought it was going to be. I was so sick of bein' sweet and fake. I'd gone more Barbie than Barbie herself, but it was so exaggerated I thought people would find out I was an impostor or at least see the funny side. Sadly, sophomores copied my look; the mushroom cloud hairdo, personalized bobby socks, earrings and nailpolish. They look like my cloned Stepford siblings.

But I was no Goody Two Shoes. Jessie Duke was one of the biggest drug-takers and party-goers at Sleeping Indian High and took great pride in it. There was nothing better than cheerleading stoned at a football game with a crowd of two thousand boys begging you for another high kick.

Just when things were gettin' good, I felt like messing it all up. I was on best behaviour so that I could be Homecoming Queen. It was the ultimate prize, my Best Actress Award. I had been following my do's and don'ts list next to the vanity table for nearly a year and a half. So far everybody had been fallin' for my Method acting, except for Caitlin and the Sugarfoot girls but they were practically invisible or pregnant. I can't even count how many times I dreamt of my acceptance speech when I would be crowned.

There I am in my lavender ball gown, with the longest and fullest and curliest hairdo in history. I have red, glittering, Dorothy shoes on. The bleachers are packed with three thousand admirers. My mother is sitting right in front petting Sammy Cat. The Homecoming parade is about to commence. The five other nominated runners-up are driven around the football field by Ken Barbie jocks, in Corvettes, knowing in their hearts they have lost to Jesusa the Great. I am delicately perched on the rump of a Jag with instructions to wave to the crowds who have voted for me.

The winner is announced over the outdoor speaker just before the football game kicks off. As fireworks blow off like nuclear bombs, I graciously accept the crown from the previous year's queen and the yearbook photographer snaps pictures obsessively. Pure fame.

But a cheerleader had to be a role model, Katherine Hepburn/Jane Fonda-flavoured frozen yoghurt. Like the dude jocks, you had a lot of pressure placed on you by the football coaches and cheerleading advisors. Of course Benny knew half of them because he was the coach at Desert Rose High School.

I felt like such a imposter prancing around the hallways shouting, "Scalp 'Em, Sleeping Indians". I ran for class secretary which was the biggest joke. I painted posters, gave speeches, and went to meetings about picnic fund raisers with all the Mormons. As far as studying and getting good grades, the teachers turned a blind eye. Except for year books, I don't remember lookin' at one book in three years. If you were a high school star you could leave class anytime you wanted to get some doughnuts at Winchells'. I always got A's without doin' a damn thing.

Bein' a Goodie-Two-Shoes didn't necessarily prepare you for real life. You'd hear about kids from the élite class who graduated a few years before who couldn't handle being on the other side of the football fence. You'd see them wearing their Letterman coats for years after.

This one ex-football star became a cop almost straight outta high school. He'd be on patrol around Sleeping Indian making sure kids weren't drinking in the parking lots but all he was interested in was trying to get chicks in the back of his cop car. He would choose the girl he wanted to breathalyse and then start feelin' her legs. Like a lot of them, he married his high school sweetheart, who of course was a cheerleader and the Homecoming Queen. She had failed to turn him on ever since she handed in her uniform.

Then there was this one football player at our school who shot himself in the head at a daytime party. His best friend said he committed suicide, others said it was an accident. Like my Mom always said, Nevada had the highest rate of suicides in the country. I don't know why that kid killed himself but I know he was drinking that day.

Daytime drinking was pretty outta control.

All that rollercoaster riding was going straight to my head. I had become the most popular girl in school and I was all geared up to get crowned Homecoming Queen the following week. My boyfriend had just gone off to play baseball at college in California so I had Homecoming Dance proposals piled up in the back seat of my car. I had worn four different dresses to four different proms in the past two years. I had a weirdo secret admirer who'd been sending me flowers every day for a month. The phone was ringin' off the hook so damn much Benny paid for me to have my own line. I had gifts, love letters and attention coming outta my ears. Even though my mom was busy making more babies, she was smothering me with "I know you'll win Queen" compliments.

My senior year at high school didn't go according to plan though. I became one of those Hollywood-kid clichés. Life in the fast lane got the better of me. It's not like I became an alcoholic or a drug addict, it's just that I always had to find a bigger and better rollercoaster than the one I was riding.

Tammi and Cheri, the only other two non-Mormon girls on the squad, were planning a party before the first big game of the season. To my surprise the party took place at my house. About fifty of us had been drinkin' margaritas at my house since 10:00 a.m.

Our drinks cupboard had been cleaned out but that was the least of my problems. There were kids passed out all over my backyard. Someone had turned my palm tree into a swing. My pool had turned into a yellow cocktail of sperm, piss and NutraSweet lemonade. Benny's perfect grass had been flattened out with slam dancers. People were beer bonging out of the Creepy Crawler. Freaky Jason next door was threatening to call the cops. Couples had climbed over George's wall and were making out in his jacuzzi and playing tug of war with his Creepy Crawler. Wost of all, my hair had gone flat after I was thrown into the pool and my new fling had answered a long distance phone call from Sparkle. And we all had to be at school for a 3:00 p.m. afternoon game.

After I cleaned up what I could and put water and food colouring in the booze bottles we headed for school. I was looking forward to executing this new cheer I had choreographed over the summer. I designed a pyramid that moved forward with the bottom row of girls strapped to skateboards. My Mom and Benny would be there because Sleeping

Indian was playing against their school, Desert Rose High. Benny was coachin'. I should have done a U-turn when Tammi puked out the side of my VW at Decauter Intersection.

So we make it out to the field. Right away the other Mormon cheerleaders smell the booze. Tammi had puke all down her Warriors sweater. What really gave us away was the flat hair. It was a fashion crime. Cheri forgot to put her sports bra back on and only realized this when the fans in the bleachers shouted it out.

I checked I had my knickerbockers on before I mounted the pyramid. Tammi was at the bottom. Once I was in place on the second row, Cheri was supposed to climb up on top as quick as possible. But she just stood at the bottom laughing and shaking her head,

"I'm scared of heights. I can't do it."

The head cheerleader was gettin' pissed off, "Get up here right now, Chereeeee!" she shouted in her self-righteous voice from the third level.

"Get your ass up here, woman!" I giggled.

The whole stunt was only supposed to last for a minute. At the end, the top girl was supposed to do a somersault off the top and the rest follow with cart wheels and back flips. It had now gone two minutes and our fake Minnie Mouse smiles had slipped.

The margarita crowd in the front row egged Cheri on. She stepped up on to Tammi's back, shaking her body. The pyramid wobbled in the fading autumn sun. Cheri then moved to the next level, sticking her bony knee into the small of my back. Just as she was nearing the top of the fleshy mountain, she slipped forward and saddled the head cheerleader's neck. Just before the skateboards could roll into action, Tammi collapsed.

We all went down like a card-stack domino disaster. Cheri never reached the top of the cheerleading cake. From the Desert Rose High bleachers across the field, you could hear perfect bones crushing. The three of us rolled around in the grass in hysterics while the other girls limped over to Jennifer, who had sprained her wrist.

The envious crowd had been waiting for this kind of fuck-up for their whole entire high school careers. Even though the crowd enjoyed our Evel Knievel stunt gone wrong, the head cheerleader went to the advisor in tears. The crowd booed as the three of us were sent to the Dean's office.

We sat there silent and innocent, until Cheri threw up into his indoor palm tree. That was when he got in the school security guard to breathalyse us. *Book 'em, Danno*

All three of us were thrown off the squad and expelled from school for two weeks. I was disqualified from running for Homecoming Queen and all other school activities for the rest of the year. Instead of the pool, I headed straight for the refrigerator.

The acting game was over. Barbie had been ripped to shreds by the sharks. The rollercoaster derailed and crashed. As far as tragedies go, I know it wasn't much compared to the kid who shot himself in the head, or the beauty contestant who got murdered at the mall, or poor Caitlin who had retired to the back parking lot for life. But my story was more like a fairy tale tragedy. The great rise and fall of Jessie Duke. Beheaded before she was crowned.

THE BODY AT REDROCK

Aged 17.

I never told anyone about what I saw at Red Rock Canyon. I didn't want to get involved with going to court and causing any more controversy. My mother could hardly look at me anymore without crying. I only had a few months left of high school and I was fighting to keep myself from turnin' into a refrigerator. I'd gone back to having zeitgeber mood swing attacks all the time. I was either comotosed in front of the TV, out partying every night with Tammi and Cheri, or fighting with Sparkle, who kept driving back to Vegas when he found out I was messing around with a new guy.

Since I'd got thrown off the squad my Mom forced me to get a job at this ice cream parlour at the Meadows Mall. It was mainly to pay off my $400 phone bill from calling Sparkle in California all the time. The rest of the time I'd spend on my raft, by the pool, killing brain cells or trying to electrocute myself in order to not go numb.

I'll never forget the first time I saw the body lying there. Rotting, fly-infested flesh. Part of me doesn't even want to try and explain what it was like cos my sad range of words could never do it justice. It looked like Road Kill is all. It wasn't a fleeting glance of a run-over hedgehog, it was a five-minute, biological investigation. The body was melted against a cactus, which reminded me of this Salvador Dali postcard I once had from my dad in England. It was all twisted and melting like that clock and there were ants crawling all over it. Dry blood was cracking along the dried-up desert wash. And with all the red rocks engulfing us, I felt like I was being lowered into hell.

If I had seen the funny side, I could have pretended I was Captain Kirk, standing next to Spock, examining the remains of an alien monster on another planet. The setting was just like that with lots of fake-lookin' boulders about to cave in on me. When I try to visualise that day, that body, those kids, it just seems too much like a movie.

It was a school day in March. Bathing suit weather. I had just finished second period English, so it was about 11.00 a.m. I was standing in the back parking lot, looking to score some weed. I didn't normally mix with the stoners in their territory, where someone from school would see me, but at that point in my high school career I didn't care.

Since becoming Homecoming Queen was another cruddy failure for my scab box, I decided I would spend the rest of my high school days going nuts on coke, weed and vodka. The back parking lot was where my long-lost childhood buddy Caitlin parked her car. She had inherited Toby's clanker. I barely spoke to her anymore. Right when I became a cheerleader, the rule was, "all stoners, losers, low riders and weirdo nerds stay with their own kind". There were no speed bumps in the back parking lot, so they could do drag races in their low riders. In the front parking lot all the rich college-bound preppies and jocks parked where there was good security and very large speed bumps so nobody could zoom off in their cars or crash into their bumpers.

I had two free periods before my biology test and I wanted to score some doobie-do. There was this girl I used to baby-sit when I lived near Sugarfoot. Her name was Judy and she was only 15. She acted much older, like she'd seen 50 times worse things than I had. Her and her boyfriend dealt weed out of the back of her truck.

Judy's father was a weird cop and her mother was a professional slot machine winner. She was a part of a cheating ring that had been going since the 70's before the slot machines turned electronic. These crooks used to go around opening the back of the slot machines and fixing the fruit symbols to hit the jackpot. Judy's dad tried to freak me out when he took me home after baby-sitting by asking if I was nervous the whole time. Her Mom was in jail now and Judy wasn't living with her father anymore.

I waved to Judy in my cheerleading outfit and skipped over to them. Even though I was kicked off the team, I still wore the outfit to piss the Mormons off. I paid 200 bucks for it, too damn right I was gonna wear it. Judy was one of the few stoners who gave me the time of day. As portrayed in Hollywood teenage films, all stoners hated the jocks and vice versa. But I was a bit of a cult hero since I had been kicked off the squad. She rolled her seriously tinted window down.

"Can I have a dime bag?

She ordered me to get in the cab of the truck as if she was the baby-sitter now. So, I jumped in there with all these long-haired, heavy-metal dudes.

Before I knew it we were on Highway 101. My unhappy hair tangled around my face. The sun and chlorine had poisoned its lusciousness and left it split and dead to the fucking root. That Barbie bounce had gone. The feeling of wind whipping at my face made me feel young again. I want to feel young again. I closed my eyes and conjured the memory of riding Timmy's speed boat. Escape to the bottom of the water.

Escape.

Escape.

Escape.

The doobie passed my way. The cherry fell into my lap and burnt a hole in my sweaty, cheerleading skirt. I relaxed and let my skirt blow up around my waist, revealing my has-been underwear. I wished I could have that underwear with the days of the week. I wished for control, to have my days mapped out for me. I wished for a new addiction, something new to gobble up.

Stoned as a desert floor, I didn't care where I was going. I took off my cheerleading sweater to tan myself in my bikini top. The stoner dudes loved this as we vibrated over the cracks in the highway and Las Vegas disappeared into the horizon. I told them lies about how much I love Ozzy Ozbourne and Mötley Crüe so they'd think I was an O.K. jock.

We turned off on to a dirt road. And then on to another dirt road. Before long we were nowhere near a dirt road as we wheeled haphazardly rock over rock. Judy had four-wheel drive so she flattened out her own route. Judging by the flame coloured boulders, I figured out we were in Red Rock Canyon. I hadn't been to Red Rock since I was a Girl Scout pickin' up trash. Back then it was mainly used by locals, but now bus loads of tourists crawled all over the famous rocks .

The stoner on the left said, "It's so cool that Judy let you come with us, did she tell you about what happened already?"

" No, what are we doing up here?" I shouted over the spinnin' wheels.

"They gotta dune buggy that we're gonna drive to the body". I didn't fully make what he said cos of the rattling of the truck.

We pulled into this cave and there was the dune buggy he was talking about. It looked just like the "The Love Bug" without a roof. Bouncing around in a Dune buggy when you're stoned was the best! It wasn't the same if you were straight. All strapped in, we took off with a whiplash. Judy's boyfriend took our lives into his hands climbing up and crashing down, flyin' in and out of ditches and hills, side-windin' on the crag of 10-foot cliffs. He mounted the smaller boulders with gritted Jack Nicholson teeth, two-wheelin' around huge Red Rock boulders. It made me think of Shaggy and Scooby Doo and the gang in their dune buggy.

Then my head hit the padded crow bar. I felt all of a sudden edgy as my inner organs juggled up and down, bruising each other. And then I felt the shark fins in my head. Mistakes were as common as my monthly periods I expected them to happen, outta my control. The cotton mouth was unbearable. I was dying for a drink. My neck was jolting and cracking in circular motions like a Jack in the Box as I tried to tell the stoner crammed to the left GET ME OUT! He didn't care what I was trying to say. He freed his hips and actually stood up, wrapping his body around the crow bar, hanging there as if he were riding a buckaroo."Hey, look, one hand!"

I had to pee so bad my eyes started to water. I yoga-counted to ten, holding my breath, trying to exhale my bladder. The suffocating wind was like steamed towels being layered over my face. I could barely close my mouth to hold my breath so I *switched*.

I am strapped to my upgraded First Class 13A seat
I have just fallen out of the airplane and I'm flying through the sky
my twenty foot hair stretches out like a palm tree parachute

I am an escape route expert, flippin' in and out of my favourite actresses.
I am a victim, Marilyn Monroe, man-handled, misunderstood and abused
I am a hero, Judy Garland, waving to a crowd full of fans
I am a baby, Shirley Temple, crying for attention
I am a queen, Katherine Hepburn, brave warrior

all of a sudden I drop down through the clouds
plunging into the ocean
down down down
I come up up up
spring to the surface like a space capsule
in bubbles and white caps

as in all my dreams
the same blood thirsty sharks appear from nowhere
I'm diced in half and then sliced
again and again
like a garbage disposal
there goes my leg and my left arm.
I just sing at the top of my lungs -
boogie, cross that line. hey! It's touch down time!

Finally the buggy jolted to a halt. I waited for my organs to finish reverberating.

"Here he is." Judy shouted, jumping up and down, like the cheerleader she'd never be. The others wandered over to where she was standing. Wiping the dirt from my cracked lips I waded through the sand and crouched behind a tumbleweed. Stoned and shaken from the ride, I lose my balance and planted my butt in the hot sand.

I bounded towards the others. One of the backseat stoners was throwing up under a Joshua tree. As I got closer I pushed my sunglasses up and there before me was this deader-than-dead, blood-caked man, spreadeagled, arms propped upwards against this huge cactus. Like the scarecrow outta Wizard of Oz, he coulda come alive at any second. The blood was purple. Exactly how dead bodies look on film.

I was petrified and stunned, drenched in sweat. Nobody moved or said nothin' for like five minutes. And then the stoners circled the body, leaning over cautiously pointing at different-sized stab wounds. All that came out of my mouth, over and over, was,

"Oh, my God! Oh, my God!"

I counted the wounds all around the face and neck; eleven stabs to the face, eight stabs to the neck. They weren't deep; tiny, neat marks, like potato pricks before it goes in the microwave.

The rest of his body was such a mess of bullet holes, I stopped counting.

"Oh, my God!" I said out loud for the tenth time.

"Shut up girl!" Judy, with her sorrowless shark eyes was just sittin' there on a red rock, sucking on a joint.

I thought I had the right to confront the brat I used to baby-sit. I went over to her and broke the silence,

"How long have you known this body was out here?"

She sassed back, "Since we brought him out here, retard." I pulled my lipstick out of my sock and applied it over and over as if it could gloss over my nervous disposition.

"What the fuck have you done, Judy?" Her and her boyfriend had given the drifter some kind of devil-worshipping death ceremony.

"We met him down town in the parking lot of the Horseshoe. He was just a scummy drifter, bragging' about his winnings like he was real laid back and all. We got him stoned and he bought a quarter bag of weed. When he pulled out that wad of hundred dollar bills there was no goin' back. We knew he was up for an adventure. We were like telling him about the Red Rock Caves and how there were all these devil worshipping sacrifices up there. We were, like, yah duuuude, come take a ride in our dune buggy. It's so cool when you're stoned... And the rest you can see for yourself. Like you used to say, baby-sitter, 'You have to have a real love to do this'."

"What are you talking about? Anyways, I bet you didn't do it, you probably just found it out here. Probably a Mafia job."

She teased me, almost singing the words, "You have to have a real love..."

And then I remembered. This was a Sadie Mae quote from that book *Helter Skelter* on the Charles Manson murder trials. I used to read out passages at bed-time, when I baby-sat Judy. It was when I wanted to kill my stepdad, so I always had it, like a manual.

I spoke to her with less authority now.

"How long has he been out here?" Trying to be the cool clone from my Sugarfoot days.

"Five days. We're still making money." You could tell she was real proud of her campfire tale, talking as if someone else had murdered this guy. In detail, she acted out how long it took him to die and how he staggered around begging for his life.

"I don't believe you." I couldn't look at the body anymore, I just wanted to leave.

"If you don't believe me I'll show you our cave full of carcasses." She pointed yonder.

"Just shut up, Judy! You're making me sick!" I wanted to tell her off like I had when I was her baby-sitter, but she just kept on describing the dissections and how good it felt killing a real human being. I felt kinda nervous. I didn't really know those back parking lot freaks at all. I had no idea what they were capable of.

"My daddy was right. There's no high like killing someone, taking someone's last breath. That's the best. It's so cool, Jessie... But you'll never know cos you're so fucking straight-laced, Miss Apple Pie Cheerleader."

"Shut up" I yelled.

It echoed for a few seconds in the canyon. They turned and gave me the evilest, shark-eyed look any screwed up American kid could give. I was insane for shouting at a devil-worshipper, bein' in such a vulnerable position and all.

"A cheerleader would be the ultimate sacrifice."

I tried to stay cool.

"Ha ha honey! I'm not a cheerleader anymore. Believe me I hate them as much as you do. Look, I'm sorry, I'm just a little shocked. It's not every day you see a dead body. I just can't believe you could do this. I'm just freaked out. But, umm, I'm impressed. Charles Manson would have been proud."

"I brought you out here cos I thought you'd understand. "

"I do. But why are you bringing people out her to see the body? You're gonna get caught. Someone's gonna tell on you, girl."

"Don't you worry about that. Come on, let's go."

No longer smilin' stoner style, I didn't say a word the whole trip back. Oh, but that evil sun kept smiling. Bangin' organs and bruised hips didn't hurt, I was just grateful the stoners didn't attack me.

When we entered the cave where Judy's truck was parked we climbed out of the buggy in silence. Judy demanded twenty bucks from me. "What for?" I replied cautiously. She dangled a dime bag in front of my face and whispered, "Twelve bucks for the weed and eight for the viewing, and if you say anything I'll slice your face off. I know where you live. I've been in your house before while you were sleeping in your pink princess bed."

I gave her the money immediately, trying to figure out what she had just said. And then I remembered. A year before my stepdad had seen someone on our roof outside my bedroom window. At first, I thought it was my boyfriend but then the next morning I opened my window and found a skinned cat with its stomach hangin' out. It wasn't my cat, but I thought maybe Sammy had dragged it there. Why would Judy do something like that to me? I used to be her baby-sitter. What the hell happened to her?

We arrived back at about 2:00 p.m. As we exited off the highway, I could see the cheerleaders practising for their next game. It was basketball season. All those Mormon girls with their untouched pussies. Fuck them. And fuck the whole of Las Vegas with all its money-hungry nutcases. I jumped from Judy's truck. As I turned to go, she rolled her window down and called to me in her stoner drawl, "Keep quiet or I'll slice your face off and give it to the devil to wear as a mask."

I stood there gripping my biology book in one hand, the plastic bag full of weed in the other. I watched as some other potheads climbed in the back of Judy's truck and zoomed off. Why did she take me up there and show me that shit? Surely she must have known I couldn't keep it a secret?

I decided to go to biology so I could concentrate on something else. An hour later I was sitting there with a frog cut open in front of me. I had managed to get its flesh pinned back but I couldn't do anymore. I was frozen and I couldn't wipe the body up at Red Rock out of my memory. My nerves were shot. I ran out of the classroom.

Back at home, I pulled the blinds shut, blasted the air conditioning and fans and covered myself in blankets in bed. On TV was this movie called *Street Car Named Desire*, Marlon Brando and Vivien Leigh from *Gone with the Wind*. I locked my door and waited for my nice *Little House on the Prairie* mom to come home from her school.

In the next few days rumours were flying around school. But I kept my mouth shut. Everyone was whispering in locker rooms, underneath desks and in cubicle stalls. Judy was famous at school, something no stoner could achieve unless she had a black boyfriend. Everybody was saying how they were takin' friends out to Red Rock Canyon and charging eight dollars to see the body. They had told practically everyone at school that they had killed the tourist and taken his money. That poor sucker was out there decaying for more than a week and a half.

Finally someone must've told the police or someone cos the following week I watched on TV as Judy and her boyfriend were arrested. It was in all the newspapers. I couldn't believe they confessed right away.

The police came to Sleeping Indian and interviewed practically every student. By now Sleeping Indian High had the worst reputation in Las Vegas. In the end the police had like fifteen kids give evidence against Judy and her boyfriend. I just ignored the whole thing. Pretended it wasn't happening. Went swimming. Went out to lunch. Gave myself shock treatments. Went out partying with Cheri and Tammi. As usual, after a week or two it was old news. After all, they were stoners and he was just a bumming tourist whom nobody cared about. Something bigger would always replace the headlines. Judy and her boyfriend got life in prison for first degree murder.

Melting Make-up, Sun Cancer, and U-turns

Just as I was opening a bag of sunflower seeds the sun spoke to me through my beat box:

hey Miss Las Vegas
you think you're so outrageous
you sad Toni Basil wannabe
you're not the only chick heading for L.A.
50,000 other bubbly-assed cheerleaders are already there in Emerald City
who know how to body pop and moon walk
with legs and boobs three times as sexy as yours
you weren't the only latch key kid
who was brought up on Special K Captain Kangaroo cartoons
who got voted best-looking and most likely to succeed
turn your sorry-ass car around
there is no Wizard of Oz
like your mom says,"get over it and get on with it"

Miss Las Vegas-
Who the hell are you, asshole?

The Sun-
I've been watching you baby doll
you're the rollercoaster girl
you piss in the streets and laugh at oncoming headlights
as they swerve to miss your butt cheeks
you're so crude rude and nude
you want the world to know your sweet sour lemonade face
even if it's on a billboard advertising the dangers of bulimia or drug abuse
you want your own line of frosted lipsticks and hair dyes
to be marketed as Jessie Duke's make-up pets

you think you got high school fame
because 3,000 mall brats know your name
hey Kool-Aid kid that ain't no real taste test
you're as special as the 2-for-1 offer at K-Mart.
looky here baby doll you've past your sell by date
at 17 you've done one too many jump splits

The back seat of my topless VW was overflowing with bouquets, marriage proposals and pom poms. "No Wimps" blazed across my chest. Due to the lack of airconditioning and shade, I was holdin' my own wet t-shirt contest. With a bag full of ice I packed cubes into my sports bra in order to keep my temperature from rising. Truck drivers passed and tooted their horns as I shook my fist at the sun.

Miss Las Vegas-
I am Jessie Duke
I am gonna boogie cross that state line
I am gonna be an L.A. Raiders cheerleader
and you can't stop me mothafucka'
because I'm a #1 neon sensation
and I got the necklace charm to prove it
the next Houdini
the next Monroe
I am the wild west golden girl
glowing with nuclear sun cancer

The Sun-
L.A. don't need anymore cliché-kids with no talent hairdos
we're all full up
so turn your shitty car right around
before I disintegrate it like a Space Invader
with my ray gun

Miss Las Vegas-
SHUT UP!!! LET ME THINK!!
Once we get over the San Bernadino Mountains it'll be downhill from there.
I think I can I think I can I think I can I think I can.
I can drive faster than the sun can.

I needed more gas so I got off at the next exit...

I was leafin' through my yearbook messages to remind myself I was a First Class chick.

Live every Moment.
Adam, Student Body President class 88

The year has passed and grad has come, but now it's time to have some fun!

I think if you had a price tag I'd buy you in a second.
Scott "Sly" Sylvester Class of '87

Surpass the rest to be the best.
I'm sorry you didn't make Homecoming queen. It just wasn't meant to be. To tell you the truth I felt kinda bad when I was crowned. Life has a funny way of working out.
Love you forever and ever. Laurie

I really don't want to diss nobody but I think I drank too much Bacardi. Joey Lopez

You're a pretty partying chick, get fat drunk. Rick?????

Jessie, my princess, I'm sad to separate in such sweet sorrow. I learnt that in American Lit. class. I've really had a lot of fun growing up with you these years. A lot of fun. Please don't ever forget the 87 Seniors. Scott B. 87

"Thanks for screwing me around. It made me grow up. It was still fun while it lasted but I'm glad it didn't cos my girlfriend is nicer than you. Robert D.

I would like plans to wed.
Jerry Crow. (Agent Orange rules dude)

You're so fine, stay that way.
Aaron

You are one of the nicest girls I know because you're not stuck up. Have a blast. Danny the Dude.

Twenty miles west of Vegas with three hundred more to go.

"I'm headin straight for L.A., dude." The cute gas attendant nodded his head as if he'd been there before. He was flexin' his pecs as he leaned over to Windex my front window.

"And noooobody knows... I'm blowing this shitty pop stand. I've had it with stepdads, heartbreaks and the fucking burning sun. I want the ocean and rain... maybe that will cool me down."

As I pulled back on I 95 highway, I flipped through the yearbook and arrived at my favourite page. The 'Best' Page. It's the traditional section where the *Most Popular* jocks and jockettes are photographed into categories: Best Legs. Best Couple. Most likely to Succeed. Best Smile. Best From Behind. Biggest Flirt. I got Best Looking...

It's the ugliest and prettiest photo I've ever seen. So innocent and so old. Joan Collins and Shirley Temple. The edge of the photograph cuts off the top of my bird's nest. A nuclear weapon looks as if it's just blown up beneath the Aqua Net Hairspray. More than fifty Cowardly Lion curls cascade around my crooked smile. Even the eyebrows look wrong, coloured in a feeble attempt to achieve that outta date Brooke Shields' look. The lips are swollen and cracked and filled in with white gooey whale's blubber. An old wart is made to look like a beauty mark. The whole face looks as if it's been bitten by Black Widows. The expression says AGONY as if I'm sitting on a perverted Santa lap. Grandma's pearls and Mom's silk blouse. I look just like a Stepford wife. I disgust myself but I know it's not my fault. I grew up in a town that encouraged beauty contests, big hair and basic thinking. I'm like Blanche Dubois from A Street Car Named Desire, *a victim of circumstance. Lady Luck's never been on my side.*

My ice chest was full of Benny's Budweisers, soggy grapes and NutraSweet pills. Dead cat Sam was in the trunk. I was supposed to be meeting my boyfriend Sparkle in Barstow in three hours. He was coming to L.A. to hold my hand when I try out for the L.A. Raiders cheerleading team. After long distant pep talks on the phone, my baby convinced me to "go for it," to "soar with the eagles" like our coaches told us to. Ever since I met Sparkle I'd been telling him how I was gonna go to L.A. and be an actress. Trying out for the L.A. Raiders wasn't exactly the same thing, but it was a start. So after a few reruns *of Happy Days* and *Laverne and Shirley* I hit the road solo.

THE SUN-
hey fat chick
your make-up is dripping off
and your hair is sticking to your back
oh no! your curls have dropped
those ain't no beauty spots on your arm
they're cancer cells

I tried to shut him out. My brain felt like a trash compactor - a zillion thoughts crushing into each other... Reading about that murdered girl who was a top ten Miss Teen finalist was what made me decide to escape to L.A.

I was working that night in Swensens when it happened. She came into the coffee shop with her Laura Ray hair and I congratulated her on making it into the finalists. I myself had just been knocked outta the race. Then that very night she was strangled in the Meadows Mall parking lot by some guy posing as a photographer. That could have been me.

THE SUN-
Oh, you're such a fuckin' drama queen
I'll tell you what it's about...

Miss Las Vegas-
Shut up! Shut up! Shut up and set would ya!
nobody likes you
we all wish you'd go the fuck away
you're nothing special either
there are millions of suns like you
you're just the meanest and the closest

THE SUN-
your brain needs a weed eater
a Creepy Crawler vacuum
too many fried brain cells
you mama tried to feed you Stephen King
but the only words you read are instructions on pregnancy tests
credit card applications and magazine horoscopes
go home
ask Siegfried and Roy if they'll give you a job cleaning out tiger cages
you're a real good pooper scooper
or you could sit in the casino's money vaults counting money for a livin'
or you could get a job bein' one of those professional wedding watchers

Miss Las Vegas-
I think I can I think I can
come on little red engine
I think I can I think I can
come on little red engine

THE SUN-
don't pretend you can't hear me
for two years you made progress
you were nearly there
you'd been on such a roll
you nearly got your high school Oscar
but your addiction to messing things up let you down
you fell on your ass
and your dreams went crashing down with the cheerleading pyramid
so party it up Miss Las Vegas
go jet skiing at Lake Mead
you won't make the L.A. team
you have to be 5'10" and you have to give a speech about
your most redeeming qualities
you haven't got one that lasts for more than a day
you have to show them your yearbook
show them how many pages you appeared on
you'll have to prove you were homecoming queen
getting Best Looking isn't enough
they want to know if you have staying power
you need staying power in L.A.
not a Charm School certificate
you haven't even been practising your Jane Fonda work-out routine
you hate yourself and it shows
do you think they won't notice that wart on your face

Miss Las Vegas
O.K! I'll go back!
you've won... fuck head! you've won!
you've made me feel like a cockroach, a chicken shit
you've turned me to a cancer-stricken sun-spotted raisin
so now my personality is formed
it's truly fucked up and there's no changing it
no matter what Woody Allen says
once it's there it's there for life
I'm only 17 and I'm so hot and tired
even putting on my bathing suit whacks me out
I don't want to be cheerleader anyway
it was all supposed to be a joke
now the joke's on me

I parked my car in front of the *Welcome to California* sign. I waited for the sun to say yet another smart-assed comment, instead he set. I looked in the rear view mirror at my melted green eye shadow. Then I pulled on the chunks of thigh fat spread across my sweaty seat cover, counting the rolls on my belly.

I took Sammy Cat out of the trunk and wrapped him in my try-out t-shirt with JESUSA *13 PICK ME printed on it. My dead cat smelt like the body at Redrock. I didn't feel nothin', as Sam's tongue and eyes hung out. I buried him under the sign like he made me promise when he was a kitten.

I did a big fuckin' illegal U-turn, and headed back home. So much for my great escape. California don't want no wimps.

I shouted at the sun one last time.

I'm tired of nuclear contamination
double dating, frozen burritos, and diet milk shakes
tired of planning what to wear and sleeping in curlers
tired of talking on the phone and three way mirrors
one of these days I'll do it
but I'm not ready for Hollywood yet

these are and will always be the four quarters of my nightmares and my daydreams
first I will rise and be a hero
and the crowds will make me a queen
then something small will hurt me
and a crushed victim I will be
as victim bored I will bang my head
as victim I'll be helpless
until someone says poor baby
nobody says poor baby
I gotta stop doing U-turns
I gotta stop doing U-turns
I gotta stop doing U-turns

CAR HOPPING THE LIMOS

I am shark bait SEX on wheels yah yah yah
I am sexxxxxx in culottes yah yah yah
I am SEX on ankle strap rollerskater sandals sucking on my hair
yah yah yah
I am sexxxxxx to the Whoudini beat yah yah yah
I am SEX that can't be had that will drive your bulging *meat mad*
yah yah yah
you want me baby with my trash compactor tan lines and my padded strapless bra
you want me baby
cos I'm the 21 century MINX
car hopping the limos car hopping the limos yah yah yah

A polluted storm stampedes from the Rocky Mountains. I'm waiting for Cheri to pick me up in her new Camero so we can go limo-hopping. Through the dusty window the drive-in movie screen sways in the black acid rain. Stallion clouds drifting in, filling the mountain crags like leaky water colours. But somehow the rain never reaches your face. It disintegrates in the invisible gasses, before it hits the ground. I don't care. I want to be entertained. My lavender finger nails and prickly stubble of freshly shaven legs look good in the mirror. Golden skin. Mommy's little girl all perfumed and shampooed, washboard stomach and arched back tight. tight. tight. Freshly factory packaged panties washed with fabric softener make their bulges beat in agony. You can beg and try to out-smart the pussy posse but we're not as dumb as we look. That's the beauty of a bimbo.

Cheri honked her brand new horn on her brand new Camaro three times. I flicked my bedroom light twice in response.

"I'm coming, girlfriend. I'm coming, girlfriend, honeychild! I wanna scoop up the whole of Vegas and study its losers in the palm of my hand, shake it up like a clear plastic snow ornament. I wanna be in every alleyway, elevator and limosine, all at the same time. I am soooo thirsty for adventure." I kissed my reflection goodbye, then hurdled babies' diapers and safety nets down the slippery, orange-carpeted stairs, past the photo gallery of sulking adolescent smiles. The Goodmans were microwaving milk bottles. As usual, they barely noticed my stunning presence.

"Bye *Mommy Dearest*!" I said as I grabbed a few nasty Coors outta the fridge.

"Be home by midnight."

I knew she was too caught up in her own world to put any real effort into playin' concerned parent.

"Mom, let's say 1:00 and I'll clean your car for free." Her cleaning chores were more important than keeping me off the streets.

"O.K. you gotta deal, but don't drink and drive," she shouted as I slammed the front door, beer tucked in underpants.

I was in a good mood that night cos my ol' peckerhead, Sparkle, was comin' home the followin' weekend for the summer and I'd be gettin' a good fuck. I sank into the passenger seat of Cheri's bass-boomin' hot rod. Rap had invaded and we wanted to be black! We headed to the west side to score some weed singing Cameo at the top of our lungs:

"Word up!" We wore sunglasses like Run D.M.C. Cheri stopped at the Rancho 7-Eleven so she could try out her brand new fake ID. She came out with a six-pack of Corona and a pocket-size whiskey bottle. On the way to Tammi's we passed Caitlin's concrete tent. I hadn't spoken to since I became a cheerleader.

To make our limo-hoppin' team complete, we screeched to a hault in front of Tammi's mansion. Her pool put mine to shame - a concrete island with a jewel of a jacuzzi slap in the middle. A little wooden bridge connected it to the outer pool deck. Her neck of the woods had massive circular driveways, displaying several flash cars. Even though Tammi only lived a mile away from Caitlin's ghetto, her neighbourhood had its own private police unit because Debbie Reynolds, Tom Jones and Liberace all had homes there.

Tammi's grandfather invented *the* Weedeater, so she was loaded. Her walk-in closet was my shrine. All the latest Esprit and Camp Beverley Hills clothes and shoes, sectioned off into colour wheels. She had her own en suite bathroom with jacuzzi and bidet. When she ate dinner with her mom and stepdad, I kneeled in the plush peach carpet fighting my desire to steal a belt or an earring. In those last few months of high school, I was spending the night at her place cos it was easy to sneak out. Tammi had her own separate driveway and garage on the side of the house.

Headin' downtown on the freeway, we passed the sign for L.A. After high school we kinda planned on moving there together. The pussy posse were in love with L.A. But for now it was time for limo-hoppin'. Cheri's stepdad worked for a limo company so I knew almost every model in the brochure. The Elizabeth Taylor, the Sinatra, the Liberace, the Tom Jones. We'd been in them all.

The three of us were a bittersweet cocktail of Charlie's Angels and the Dallas Cowboy cheerleaders. We had traded in our pussy pants for hooped culottes that looked like our ol' cheerleading uniforms. Getting loaded and acting out dares were our daily jobs. Sundays, we'd spend out at Lake Mead hitchin' jet ski rides. Monday to Saturday we met at Tammi's house. From midday after school, to 2:00 p.m., when the sun was its evilest, we deep fried ourselves in Crisco cooking oil and watched *All My Children* by the pool soothing our hangovers with joints and vodka Kool Aid.

Downtown Las Vegas. Wheeling over speed bumps and beer bottle glass, we reached the top layer of Horseshoe parking lot. Super Big Gulps filled with whiskey and diet coke cooled our fiesty crotches. After the piss contest and drip dry, we skipped to the elevator, hop-scotching cowboy spit and cracks. House keys and lipstick jiggled in our bras.

"LL Cool J is really Hot. Hot. Hot." Our voices echod in the four-storey parking lot. Saturday night was the best night for limo hoppin'. Guys with big, hairy chests flew in from San Diego and Phoenix ready to spend their pay checks as if it were their last.

We wanted some action, not sex, just a little tongue. To straddle and be licked on the neck, under the ear lobe... the tingling feeling of kissing someone for the first time. To meet new guys every weekend and then never see them again. Vegas was great for that, there was always a new batch of dudes.

As long as you didn't have sex with them, you never got hurt. Sometimes poor Tammi would get so wasted she couldn't help allowing some love muscle in between her legs.

Scamming, getting hot and bothered, dying to fuck but always stopping at the crucial moment was the name of our game. It ain't an easy game to play. But it was much more fun just feeling them press up against the cotton crotch material, that way you don't get used - they get used. Prick tweezers in a limo play-pen. The kiss of a weekend stranger and if they're real cute - a dirty fingernail poke downtown.

Time to fuck with the tourists. After our ritual free pictures taken in front of the glass horseshoe made up of a million dollar bills, we power-walked through the Horse Shoe Casino pinching butts, blowing kisses and pretending to grab bettin' chips as we passed the crap tables. I winked to the suited Mafia men monitoring the tables. The brutes winked back and then glanced at the eye-in-the-sky cameras.

We were the brazen hussies, saloon girls flaunting flesh at the O.K. Corral, looking for some action so we could tell a good story at the local salad bar. We walked in and out of Sassy Sally's, The Golden Nugget and Glitter Gulch. Bargain this. Big boob that. We'd sit down at lounge shows until we got our IDs checked and thrown out. Security kept movin' us on. Usually we gambled, but we had our fake ID's confiscated the week before and only Cheri got a new one from her sister.

A boring white limosine pulled up as we were standin' on Golden Nugget corner, as if we were selling gutter-mouth, girl-scout cookies. Thickly coated Lipsmack stuck to the straws of our Big Gulps. It's Cheri's dad.

"Can you drop us off at the Strip, stepdaddy?" Cheri had him wrapped around her pinky.

Through the tinted limo window, *The Jetsons* cityscape whizzed around me like a cotton candy Pac Man maze. My mind was like a Space Invaders screen - rows of brain cells bein' shot down. What could I see? Escalators and elevators made out of gingerbread. Joke building after joke building seemed to be laughing at us victim humans.

Everybody ignored the wind storm. Dirty headlights bounced off mirrors and illuminated dollar signs. $500 palm trees hid pleasure domes and lined the road like bumper-car railings. The eight-lane strip rammed with out-of-state cars, holding passengers too lazy to get out and walk. They all sat in their cars taking pictures and pointing, as if we were animals at a Safari Park.

Entertain us. Entertain us. White tiger magic .

Like Dorothy in the Poppy Fields, I felt sleepy. A melting cheese burrito in the microwave. A loser. The joke's on me. Everything edible, even the airplane's tiny flashing red lights in the sky were like cinnamon Red Hots.

Locals danced in and outta cars, happy to escape their lives just for the weekend, acting foolish, everyone throwing money away, all walking around like dumb cattle, herds of sheep. They came here to win but this town is full of losers wide-eyed baaaahing and mooing in amazement. I don't want to be a joke, Mom.

We had arrived at our pitch... Caesars Palace Entrance. The intersection of Flamingo and the Strip. Cheri started her cheerleading holler, like she was doin' a car wash.

"Come on, boys!" If we weren't so damn cute, anybody woulda thought we were prostitutes. The dust storm swept a dollar bill into my hand. The tourists took pictures as we sashayed in circles of pastel pinks, blues and yellows. Attention seeking in front of the temple of Cleopatra. "Hey guys, can we have a ride? We'll show you around, take you up to Hoover Dam, do some tight-rope walking, we'll give you a kiss and a grope."

"Come on, boys, let's see some action. We'll sit on your lap if you behave yourselves." Limo-less jet skiers from California ignored us in their big dick ginormous trucks with wheels the size of refrigerators. Tom Cruise and Rob Low look-alikes.

We welcomed visitors as they passed. Through the metal and mayhem, I spotted a Tom Jones limo and shouted out,

"Have you got any champagne in your mini bar?" A bride ruffled out from the sun roof and replied,

"Not for you, honey. You better go home to bed now." Traffic was so slow at this main intersection, so we had no problem catching the attention of all eight lanes.

"Hey guys, can we have a ride? We'll show you around, take you up to Hoover Dam, do some tight-rope walking, we'll give you a kiss and a grope." We especially liked the guys who were in their late 20's. The ones who had girlfriends or wives who just wanted to do things through fabric. Some people laughed and enjoyed our teenage brash precociousness, others frowned upon our free street theatre in front of the temple of Cleopatra. Cheri, the tall blonde goddess, me, Priscilla Presley with the Elvis snarl, and Tammi, Raquel Welch, with those Italian stallion legs.

We spotted limo number three pullin' out of the MGM casino. It was a private one, not hired. A very good sign. We begged them to roll the window down. I asked them if they were in the Mafia and they laughed. Laughed at my impudence. My stepdad wisely pointed out one of these guys would someday not see the funny side and whack me across the head. They asked us if we wanted to go to see Folies Bergère, a drag show with Diana Ross and Marilyn Monroe look-alikes. We jumped into the limo. They had stumpy gold hands, Slick-Rick suits and dark tans and... they had coke.

"Coke alert. Honey, please, come on, sugar daddy."

Once we got to the Dunes, the pussy posse dragged the coke holder to the Ladies restroom. We all huddled in the handicapped cubicle. He made some lines out on the top of the porcelain toilet tank, then I dragged him into the next cubicle and start blowin' into his ear. Meanwhile Cheri and Tammi snuck out of the bathroom with his vial of coke. When he got too frisky, I told him the other two girls had left with his coke. Forgetting he was in the powder room, Mafia man tried to yank me outta there, but the bathroom attendant came in and shouted in Spanish for him to leave.

Breathe in for ten. Exhale for ten. I backed into the handicapped cubicle waiting for my heart to stop racing. Wired and nervous, piranha baby teeth chattering, I sucked my index finger and ran it along the top of the toilet bowl lid where a few crystals of coke were left. It felt like snotty crushed diamonds lodged in my throat. I hate coke! I hate coke! I hate the fucking feeling. It's O.K. if your suckin' face but when you're solo, the muscles in your throat tighten up and the air tastes like a nuclear bomb.

I was fuming at those bitches for skippin' out on me like that, leaving me with a Mafia type who wouldn't have thought twice of dumping my concrete ass in Lake Mead. After what seemed like an hour I rustled up enough courage to mince out of the restroom. The Mafia guys were nowhere to be seen. Jeeez Louise, what made me think they would be waiting on a little tiny bag of coke.

Black sun dreams zipped through my mind as I walked back down the strip to our pitch. *Why is my brain so small ? Why is everything I think and say a cliché? What would my dad say if he saw me lookin' for limos carrying a bunch of beer guts?*

Magazines. That's all I read. How to keep your man... how to say sorry... how to lose weight ... how to avoid stress in the office... how to seduce a married man.

What the hell am I doin'? Hitting the midnight pavement, scuffing up my best cheerleading shoes. I should be at home fillin' in college applications. Here I am walkin' down the most legendary stretch of road in the world, and I can't find anyone or anything who will teach me how to smile straight and be pleased with this life that was given to me on a platter.

The world is your oyster. I don't want an oyster, when you lift it to your ear you can't hear the ocean. I wanna hear the ocean. I wanna hear the Atlantic Ocean. I wanna get away from all this technicolour.

Back at the ranch, Cheri and Tammi were nowhere to be seen, but that was no surprise. They were always disappearing together, leavin' me in the dust. They were closer than I was with either, but that was cos they spelt their names with bubble letters and dotted their 'i's' with identical lips.

I perched myself on the edge of the Caesars Palace water fountain. I felt all depressed and alone. As I chewed on the inside of my mouth I watched the old ladies steppin' cautiously off the conveyer belt that transported them from the heart of the casino to the street.

My grandmother was in an alcoholics' rehab again. A few weeks previous, my mom, who had just had her second Goodman baby, sent me over to Grandma's cos she wasn't answering the phone. After knocking on the door and calling out "GRANDMA" I lifted the plant pot where the key was kept and opened the door. I switched on the lights to find her lying on the carpet, shivering wet and surrounded in sick. Alive. Seymour the fat cat was lying next to her. Dead. There were empty whiskey bottles lying around.

"Come on, Grandma, let me help you up."

Terrified, she shook her head, still unable to use her voice box. From the rug burns I deduced she'd been crawling around on her hands and knees for days. Her phobia for heights must've gone haywire from the drinking. She couldn't even reach the phone or the light switch because she found it too scary to stand up. Then the ambulance came. She was put into Betty Ford again...

As the midnight pavement scuffed my ol' cheerleading shoes with Mt Charleston ash, I kept trying to swallow barren air. It was so retarded the way I was still holding onto them like Dorothy's magic red shoes. My trophies, representing a short stint of success.

The water fountain looked inviting with its underwater purple lights. My throat felt like a gasoline nozzle. I took my red tennis shoes off. Just as I was about to lie down in shallow water, I heard Cheri's voice boomin' out from across the Cleopatra statue. I turned round to see Tammi's fluorescent pink bathing suit poking out the top of a Liberace. Their boobs were bouncing up and down in slow motion. They scored a Liberace! I jumped in and laid on the back seat. I was finally goin' to L.A.

There were two guys with them, dressed in black. We didn't ask for names. One fat American in shorts, one skinny Englishman in leather. An Englishman in Las Vegas? Who woulda thought? As soon as I heard the Northern English accent I perked up. Mr Leather Pants was mine for the night. We each had a bottle of champagne to ourselves and Cheri lined up stolen coke on top of the mini fridge.

"I'm surprised it's not all gone" I snarled.

"Stop your bitchin', we came back for you, didn't we?" Tammi said.

The English guy was tall and lanky just like I remembered them all to be. As I told him how my best friends left me with a Mafia man, I noticed we were getting' on Freeway I 95. Cheri shouted into the starry night,

"L.A., here we come!"

I was so excited I could barely keep cool. as I sat opposite my chosen guy. I could hardly get a good look through the curtain of legs. Cheri, Tammi and the fat American dude were standing waist high hangin' out the top of the limo's sun roof. The coke rushes didn't help either, as my eyeballs rolled to the back of my head.

"What are you guys doin' in Vegas?" I said and then took a swig outta my bottle. I began my Charm School routine. His shoes said dignified but playful so I decided to use my innocent girl stance with a hint of Lauren Bacall.

"We just came up for the night," he mumbled.

"Whereya from?"

"I live in London but I'm from Manchester..."

"Oh my gaaaad, I'm from Manchester, well, Leeds but my dad lives in Manchester!"

"Fookin' hellll. How did you get from Leeds to Las Vegas?"

"I don't knooow" I valley-girled. "I might go back there when I graduate... just like disappear." I twirled my hair around my finger.

"Why would you want to go live in some grey shithole when you've got the easy life with a bloody pool an' all ?"

"But that's just the thing, dude. I don't feel like I got naathin. I know this sounds stupid but I don't feel like I have a soul, like I grew up in a soulless city. Everything's just money, money or makin' Mormon babies. O.K., so I have a pool and a convertible and I party my ass off every single day but I'm soooo bored, I've been doin' it for like the past five fuckin' years. Anyways, don't let me talk too much, I always get boring when I've had too much coke."

"What are you doin' in America?"

"I've been in L.A. signing a record deal." He slapped my hand from my manic hair twirling.

"No way!" I was in love.

"Yep. Signed and sealed!"

"Wow. Congratulations. Hey, girlfriends, we got a rock star in our limo." Tammi and Cheri couldn't care less. They were too busy making eyes at each other in the wind, as the fat American guy watched.

Pit stop. Three taps on the black window and the invisible driver pulled over. We all stumbled out. Tammi and Cheri ran off into the desert as I showed the two guys my cheer,

"Boogie, cross the line. Hey, it's touch down time." They looked at me unamused. English gentleman pulled me from the splits.

"That's very impressive. I wonder what other tricks you can perform?" But he said it in a way that I could tell he wasn't at all impressed with cheerleaders. My idea of a joke belonged back in fourth grade with the cooties. I decided to go for the Katherine Hepburn charm approach which I wasn't real practised at.

We piled back in, bladders relieved, ready for more drugs. I sat next to Leather Pants from then on.

"I bet you think I'm a Miss Apple Pie from hell, huh?"

"Even if you are, you're pretty cute." He took my hand and draped my arm around his shoulder like a pro.

"Well I coulda' grown up in England, you know. But what would you choose - a shitty little council flat in Moss Side or a big pool in the sun?"

"Fookin' hell, I'd say the pool but I don't know, Americans do me head in."

"Why, though? You make fun of us like we're all Reagan-loving hillbillies but you watch all our movies. You eat our food. Wear our clothes and then steal our music..."

"I don't steal anybody's music. Anyway, I thought you were English."

"I'm transatlantic. When I'm in England I feel American and when I'm here I feel English."

"You've just contradicted yourself..."

"What does contrad-dick...?"

"Shut up, you little coke-head and give me a kiss."

I moved closer, blushing. The peckerhead pecked me lightly on the cheek. I wasn't used to a guy goin' slow. I broke one of the pussy posse rules, never fall in love. I woulda fucked him right then and there. Instead, we carried on kissing and petting for what seemed like hours. Privacy didn't really matter in a limo because everybody else was always doin' their own thing or too out of it to give a shit.

The English gentleman was reeeeal good with his tongue. He had a way of painting the inner sides of my mouth, flickering, darting in and out, gently teasing my whole body with just the tip of his tongue, his teeth and his lips barely touching me which made me want him even more, but every time I tried to straddle him he held my hands down to my side.

"No more cheerleading moves. I want you to remember this kiss for the rest of your life." Normally I would have thought that was a dorky thing to say, but coming' from him it was pure poetry.

"Keep your eyes shut." Bossy Boots stopped kissing me for a few seconds. I kept concentrating on what he told me to... the colours of what I was wearing that night... the texture of his leather jeans... the way my underwear felt between my legs. I imagined what the limo must've looked like above, driving on the deserted highway, its white tiger magic gleaming in the clear moonlight.... the sound of the tyres spinning over the cracks in the concrete... the black jagged mountains against the star-sprinkled midnight sky.

Sprawled out on the limo floor, the girls were playing poker with fat guy's money. I felt his lips again and then smoke, the smoke of marijuana and coke burning. Ahhhh. I inhaled his smoke and held it in my lungs. I felt like I was swimming underwater with him, deep sea diving sharing his oxygen tank. Limo sounds were getting farther and farther away as I got more and more stoned in his mouth, breathing as one. Pussy posse voices bubbled on the top of the water. I could feel myself melting into the tan upholstery, slipping lengthwise across the entire back seat.

We stayed in that limo for more than five hours, kissin' and talkin'. The English gentleman was unlike anyone I'd met since I'd last been in England. His eyes were so far away and then they would come back to me like a circling airplane... and he could hold a conversation.

"So what will you do with your life, little girl?"

"Well I wanted to move to L.A. and become famous."

"How did I know you would say something like that?" He pretended to look out the black window.

"I know. I know. See, I'm sooo stupid. It's not my fault though. It's this place. It's the goddam TV. It's like I've watched so much TV I wanna be inside the TV or... I don't know. Why do people want to be famous, do you think?"

"God damn! I don't know, but let me give you one word of advice. Think it but don't say it. It's naff..."

"What's 'naff' mean?"

"It's tacky. To just want to be famous for the sake of it is just superficial and... look, trust me... just don't say it to people." I wanted to retort something really interesting for a 17 year old, something he might use in a song. If I'd been talkin' to some desert rat standing behind the counter of 7-Eleven, I would have come out with some witty comment. If I was just wooing a car full of limo jocks, it woulda been easy.

"I think I better maybe go to England. Like, get a brain."

"Yah. Who knows." He wasn't interested in hearing me talk about my future at 4:00 a.m. I fell asleep with my head in his lap.

We woke up on Hollywood Boulevard, fenced in by concrete, plastic, aluminium and freak shows. I wasn't used to the humidity and smog. Los Angeles always made me feel empty and sad - memories of taking off into the chemical sky.

Cheri with all her stamina demanded more booze. "We need to drink soon if we're going to avoid the headaches and the come-down." The last bottle of champagne came out of the mini bar. I couldn't handle the bubbles and the burps so I opted for straight vodka with only ice cubes to chase. We all did a few lines of coke each. No one wanted any more coke, but who would be the first to bottle out? We came this far to be dangerous. Luckily the fat guy suggested coffee and grub. I spotted The House of Pancakes, the exact one my mom always took me to before going to the airport and we went in. The five of us together must've looked pretty suspect.

I saw the Hollywood Boulevard street sign through the window and told everyone that when I was 2, I was found prancing barefoot up and down this very same street in my diapers. My English Prince pulled out an airplane ticket and studied it.

"Bloody hell, the time. I'm gonna have to shoot. My plane goes in an hour." He looked at me and kissed my nose. The next thing I knew we were at the airport. We said goodbye to the fat American guy and he zoomed off. Another limo bit the dust.

There was nothin' left to do but pay for tickets back to Vegas on Tammi's credit card and head back home. The girls went to the bar to see if they could get some free drinks out of some businessmen. My English dude disappeared for a few minutes and came back with a very large bottle of Coco Chanel

"I don't wear perfume."

"It's Coco Chanel - the classiest perfume for the classiest teenager in Vegas."

"Write a song about me and send it to me."

"Yah, sure. I'll do that."He wrote my name in a scruffy little black book filled with zillions of names and numbers.

"Wow, you must've met a lot of Vegas teenagers on your trip."

He gave me a snaggle-toothed smile and wrote, 'Jessie Duke from Vegas/Leeds (The Limo Hopper)'.

"You better get outta this country before your smile gets crooked."

"Thanks for making my last night a good one, I really enjoyed your company, hearing all your cute stories."

"I'll make you a deal - you never say 'cute' and I'll never say 'I wanna be famous' ever again."

"You're a good girl, now aren't you glad I didn't let you seduce me?"

"Maybe I'll run into you when I move to England." It wasn't till I heard the words that I knew what I was going to do. A wave of pussy posse panic swept over his face as I launched into my Oscar acceptance speech. "I wanna, ah, thank you for, ah, helpin' me make up my mind. I'm gonna go to England. My brain's a little fried but I'm not stupid.

"I think so many things and have no way of explaining what I'm thinkin', everything comes out as clichés, as some fucking line Bill Cosby's TV kids would say. I want to be different, I feel like I'm suffocating, like I'm on coke all the time. Sorry, I'm talking too much, it's too much coke... Ah, anyways. Well I think you're a fucking stud and I hope you become the biggest rock stud in the Universe..."

"Oh shit, I gotta go... look I won't kiss you properly because you look way too young."

He kissed me on the nose. I watched his skinny butt jog down the walkway. My contacts misted over with emotion. I knew I'd never see that guy again.

When I got back to the Goodman house, I didn't even get in trouble. I told my mom I fell asleep at Tammi's. I slept all day on my *I love Jesusa* raft, reliving the night before over and over, trying to memorise every word that was said. That evening, while my mother was videoing her babies crawling around on the living room floor, I told her I was going to move to England.

She said, "Oh, I think that's a good idea, it will get you away from that horrible boyfriend of yours once and for all. You can live with your dad." My stepfather seemed to think it was a *very* good idea.

I am due to leave in the next few months. Mom's attitude towards me has changed. There's no curfew anymore, no cleaning the house on Saturdays, just an excited preparation for my departure. For the first time I feel really removed from the Goodman family my mother has produced. There are two alien babies crawling around on the freshly vacuumed carpet. The dog is lying in front of the TV and they've even got a new cat.

Elvis Died For Me

I huddled next to my vanity table and waited to be rescued as my first love tried bangin' my bedroom door down. For once, Jason's next-door-neighbour's spying paid off. He heard my victim screams and Sparkle's fists, so he called the cops.

Sparkle had a Leo tantrum on me. In our hallway, all the glass from the family picture frames were smashed. Usually he only knuckle-dented his truck and pretended to run me over. He had never tried to hit me. If he'd burnt my house down like Brooke Shields' boyfriend did in *Endless Love,* maybe I would've stayed. The fact that he tried to bash me up didn't prove his love in the right way.

Just my Mom came with me to the airport. She had sold my VW Beetle to pay for the airplane ticket. Benny gave me a money belt, a pocket knife and a can of Mace. No big send off. Grandma was still in the Betty Ford Clinic. Aunt Erica was getting a divorce. Cheri and Tammi were in Hawaii wave-hoppin'. Benny Goodman was learning how to be a Real Estate Agent cos Las Vegas was boomin'.

At McCarren Airport, we ate a frozen yoghurt and shared a mocha-mint iced-coffee together. I was dressed in a pink, Camp Beverley Hills, short outfit with yellow and pink sandals. Mom looked pretty with her sunglasses perched on top of her blonde bob. She had that same brave face as always.

After we checked in, she gave me a present wrapped in pom-pom paper.

"It's a diary. Gee, thanks."

"It has cheerleaders in the corner of every page with scratch-and-sniff fruit flavours." She'd written a paragraph on the inside cover, with her teacher's pen but I was too embarrassed to read it in front of her. I put it away and edged my way up to the gate attendant.

"Well, I hope you know what you're doing." She seemed a little lost for words as she applied lipgloss.

'I haven't got a clue. Oooh, man! I forgot to stock up on lipgloss. You can't get Lipsmackers over there!"

"Take this one, I'll buy some more and send you a few in the mail."

"Thanks. Mom, you're not going to have any more kids, are you?"

"No, that's it now... God, I can't believe how quickly you've grown up." She exhaled heavily. I could tell she was struggling to find the right cliché... waiting for,

"Well, you know, parents aren't supposed to be good". Luckily it never came. We hugged. It was quick but as intense as a Jane Fonda butt lift.

As I was walkin' up the ramp to the plane's mouth, I turned around to wave goodbye. For the first time, I wasn't afraid of breaking down into tears, or of her not being there when I looked back. I didn't have one goddam emotion left.

To my surprise she was crying real hard. Her whole face was beetroot red and mascara stained. I gestured to her to put her sunglasses back on. I quickly waved and carried on walking, thinking her favourite expression - "get over it and get on with it".

The plane is taking off once again. I'm doing my breathing exercises as if I'm about to have a baby. The plane does a U-turn in the sky as if it might land again. I look down at the pockmarked brown earth, half hoping there might be a crowd with banners waving me to come back. There are cranes everywhere and the Strip is clouded in a disarray of dust puffs. There's the drive-in movie screens. I feel like every single character out of *The Wizard of Oz*. The Tin Woodman lookin' for a heart, the Cowardly Lion wantin' courage. And the Scarecrow lookin' for a brain. But most of all - Dorothy trying to get back home.

For the first time in my life, I order a gin and tonic from the air hostess.

"Excuse me, I have a leg problem..."

"Sorry, First Class is full, you're the third person who's tried the leg one."

These moms don't seem as pretty as they used to be. Their calves are huge and you can hear their inner thighs swishin' together. As I look out the window, my Mom's face flashed like a ghostly neon sign. I open up the diary and read the message.

Well, you're finally spreading your wings. Remember Jonathan Livingston Seagull? Don't go smashing into any cliffs. But seriously, you will come to many crossroads and have to make many decisions. You know I had to make the same decision you're making. I left my boyfriend and all my friends, and Beverly Hills, but I'm glad I did it because you wouldn't be here today... there are so many other things I'd like to say, but as usual I'm running late. PS. Don't get married!!!!

My first entry in my England journal. June 5, 1987.

I want to get as far away from America as possible. It stinks of falsity and shines white teeth metal jaws. Heart and guts slapped down on the table. So goddam open and loving. Free filter coffee refills and parking.

goodbye to all the raspberry milkshake insecticide high school sweethearts
goodbye to all the creepy men with dick problems and 36 flavours of ice cream
goodbye to the sunburnt swimmin' pools and slumber parties
goodbye to a town full of dreamers schemers losers and flakes
goodbye to the cotton candy palm tree hairdos and champagne water fountains
goodbye to the sun

and so now I'm hungrier than I've ever been
I want to fondle Marilyn Monroe's breasts in flaming fame heaven
I want a hotel casino to be named after me
I want little girls to read biographies about me
I wanna talk to Howard Hughes and Liberace
ask them - how does it feel to be special, how does it feel to be special?
I want to win an Oscar for the best performance of my hicksville life
I want my ego to be blown up from a satellite and have it sprinkle the planet like confetti
I want to be colour blind.
I wanna fly with Elvis' soul
rocket through the white sky straight up until it goes black.

Elvis died for me
Elvis died for me
Elvis died for me

Airplane. Ten hours later. ✈

The sun has come up and I have filled this crappy journal. I'm half tempted to just leave it on the plane with the rest of my past... but I think it might make good reading in twenty years time.

The captain has told us we will be landing in twenty minutes.

"Did you finish your letter?" The hippy girl's back to her perky, nosey self.

"Yah, I think I did... my hand is fuckin' killin' me."

"My head's killin' me. Here - you wanna painkiller?"

"No thanks, I don't do pills."

"I love them."

"My mom used to pop pills, so I keep away from them."

"So did you write a nice letter or a mean one?"

I was too whacked out to be unsociable. It was the last conversation I intended to have with an American for a long time, so I carried on as if I was sayin' goodbye to my old self.

"I don't know. It kinda started out as a mean letter to my mom. I was gonna tell her what a bad mom she was and all."

"Ya, I know that feeling." I hate it when people tell you they know exactly how you feel.

"But I was just goin' round in blame U-turns."

"Blame U-turns?"

"Yah, like it's her fault, then it's all my fault, then it's the sun's fault and then I'm back at square one, trying to remind myself what the crime was.

"I've, like, had a privileged life and shit. I mean, what the hell am I complaining about? Everyone's fucked up to some degree. Right?"

"Ya, you can say that again. You're just like me - running away from it all. My Mom's such a bitch, she's always trying to run my life... God, my boyfriend doesn't eeeven understand... nobody understands what I'm going through."

"Honey, I don't mean to be rude, but you don't know me at all."

"Yah, but it's like you said before, when you read that thing out to me. You said: 'People spend their lives either running to or away from something'."

"Well, I don't know, that's just what my dad says. I don't know jack shit about nothin'. That's why I'm going to England. I'm gonna get smart."

The plane lowers through the black clouds. I'm so happy to see rain. I'm so grateful to see green fields even if they are dark and gloomy. The hippy sitting next to me is biting her nails so I get my make-up bag out. Concealer. Mascara. Lipstick. Blush. Mirror.

"Why do you put all that make-up on?" I can feel her watching me. I try to think of a good answer. But I can't.

"To cover my scars."

"People in England don't wear make up."

✈ ✈ ✈